WAR
FORGED
BOOK 4 OF THE GIFTING

War Forged

The Gifting Series #4

Being kidnapped by aliens does not sit well with Quinlan. Not only would her seven guardians give her hell if she doesn't attempt some sort of escape, but she refuses to be at anybody's mercy. With her practiced military skills, the help of an underground lounge singer and a personal assistant, she takes over the alien slave ship. Not knowing how to fly the damn thing, she sends a distress signal. ...The rescue comes swiftly in the form of a bronzed man with exquisite ice-blue eyes. Leaving her to ask the true question: has she just given up her newfound freedom for a gorgeous man who seems determined to have her for eternity?

As Elite Supreme Commander of the Etterian Forces, Xan answers a distress call in Earth English. That is all he did. The female who captured the slave ship shows remarkable skill, making her a warrior in her own right. Said skills should be respected and honored. Except she is his Dar Eth, calling forth the Ethera—the soulmate bond. How can he protect his female when she can do so herself? What can she possibly need from him? What can he offer a female, not Etterian but human? Not that he can think clearly in her presence when she scents so good and makes him want to kiss all of her.

Maker help him.

This is a work of fiction. The characters, incidents, and dialogues in this book are of the author's imagination and are not to be construed as real. Any resemblance to actual events or persons, living or dead, is completely coincidental.

Published by Sevannah Storm.

First Edition 2022

Cover Art by Sevannah Storm

https://sevannahstorm.wixsite.com/website

Version_1

Also by Sevannah Storm

The Blood of Legends Series

The Huntress

The Healer

The Gifting Series

Soul Forged

Fate Forged

Sun Forged

War Forged

Star Forged

Shadow Forged

Earth Forged

Lust Forged

Standalones

Xiaxan Fox

Ire of Silver

The Shikari

Sol Survivor

Contents

CHAPTER ONE

Etterian Battleship, Phoenix
Communications Room
12254 Years, 5ᵗʰ month

"WHAT HAS YOU SO irritable?" Oyaz asked his Supreme Commander Xan. The male was unpleasant today, to say the least. After all the diversions he had partaken within the last week, this expression should not be on his battle-bond's face.

Xan's dark blue gaze shot up to meet Oyaz's. He grunted, acknowledging his irritability and the question. "I regret you did not meet them, Oyaz," he mumbled as he tossed his data tablet onto the table. He rose to his six-foot-six height and stood behind Pilot Msar, staring into the large display vids that projected the passing stars.

"Are you referring to the Earthian females, Supreme Commander?" Msar glanced at Xan before breaking eye contact.

If it was possible, Xan's expression darkened.

"You have the comm, Pilot Msar." Oyaz gestured to Xan to follow. "We will spar. Expenditure of energy is required for such a situation."

"And what situation would this be?" Xan trailed along the narrow passage, his shoulders wide enough to touch the sides.

"Dealing with the encroaching void." Oyaz's words were met with silence. He had hoped it wasn't true, not yet. "How bad is it?"

"I am fine. I am far from being Remi," Xan growled, his scrunched face conveying how displeased he was to have such a discussion.

Oyaz snorted. Remi was the Base Commander of Aluna, their northernmost base on the planet Gikaet—once a perpetual war zone. A four-year service on Gikaet served as a rite of passage for all Etterian males. Older than Xan, and yet, Remi managed to ward off the darkness consuming his soul. Why was Xan struggling then?

"You did not see them. You did not touch them," Xan roared.

Oyaz frowned. "You said they were like *damu* in size, Xan."

"Their size does not concern me." Xan sighed, turned in the quiet passage, and leaned against the bulkhead.

"I have seen the image of the one they call Lady Ava," Oyaz spoke into the silence. "She is beautiful," he admitted before breaking into a grin. In the sensual garments she had worn, even a six-eyed, twelve-tentacled Algri would have looked attractive.

"And she was gentle, soft-skinned, kind..." Xan activated his O .D.I. calling up an image of Lady Ava—a black-haired, green-eyed Earthian female. She was partially covered, with strips of transparent and colorful fabric. The image switched to another Earthian female who battled a sogair in the Yithian Arena. The snarling, razor-toothed, sharp-clawed, blood-red creature with incredible speed and agility, landed on top of the pale-haired female.

"So, this irritability is because you want a Dar Eth?" Oyaz arched a brow at his bond whose bronze skin darkened. Whether in embarrassment or anger, Oyaz didn't know. "You do know that finding your Dar Eth is impossible—?"

"Of course I know that. But three, in as many months? All human?"

"Human? Not Earthian?" Oyaz paused as his O.D.I. fluttered his eyelashes, flashing images of humans in all shapes and sizes. His breath hitched. Their coloring varied, whereas Etterians were all bronze-skinned and dark-haired.

Xan ignored him and strode to the common.

Oyaz could not fault Xan's irritability. He too yearned to find his life force, his true mate, the female to spark the Ethera within him and thus cease the growing void in his soul. Regardless, Etterian males had to remain resolute for the survival of their race. They were allowed emotions until the age of four. After which, they learned unarmed combat and self-control to restrain their baser instincts. They trained, continually, exercised control in all situations, including the one he now found himself in.

"You do not like your eye color is what you are saying," he teased. When an Etterian experienced the Ethera, their eyes reverted from indigo to the color at birth—a pale blue. The change served as a physical manifestation of the Ethera's presence. It was also said to be excruciating. Emotions, stored from their youngin-days coursed through their bodies, renewing neural paths along their brains and hearts.

"Alodon's balls, Oyaz, I would take a female over my eye color." Xan stomped to the weapons bulkhead, his jerky movements angry, frustrated, determined. It did not surprise Oyaz when their males dove out of their supreme commander's path.

"No, not the spears of agility," Oyaz called as Xan removed the blinding-white stone spears from the bulkhead and tossed him one. "Last time, I nearly lost an eye." He caught the heavy weapon in mid-flight. The slap of the haft hitting his palm echoed through the common.

"It would have grown back." Xan chuckled as he marched to the center of the common, where the large sparring mat was embedded in the floor.

"After a few weeks of blindness." Oyaz scowled as he spun the spear in one hand to test its balance. "I do not understand why you insist on improving this skill."

"It is your weakest." Xan launched an attack.

Oyaz dodged the thrusts and lunges. Xan kept him on the defensive. He dodge-rolled past Xan and kicked him in the backside. The male didn't budge an inch. Oyaz huffed and sidled toward the weapons bulkhead. He tossed Xan his spear and took two more from the wall.

"Truth?" Xan taunted.

Oyaz gritted his teeth. When he had suggested sparring, he had meant unarmed combat as it exerted the most energy. Having his backside handed to him had not been the plan.

With a spear in each hand, he spun them around his body while lunging toward Xan with each rotation. His supreme commander dropped to his knees and thrust upward to strike Oyaz in the center of his chest, spinning the spear at the last minute so that the butt hit him. Oyaz grunted and ignored the throbbing to flip backward, crossing his spears as a shield. He landed on his feet and dropped into a defensive stance, one spear in front of him, the other over his head, both aimed at Xan.

"You are improving, youngin." The almost imperceptible twitch of Xan's mouth eased the burden on Oyaz's shoulders. At least his irritability had faded. Sparring was the only thing that seemed to raise Xan's spirits.

"Baiting me, Xan? Are you concerned? Nervous?" Oyaz offered an arrogant grin.

"Are you on the attack, or are you planning to stand there and look at my handsome face?" Xan asked, calling forth a few chuckles from their avid audience. Their males stomped their feet in encouragement, their gazes fixed.

Oyaz tossed his spears at Xan and launched himself into the air, colliding with his battle-bond's torso to take him to the floor. His body slamming into Xan's should have winded his supreme commander, but it didn't. Xan hit Oyaz with a hammer fist to the back of his neck. He grunted as his hold loosened. He couldn't help but smile when Xan tossed him into the air, then yanked him onto the mat. His battle-bond's laughter was worth the pain Oyaz would be in for the remainder of the day.

Chapter Two

NOTHING OUT OF THE ordinary alerted Quin, not a creak or muted pad of a footstep reached her. Someone had intruded in her home. The air thickened, tensed, as if frozen in a moment of time. She knew no other way to explain it. Perhaps it was her hypersensitive instincts, bred to be paranoid. She stilled, slowing her breathing as her bedroom door opened on silent hinges. When they left her as they always did, making it squeak would be first on her agenda.

It took all her control to remain relaxed despite tuning her senses on the intruder crossing her bedroom floor. A familiar cologne tickled her nose, and she almost barked a laugh.

"You breathe like a gorilla." She opened one eye and focused on her oldest brother.

Lucas grunted despite his grin. "You should've heard me at your front door, sis."

He opened his arms wide. She bolted into his embrace, slamming her face into his T-shirt-covered chest. Tears prickled the backs of her eyes, but she didn't release them. Crying was for sissies—they, her three brothers and their four friends cum guardians, hadn't raised one.

"I thought you'd never wake up." He grinned, his yellow-blond hair the same as hers. Shaved as it was made it appear darker than their high-school days.

She remembered when his locks had brushed across his face making all the girls swoon. *Now look at those swoon-worthy locks. All gone.* But no hair enhanced the cut of his jawline. All the Walsh brothers shared that trait.

"You could've called first." She pushed herself out of his arms, tempted to punch him on the shoulder.

"What's taking so long?" Garrett hovered in the doorway, leaning his great bulk against the frame.

Shit, he is gorgeous. Tall, dark, and handsome, he filled his pilot suit like no man should. He'd been her next-door neighbor for as long as she could remember. Until he volunteered for the Air Force, now he cycled through bases. When she was younger, she'd had such a crush on him, but he'd never shown interest. Any lingering 'love and hope' were for nostalgia. Of all her guardians, he was her favorite; her brothers excluded, of course. Well, maybe not Aiden, her youngest brother; she barely tolerated him.

Lucas rested his chin on the crown of her head. "We could've stomped like a pride of elephants."

"Herd." She laughed and squeezed Lucas's shoulder. "Happy to see you, brother."

Nine months had passed since his last visit. She'd shared her displeasure at their neglect when Garrett had taken her camping. *Now that had been fun.* All they'd done was camp, fish, and hike. The normalcy of it was rare. He hadn't made her crawl through mosquito-infested water, nor had he camouflaged her in leaves and mud that made her skin itch for days afterward. They'd just camped, breakfasted over a fire, and stared at the stars in the evenings.

She skipped across to hug him. "Hello, Garrett, my big teddy bear," she said as he tugged her against his chest. "So, two of you? How did that happen?"

She buried her face into the curve of his neck as he cuddled her closer. Her height was perfect for such a hug from her guardians but not from the men she dated.

"Three," Wyatt called from the kitchen. A familiar crunch of an apple followed. "You have nothing in the house. Where's the food, Quinny?" A full mouth muffled his words.

"Wow, three of you? I'm so going to feel it," she muttered.

With a final squeeze since she didn't know when next her hugs would come, she released Garrett. She slipped around him, scraping her fingernails across his rock-solid torso as she headed for the kitchen. On the passage wall, she paused to straighten a framed digi-photo showing their makeshift family at a shooting range. What made it special was that all seven of her guardians had been there. Lucas, her eldest brother, held out a rifle to Aiden. Her middle brother Mason cradled a beer while chatting to their lifelong friends, Carter, Garrett, Wyatt, and Josh.

"Do you think she'll like what we've planned for her?" Lucas asked Garrett as they trailed her.

She grimaced. No, she wouldn't like whatever they wanted to do for their furlough, but they never bothered to ask her.

"No," Garrett chuckled.

Yup, the one man who understood her but even he didn't want to date her. Wyatt bit into another apple and held it there while crushing her in a hug. He needed her the most and saw her as a brother, best friend, confidant, and accomplice.

Sighing, she squeezed him back because if she didn't, she'd be stuck like this for longer. When she whispered she'd make bacon, he released her with a nudge toward the stove.

Coffee was first, and she set the machine to make its maximum number of cups. Her insides churned, forming a knot. Despite knowing what hell was coming, she grinned like an idiot at her guardians visiting her. In times like this, she didn't ache with loneliness. That would slam into her after they left.

As the coffee percolated, she started on the imported bacon. She'd been saving it for a special occasion, and this seemed about all she could have hoped for. They assumed couches in her rarely used living room, discussing work, life, and goals. She listened with one ear, not learning anything new other than she'd be left behind, as usual.

Her ankle twinged as she danced to the coffee pot, reminding her of all the times she'd been injured on their escapades. They'd hie back to their bases, stranding her with some malady, in effect, ducking the consequences. Anger surged, stiffening her posture until she was ready to punch something. No, not this time. She'd be damned if she took the brunt of their 'bonding' sessions. No more meekly going into the fray for her.

"Okay, out with it." She served the coffees and, once done, faced them with her arms folded across her chest. "What's it to be this time? Will I be stabbed, punched, shot at, thrown off a cliff, or dunked?" She threw up her hands with a groan, imagining the torture they could dream up. "Never mind, after breakfast, just...leave. I'm not interested."

Lucas swept out an arm, gesturing to the room. "But three of us on furlough, squirt, what are the odds—"

"That I'm cursed? Those odds are pretty good." She folded her arms across her chest. Garrett's gaze lingered on her unbound breasts in the tank top. She wanted to challenge him with a glare, but he glanced away.

"It's paintball." Wyatt gaped, his eyes wide. He couldn't handle it when she wasn't 'sweet' or 'amenable.'

She'd had enough. "I don't care." She stomped to the kitchen to serve the bacon, bundling strips in paper towels before shoving a bundle at each one. "Go. Have fun." She hugged Wyatt, who'd delved into the bacon like a starving man. The next hug went to Lucas, then Garrett. "Send me a digi-card." She swung open her front door.

"But Quinny—" Wyatt's gray eyes darkened while he chewed.

"It's for charity, squirt," Lucas said, then grinned when she released a string of curses along with the violent slam of the front door.

"I don't know why you're not enjoying yourself?" Lucas called from behind the V-shaped bunker where the three of them 'hid.' The plan was to lay low and have Quin do all the work. After all, they did this for a living.

She snorted from across the tire-strewn yard. "I hurt for days after your visits. I know things women shouldn't. I can't even find a man who'll accept that I can kill him with his dessert spoon. I need to have a relationship, one that's not in passing or includes bodily harm."

A ball splattered green paint too close for Lucas's comfort. "Relationship?"

"I'm so willing. It's the lack of decent men, I tell you. And it's not that I'm not trying."

Was there a whine to her voice? He chuckled. When last had she used that tone?

"Are we talking sex, squirt?" Wyatt burst to his feet and fired a few paintballs before dropping alongside Lucas, sprawling in the dirt without concern.

"Sex? What sex? Are you insane? If I wanted to find it with just anybody or thing, I'd have opened Victor." Her voice came from a higher point as a few balls exploded paint an inch above Wyatt's head.

"Victor?" he mouthed, arching a brow at Lucas.

"Her vibrator." Lucas grinned as he held his gun over the plastic barrel and fired a few shots in his sister's direction, not aiming or planning on hitting anything.

"She has a vibrator?" Garrett crouched behind another barrel.

Lucas shot him a glance, wondering when his friend would grab his balls and ask Quin on a date. "Of course she does. I bought it for her." He shrugged, ignoring Garrett's look of dazed fascination. "It's an abnormally huge one too." He puffed out his chest. "Only the best for our sister."

"She *named* it?" Wyatt shook his head.

"*I* named it when I bought it as a joke." Lucas peeked over the bunker as she somersaulted over an obstacle, landing on her feet with ease before disappearing behind tires. "Shit, I never taught her that." He ducked his head again.

"It looked like a Carter-move," Wyatt spat.

Carter was the operative in their *family*. An assassin was a better designation. Agent provocateur according to Carter, not that any of the actual soldiers in the family gave a damn about his opinion.

"It looked badass. I should have her teach me that." Garrett smiled as he reloaded his magazine.

"Why haven't you opened Victor yet?" Lucas tilted his head to listen for movement. "I should be offended you don't like my gift." He laughed as only a brother would do. Anything to embarrass a beloved sister, right?

"I refuse to lose my virginity to an inanimate object." Her grunt preceded a ball splattering to the left of Garrett's head.

Cursing, he ducked lower.

Lucas frowned. By the pained expression on Garrett's face, her words hit him harder than the near miss.

"There are children here, Quinny." Wyatt waved at the passing kids and their mothers.

"If you must know, my longest relationship has been with Victor, and I'm fond of him. I haven't unpackaged him yet, but he's a good listener." Her words came from another direction.

Lucas shuffled on his backside to peek over the other side of the bunker. She was covering ground with efficiency. He didn't know whether to be proud or concerned. Her techniques were better than the men in his squad.

"Anyone of us non-biological brothers could take one for the team, dammit." Wyatt dove to the ground and leopard-crawled to a new position as balls struck the top of the bunker, raining paint. When another two balls near-missed Garrett's head, Lucas realized she was toying with them.

"I'll do it," Garrett yelled as a ball whizzed past his ear.

Pht pht pht

Fire throbbed just above Lucas's heart. He dipped his chin and scowled at the bright green splat on his armor. A shadow fell across them. He squinted at Quin crouching on the wall of their bunker.

"I don't want pity sex." She leaped off and tossed the rifle at Lucas's feet. With a dismissive wave, she strode off. "That's it, I'm done with this bullshit."

He lay there stunned. A glance at Wyatt and Garrett revealed a precise kill shot to each of their hearts.

"Shit." Wyatt jumped up to stomp to the 'base,' known to civilians as the reception.

Lucas stared at his sister's disappearing back, hating the sensation crushing his chest. "What have we turned her into?" He scooped up her gun, her original magazine half empty. "She's not happy, and I don't know how to fix this." He strode to the 'base' with a grumbling Garrett trailing him. "When she was younger, a teddy bear, a strawberry milkshake, hell, even a hug would've solved everything. Now, I just don't know. You might *have* to take one for the team, Garrett."

"You heard her, Lucas. Besides, I'm moving bases again." He ran a hand over his face, his anger and frustration in the jerky twitching of his fingers. "I can't believe I'm saying this, but she needs a man who'll stick around."

Lucas frowned. "You've wanted her for ages."

Garrett jerked back, then tried to hide his shock. Had he thought his obsession had gone unnoticed? There were no secrets in a military family.

"That's true, but I also love her."

"Not as much as you love flying, though?" Lucas pinched his lips when Garrett nodded.

"Regardless, I want her happy too, and if it means with another man..." He winced.

Lucas wasn't going to force someone to date his sister. She'd made her stance on this clear. An authentic relationship couldn't be bought or coerced. He thumped the guns and protective gear onto the counter, then strode to a pacing Wyatt.

Quin wasn't with him. "Where is she?" Lucas peered through the glass doors to where he'd parked his car.

"She's jogging home, said something about us disrupting her schedule, dooming her to a sexless life, and generally being a pain in her ass." Wyatt cupped his cheeks, his eyes darkening with sorrow.

"What has you so upset?" Garrett handed in his rifle and goggles.

"She's my home." Wyatt tilted his head, his gaze afar while he held open the glass door. "Maybe parachuting over the gorge wasn't such a good idea."

"Isn't that when she sprained her ankle?" Lucas climbed into the driver's seat of his car.

"Yes, and like I said, it was a bad idea." They remained silent before Wyatt made another suggestion. "I'll take her hang-gliding with me over the canyon. She'll like that, right?"

Garrett thumped his head on the window.

Lucas groaned. To Wyatt, Quin was the one constant in his life, and when her behavior was out of the ordinary, he was unable to deal with it. "Maybe not this time, Wy."

"Yeah, I thought as much."

Lucas glanced at the man in his rearview mirror and would swear under duress, there were tears in his eyes. Shit, this was bad. And as the oldest, they looked to him for guidance. He faced forward and tightened his fingers on the steering wheel.

What the hell was he going to do?

QUIN BURST THROUGH HER front door, allowing it to slam shut behind her while she bent over, hands on her knees, to suck in great gulps of air. Sweat dripped off her chin and had plastered her T-shirt to her like a second skin. Her jeans weren't the best for running, but at least her sneakers had served their purpose.

Despite her trembling legs, she could run another thirteen miles with the fury in her veins driving her. Fuck her brothers. When would they learn she wasn't a mini-soldier to drill and train?

Huffing, she toed off her sneakers and kicked them aside. She grabbed a bottle of water out of the fridge and took a long pull, relishing the chilled liquid sliding down her throat. For a moment, she pressed the bottle to her cheeks, hoping the condensation would cool more than her temperature. After another sip, she peeled off her drenched T-shirt and sports bra, tugged off her socks and jeans, and threw the bundle into the washing machine. The cool air on her damp skin brought a sigh of relief.

"Should we say something now, Lucas?" Wyatt laughed.

She yelped and grabbed the kitchen towel, holding it in front of her. "What the—?"

"My eyes, they're bleeding." Lucas chuckled.

"Lucas." She slipped behind the counter to hide her lower half better. With one glance, she calculated how much more she'd reveal if she bolted for her room. Raising the cloth to cover her breasts, she glared at the three grinning idiots.

"Sorry, babe, we came to apologize, but we could stay for the show." The way Garrett ran his dark gaze over her left her with no doubt to which show he was referring.

Bloody hell. They'd sat in her living room, watching in silence as she'd stripped. *Why didn't I hear them? Feel their presence? Shit. I didn't notice Lucas's car.*

"Apology accepted, now get out." She pointed at the door, and in doing so, the corner of the kitchen towel dropped to reveal a nipple. Cool air bathed it, puckering it. A shiver followed. She righted the towel and gritted her teeth, ready to kill them.

"Like I said, a show." Garrett sounded harsh.

Her brother rose, and with a huge grin, strode to her front door, opening it before saying one last thing. "We'll pick you up at seven, sis, for plain, old, boring dinner."

"No knives, bullets, poison... Just dinner." Wyatt jumped up and marched out of her house. At that moment, she loved him the most.

"If I could, you know I would, Quin, in a heartbeat," Garrett traveled his gaze over her bare shoulders and pebbled nipples peaking the kitchen towel.

"I know, and I love you for offering even though your heart's not in it." She flashed him an understanding smile and slumped when the door closed behind them. Had Snow White felt the same with seven irritating, smothering, and frustrating guardians? With heat still burning her cheeks, she tossed the kitchen towel in the washing machine and went to shower.

"YOU LOOK BEAUTIFUL," WYATT greeted her as soon as Quin stepped into her living room. Ten minutes ago, they'd entered her house and helped themselves to the beers she kept in a small fridge in the garage.

"Thanks, Wy." The yellow silk dress fell to the floor, with a slit from ankle to mid-thigh, exposing her left leg when she walked. In it, she felt feminine...beautiful. She had taken the time to shave. The dress, paired with pale gold ankle-strap, peep-toe pumps, was smart enough for an expensive restaurant. When her guardians said dinner, she never knew what to expect. So, she chose to overdress rather than underdress.

"You look handsome too." Quin smiled at Wyatt in his gray slacks and a dark-blue collared shirt that enhanced his broad shoulders. He was the typical tall, dark, and handsome man most women had heart palpitations over. He flashed her a charming smile between bites of an apple and sips of beer.

"Wyatt's right. You look heavenly, Quin." Garrett slipped his arm around her waist and spun her, sending her unbound curls wild.

She laughed as he twirled her before bringing her to a gentle stop. She stepped back to make her perusal obvious. He wore tailored slacks in dark blue, molding his long legs. He paired it with a crisp white shirt that clung to his arms and shoulders. With those muscles on display, she should complain on behalf of women. Tonight, she'd watch said women drop like flies.

"Damn, Garrett." She grinned, raising her gaze to meet his. "Just let me get my taser. You guys might need it."

"And me?" Lucas called as he swaggered from behind the kitchen island. In his black slacks and black-velvet-flowers-on-black shirt, open at the collar, he could've posed for a men's digi-zine.

"Meh," she teased, giggling when he wiggled his eyebrows. "You look like Dad."

"You look like Dad too." He barked a laugh before hugging her. "Ready to go, squirt?"

"I hope so." She grabbed her pale-gold clutch and followed him to his car.

Wyatt tossed away his apple core and licked his fingers. "The view from behind is better."

"There's a compliment somewhere in that." She slid into the front seat. Silence descended on the car ride, but it wasn't awkward. "Your furlough ends tomorrow, I assume?"

"Moving bases," Garrett said, "and Wyatt's got a course to attend on something or other. Lucas's going to Mars for a month, maybe longer."

"Well, I hope I'm back by then. I'm traveling to Uruguay next week for a travel digi-zine. I thought I'd do more sightseeing, stay a little longer. I'm undecided."

"It's a beautiful country." Lucas parked the car.

"I was in Africa about nine days ago. The sunsets were the best I've ever seen." She twisted in her seat to face him.

"I won't panic then if you're not home." He threw her a quick smile.

"You? Panic?" she teased as she opened her door to slide out.

"You're too quick for me," Wyatt whispered, closed the door, and offered her his arm.

She smiled and looped her arm through his, slipping into an easy stride alongside him.

The restaurant claimed the bottom floor of a skyrise building—its glass-solar panels shimmering in the domed lights contrasted with the weathered-stone detailing and antique wood doors. Warmth from art deco lanterns poured through the windows onto the walkway. The impression was almost ruined by the massive neon signs advertising fashion or food lining the roads and buildings around it. She couldn't shake the thought that the place had been ripped out of time and space.

The maître d in a tailored suit offered a bow, then ushered them to their table. Despite the upper-society vibe, the waitresses reacted the same no matter where her guardians went. They fell over themselves to serve them, throwing Quin jealous glances until she let slip that these were her *brothers*. Then, of course, she received better treatment. As the perceived gatekeeper, the sister had to like them first. She snorted and ignored the glance Garrett cast at her.

As the evening progressed, each dish a mouthwatering delight from the tofu-prawn starter to the real steak, she couldn't hide her amusement. They were on their best behavior, their attention on her as if she was a newborn baby. The air had thickened with unsaid words like they were acting out roles with unfamiliar lines.

But loving them as she did, she couldn't let this continue, no matter how sweet their intentions.

"Thanks for dinner, guys, but I'm calling it a night. I'll take a taxi." She rose to her feet. "If I hurry, I might make the last kickboxing class."

Lucas gaped at her.

She winked and gestured to the hovering waitresses. "Go get your 'no-strings-attached,' and I'll see you whenever." She kissed him, then Wyatt on the cheek.

Garrett stood to hug her, squeezing her hip at the same time. "Be safe, Quin," he whispered before kissing her temple.

She waved and left, realizing that the moment she stepped through the wooden doors of the restaurant, any opportunity with Garrett would be lost forever.

And yet, she didn't look back.

Chapter Three

Etterian Battleship, Phoenix
En route to Earth
Xan's Officers Quarters

XAN STARED AT HIS O.D.I. in disbelief. He'd received a message from King Xeus's battle-bond, Adviser Cales. A Yithian male named Kbal and his commander Pyo were looking to overthrow their king, Urio. Of all the species Xan had encountered, his thoughts were not favorable toward them. They lacked honor which was the crux of it. Had their attitudes, their values been similar to the Maloidians, then perhaps Xan might have been more forgiving.

They had one universal belief, their superiority as a race but underlying this was their greed. A Yithian would sell their spawn for tokens. Maloidians were not so extreme, and they were far more approachable. Their sense of humor coupled with their love of a good bargain made dealings with them enjoyable and challenging. They also respected other cultures and attempted to compromise. Etterians had the brawn, the power, the technology, and the honor, not to mention detailed navigational charts. No species could hope to best battle-honed Etterian males without utilizing deceit.

But Yithians refused to accept this.

King Xeus had tentatively given his support to this Kbal, but Xan knew his uncle, that he was biding his time as to how this would play out. Cales had notified all Etterian commanders of the possibility a Yithian vessel might make contact and demand to speak to Xeus.

Xan cursed as he swung his long legs off the bed, having realized sleep would be elusive this night. He sat there in his sleep pants, his head in his hands, not knowing what to do. If he left his quarters, it would worry Oyaz.

He grunted and lay down again, activating his O.D.I. to call up Lady Ava's image. He violated protocol to gaze upon Warrior Kanzo's Dar Eth, but something drove him. A hopelessness he couldn't control, perhaps?

Lady Ava had the black hair of an Etterian female, but her pale green eyes set her apart. Not to mention her size and fragility, as well. Her curves held a sensuality he found enchanting. Her voice was melodic, and her scent had been...appealing.

Lady Jacqueline was a different human female in that her white curls reflected the sunlight like a supernova. Her eyes were a bright blue, a different hue than the dark-blue eyes of an Etterian. She was Supreme Commander Ulriq's Dar Eth but taller and more muscled than Lady Ava yet still appearing as soft.

In both images, their faces were expressive, revealing a variety of emotions, most of them he was incapable of identifying. It was the intensity that called to him. Lady Oriana, Prince Enyl's Dar Eth, had hair the color of Etteria's red oceans and eyes the color of their Ferusi crystals.

Etterian males had never concerned themselves regarding their Dar Eths appearances since all Etterian females were black-haired and blue-eyed. Now that they'd discovered Dar Eths from a species that had variety, it was a new and intriguing concept. Xan longed for his Dar Eth, that yearning burned within the cells of his body in every waking moment.

He was too exhausted to concern himself with a possible Yithian rebellion. Before meeting Lady Ava, he would've received news of a civil war with enthusiasm, as an opportunity to test his battle skills, his control, and Maker willing, lose his life in glorious carnage.

He wondered if this intense yearning was the last burst before the void consumed his soul—the darkness where no emotion existed. Descending into such an abyss would drive him to sacrifice himself, tossing his meaningless life at the mercy of an alien creature or a Gika soldier. It was honorable to die in battle.

A Gika, fully grown, could spit acidic saliva in sufficient quantity to dissolve an Etterian warrior. It was for this reason that all the warriors wore suits which were metallic-and-fabric-layered armor, pre-soaked in acid deterrents. The immense satisfaction in striding out onto the eternal battlefields of Gikaet, suited, and with a greatsword in hand, summoned addictive and unidentifiable emotions.

With a frustrated growl, he bounded off the bed, strode toward the display vid, and moved his chairs against the wall with a stroke of his finger. Their magnetic bases slid across the floor as he shifted them on the display vid. He fell into his routine exercises, doing the steps every Etterian male was taught to control his emotions, to focus his thoughts. Only when his knees trembled and sweat dripped off his chin did he cease, striding to the cleansing room to strip off his sleep pants and step into the cubicle.

As the water streamed over him, he lifted his arms above his head to press his palms to the white bulkhead. He lowered his forehead, relishing the cool paneling against his temple. He had one thought driving him. He had to find his Dar Eth soon.

Chapter Four

QUINLAN JERKED AWAKE. THE darkness gripping her chest announced something was wrong. She didn't move but kept herself immobile, trying to sense her surroundings. The surface she was lying on was hard, cold, smooth, and unfamiliar. It didn't have the porous texture of a tiled floor or the granular feel of pseudo-wood. Perhaps a screed floor? No, it was too smooth like polished metal.

The air smelled stale—a miasma of decaying organic matter.

No other sounds reached her. No gorilla breathing from Lucas, no barking dogs, no humming of the dome, just dead silence. She did detect a low vibration with a slow-fast-fast murmur.

She opened her eyes and wished she hadn't. The sharp pain lancing through her skull made her wince. She massaged her brow to try to ease the throbbing. *What—?*

"Don't make sudden movements," a woman said from the shadows.

26

With a start, Quin sat up, spinning to face the feminine voice, and frowned. *Where am I? Why is it so dark?*

A sickly yellow light along the bulkhead didn't reveal much. As her eyes grew accustomed to the darkness, an idea of the room formed. She was in some sort of cubed cell. The walls were a dark gray, looking like brushed metal, so she'd been right about that. But there were no bars, just a solid-looking door that reminded her of a submarine's airlock. This didn't bode well. It implied air pressure could come into play. She sharpened her gaze on the rounded 'edges' of the cell, only to realize it could be jettisoned. But into what? Water? Air? Space? Perhaps she was in a gas chamber of some sort?

"Where are we?" She ignored the nausea churning her stomach, which the yellow light worsened. Although no sharp lights did soothe her headache. She glanced around the room and settled on a slumped form in the 'corner.'

"Some sort of spaceship. You were the last...victim."

They could be jettisoned into space? Shit.

"How long ago?" Quin grimaced.

They were in a capsule and could expect one of several outcomes, none of them good. They'd need to escape. The longer she waited, the farther away from Earth they traveled. She had to act now. Driving her was the knowledge that if she didn't escape, her guardians would never let her live it down.

The shadow shrugged. "About a day. Time is immeasurable here."

"Are you telling me aliens or pirates kidnapped me?" Quin's voice rose. "And why the hell are we whispering?"

"Yes, to the aliens. Yithians, slave traders, if they're being honest. And I'm whispering because I don't want to give them a reason to visit." She gestured to the form in the corner and shuffled into the yellow light. "That happened last time."

"Who's that?" Quin studied this woman's face for any subterfuge or indication that this was a joke.

Dirt streaked her cheeks and her hair hung limp and stringy, but her eyes were pretty. This was a woman who would have steered clear of Quin. Who was she kidding? All women avoided her, so maybe she was the common denominator? Maybe she had a resting bitch face or gave off an unapproachable vibe? She shook her head, scattering her thoughts.

"She's Macera Mitchell," Pretty-eyes said. "She demanded freedom, and they hit her with some sort of yellow ray gun. She's breathing but still out." She gave a sad chuckle. "Damn woman poked Scarface in the chest and called him Fish-breath. It was a dumb thing to do, but it took guts."

Courage was good. If they were to escape, they'd need it in buckets. "How long have you been in here? As best as you can tell."

Pretty-eyes rubbed behind her ear with a wince. "I've had five protein bars, so maybe five days. They've given me water, but it wasn't much." The woman stood up to lean against the metal wall. "I was the first in this cell. They held me down and forced something into my ear so I could understand them. We don't speak Galactic. It hurt like hell, still does." She shrugged, but the way she gripped her upper arm told Quin her indifference was fake.

"Are there others?"

"Yes." The woman dipped her head, resting her chin on her chest. "Sometimes, when the door opens, I hear screams. Some of them sound human."

"All right, so kidnapped and held captive." Quin ticked it off on her fingers. "What do they plan on doing with us?"

"I asked as soon as they confirmed the interpreter was working. They said something about their champion human having escaped their arena, and they needed a new one."

"Okay, but why women?" Quin rose to her feet, testing her balance and checking for injuries. Losing the use of a limb would be a hindrance. Her Wyatt-sprained ankle clicked as she twirled it. That adventure hadn't been fun.

"I'm Cyndi Stanford, by the way." Pretty-eyes's voice was reedy, exhaustion saturated her sigh. How long had Cyndi been alone with these aliens? Quin's lip curled downward at that thought.

"Quinlan Walsh, but most call me Quin." She grabbed Cyndi's hands and clasped them. "Tell me what happens when they visit?" If the aliens were tiny, she might be able to take a few. But a technologically advanced species could be beyond her capabilities. Still, she had to try.

Cyndi pulled away, shaking her head.

"Please." Quin gestured to the door. "I need to know what to expect."

"It's the same walking shark every time."

Quin mouthed 'walking shark' but didn't interrupt.

"He has a scar above his eye. It's why I call him Scarface. The lights go white and bright, then the door opens." Cyndi shuddered. "The gun he used on Macy looked like a toy shotgun, and it didn't fire a bullet." She flashed a fearful glance at the door. "He pressed the yellow button to shoot it. Made quite a show out of stroking it while she challenged him as if she would know what that button meant."

Quin strode across to Macy's body and checked for a pulse—steady and strong. Sighing, she stroked the woman's brown hair, hoping to wake her. If they were to escape, she would need all the help she could get. Sliding down the wall, she dropped to her backside and rested a hand on the woman's shoulder.

"How were you taken?"

"I was locking up the office. I work as a personal assistant to the boss's son," Cyndi sniffled. "Well, used to work there. I didn't even make it to my car." She sat next to Quin, close enough for the heat pouring off her to cross the gap between them.

Quin shivered, realizing how cold it was in the cell. Which meant she was coming down from an adrenaline high.

"I'd just finished a workout session." She indicated her gray tights and white sneakers. "I didn't make it to my car either. They must have snipered me. I would've noticed them otherwise."

Cyndi twitched. "What do you mean?"

"I grew up around boys. I can hold my own." She hesitated, not wishing to scare the woman. To fight in an arena was plausible. She imagined various alien species had different levels of civilization, so perhaps a Roman-like arena existed.

But Quin wasn't a stunner, not like Cyndi. She was too bossy, strong, and many other unflattering words. Six-foot wasn't so tall when her brothers towered over her. Being strong had come from wrestling with them, fighting back, and learning how to handle guns and bows. Now she stayed in form with kickboxing and sparring.

She had learned from an early age she didn't attract boys, not with seven guardians to get through. So she focused on her body. Whenever they received leave from North Korea or Mars, they would train her to justify their long absences. Freeletics was harder with Mars's gravity, and she had accepted the extra weight packs as par for the course. But no matter what she did, she didn't bulk up as she would've liked. Just more toned, stronger, but she refused to take supplements to mess with her biology. That scared her as nothing else could have.

Her one feminine trait was her hair. Yellow gold curls cascaded around her when her hair was down. It drew admiring glances, but her height and strong personality intimidated. And if there was something she hated, it was attention. She didn't need the judgment. So she kept her hair braided, and its beauty her secret alone.

She snorted. Free from under the vigilant thumbs of her guardians, and yet, her romantic life was still as dry as the Sahara.

She must've dozed off when Macy stirred, grumbling in her sleep.

Quin straightened. "Macy, sweetheart. How're you feeling?"

More muttering followed while Macy rubbed her forehead. The woman must suffer from a killer headache. The same toy rifle could have been the one to get her too.

"Like shit. Bloody shark." Macy struggled to sit up.

"You challenged him," Cyndi said. "He probably thinks you're champion material now."

"Oh, shit." Macy slumped and shuffled on her backside, then leaned against the metal wall. "I didn't think of that."

Cyndi picked at the ladder in her stockings. "Their escaped champion took down a few Yithians when they kidnapped her."

"Why didn't you tell me this before?" Macy's mouth flattened, the anger in her voice harsh.

"I'm sorry." Cyndi sniffled. "I forgot."

"It's okay, Cyndi. We know now." Macy leaned across Quin to pat Cyndi's hand. "Hi, I'm Macy." She flashed a small smile, bright in the darkness.

"Quin. Glad you're okay."

Macy's gaze traveled over Quin, who stiffened, guessing what the woman would see.

"You're gorgeous." Macy raised her wide eyes.

Quin jerked back, banging her head on the wall. *What now?*

"I know, right?" Cyndi giggled. "She looks like an Amazon warrior."

"Will they think you're the champion?" Macy's brow furrowed.

Her concern touched Quin like nothing had in a long time.

"Nah, even though Quin's tall, they're bigger." Cyndi waved her arms as if she drew the alien's outline in the air. "Let's hope they see us and think puny Earthians."

"Earthians?" Quin swallowed a laugh. This wasn't a humorous situation.

"It's what they call us." A scraping noise had Cyndi screaming to close their eyes.

Quin obeyed, the panic in her voice overriding her distrust. Cold, wet foam rained, smelling like antiseptic, but the feel of the white substance between her fingers made her skin crawl—like sand meets soap. It drenched the cell within seconds.

"I hate that stuff." From her arms, Cyndi sloughed off large dollops of foam.

"It's supposed to keep us clean." Macy wiped her face with her hand before standing up to stamp her slippered feet.

Quin gaped. The woman was in her pajamas. Cyndi wore a button-up blouse and a torn pencil skirt. She had no shoes. Quin stood, plucking at her drenched leggings before wringing the foam from her braid. Using the bottom of her T-shirt, she cleaned her face and shivered. Wet clothes, foam on her skin, and a metal cell made her freezing.

"They do it every second day." Cyndi squeezed out her shirt. "I made the mistake of looking up the first time it happened. Damn shit burns."

The remnants of the foam on the floor and walls of the cell evaporated after a few minutes, but not from their clothes or bodies. The sand-oil-soapy feel lingered on Quin's skin, gritting her teeth—like nails on a chalkboard.

"How were you taken, Mace?" Quin gave up on drying her braid, letting it rest between her cleavage.

"In the middle of the night, I went out into the backyard to chase away a stray dog digging in the trash." She sighed, the sound of it hollow. "Didn't see this coming. That damn dog is probably sleeping on my bed now, king of my bedroom."

Silence fell, settling on Quin like an anvil. Instinct screamed that Macy would never see a dog again. Quin drew in a slow breath. She'd learned to trust her gut, but what it implied didn't mean they wouldn't survive this. It could be they never set foot on Earth. She studied both women, wondering if either would mind not going home. What if either had family, friends, or worse...children?

"If we get free, would you want to return to Earth or travel the stars?" Quin watched their faces for honest reactions.

"I've wanted to see the stars, but never as a slave." Cyndi's tone was wistful.

"I wouldn't mind if I had one of those *sexy* bronze aliens." Macy giggled, the sound comforting as it echoed through the cell.

"Oh, no, Mace, you can't be serious." Cyndi teased, having picked up on Quin's nickname.

"Hell, yes, I am. They're damn hot."

"What? The shark aliens?" Quin frowned. She hadn't watched the news-vids in a while, more focused on organizing the upcoming Uruguay trip. Lucas would have mentioned the discovery of a new alien species, right?

Cyndi grimaced. "No, not Yithians."

"Quin, where have you been?" Macy squealed, her laughter contagious. "Gorgeous aliens have found us women to be just what they're looking for. Four or five women have mated, so far."

"Mated? Like with bears and wolves?" Quin widened her eyes.

Mace did a little dance. "I saw one once, on the homepage of Trash-e. Looked like paparazzi-style pics."

"Let me guess, tall, super buff, bronze-skinned, long black hair down to his ankles?" Cyndi beamed. "And sexy as hell."

"Yup, that sounds about right." Macy rubbed her hands together as if she'd relish an hour alone with the poor man...um, alien. He did sound heavenly.

"Damn, how come I didn't know?" Quin slumped. Trapped meant there'd be no sexy alien for any of them.

Silence descended. She mourned the loss of her previous life and any future she'd planned. Unless she did something about it.

"Mace, sing for me please," Cyndi asked in the deathly quiet.

Mace's head whipped up, flopping her dirty brown hair over her shoulders. "Anything?"

"Please." Cyndi clasped her hands in front of her.

Quin didn't have the heart to ask about whatever this was. Singing, along with music, movies and anything culturally significant to humans had been banished centuries ago. Sure, a hundred thousand kids had died from some sort of music-vid, but the government and churches' reactions had been over the top.

Humans being who we were, had taken things underground. There'd been talk of allowing those industries to return, abolishing the media police and the laws they failed to uphold.

Mace belted out a bubbly song. As soon as Quin recognized the archaic tune, she surprised herself by joining in. It was one her father used to sing when he thought no one was home.

With a breathless laugh, Quin hugged Macy. "You have an amazing voice."

Mace shrugged, but Quin couldn't dismiss how much better she felt.

After the song dwindled, they each took a spot somewhere in the cell and silence descended again. Cyndi continued to hum the tune, off-key, but it didn't matter.

Quin smiled.

She rubbed her eyes and cringed. Her contacts were scratchy. Not a good sign. Sucking on her finger and grimacing at the bitter foam coating her skin, she removed and tossed aside each contact lens. She didn't need those anymore, not that she had poor eyesight. Heterochromia iridum made one of her gray eyes hazel. People tended to stare. She blinked a few times. In the dark, she doubted Macy or Cyndi would notice. And if they did, it didn't matter. Being an alien slave squashed her insecurities; they weren't a priority. Surviving was.

"Did they mention sexual slavery?" she asked, then wished she hadn't when Macy curled in her shoulders.

"Yithians don't find Earthians attractive. We're arena fodder if they cannot find a champion among us," Cyndi said.

"What do they look like?" Quin pictured green octopus humanoids with fangs. She shuddered.

Cyndi tilted her head. "Like sharks, gray, slimy with black eyes too wide apart."

"Wearing some sort of body armor," Macy said.

Quin released a slow breath. No tentacles was good. "Any weaknesses?"

Cyndi scowled. "Oh, no, you don't, Quin. They'll shoot you like they did Mace."

"Just tell me." Quin lowered her voice to super-serious.

They sighed at her stern expression.

"Eyes wide to see all of the room." Macy split her fingers and pointed at her face.

"Excellent peripherals." Quin tapped her chin, so no sneaking from the side but maybe from behind?

"What about a blind spot, right between the eyes?" Cyndi tapped the bridge of her nose. "You know, like a hammerhead."

Quin shook her head. "It would be too tricky if he did have such a blind spot. A step to the left or right, and he'd see me. Anything on his body that looked soft?"

"They have genitals. Well, I assume they do. One of them grabbed them suggestively as our men do." Cyndi grimaced at what must be a horrific memory.

"Good to know." So groin shots might hurt. "And their necks?"

"Looks like a shark's, wide to their shoulders, thickly muscled." Cyndi used her hands to describe it, touching her earlobes, then the tips of her shoulders.

Shit. Quin curled her fingers into fists, tempted to rub her temple. "So only eyes and balls. That's not much."

"If we distracted Scarface, you could come from the side?" Macy indicated the corner closest to the door.

"That could work. I'd need to get his gun. Once I have that, we can blast our way through, arming ourselves and some of the prisoners, as well."

Macy gaped. "Shit, Quin, you don't think small."

Quin frowned at the fear pitching Macy's voice. "If we kill the guard, sweetheart, it's not going to help. We need access to the command room and communications. We need to send out a distress signal or message." She jumped up to pace. "There's bound to be more prisoners than Yithians, right?"

Cyndi shrugged. "So what? You get the gun, we leave, and start shooting the guards?"

"Yes, and let's take the time to get the stunned guards into the empty cells. I don't want them taking us from behind." Quin pressed her ear to the door. "Also, I think we need to check before we open cells. For all we know, there are alien monsters also captured, as part of the arena." She couldn't promise them it would go well, but it was better than waiting for their deaths.

"Like a gladiator?" Macy whispered, her fingers twitching.

The light flipped to bright white.

"Shit, I'm not ready." Cyndi's eyes widened in fright.

"Go to the corner." Quin pointed. "Mace lie down. Cyn, pretend to kick her. Mace, I want you moaning and groaning like she's killing you."

"What?" they squeaked.

Quin glared. "Just do it."

The women lunged for the corner opposite the door. Macy curled into a ball, arms over her head. Cyndi splayed a hand on the metal wall while swinging her foot, stopping an inch from touching Macy's ribs.

Quin threw herself on the floor where she had woken up and pretended she was out. Her arm over her face hid her opened eyes. She fought the urge to look at Macy as she squealed and whimpered in 'pain.'

"Bloody bitch. Why don't you die already?" Cyn screamed, fear cracking her voice as she swung a 'kick.'

Quin regulated her breathing just as the door whooshed open.

She tried not to stare at the shark-like creature that stormed into the cell. On his humanoid body, his black armor looked thick and bulletproof. If she managed to get his gun, she would have to aim for his neck. Cyn hadn't lied about that. Thick muscles met his shoulders, and he shimmered silver as if his skin was wet. The eyes were wide apart and solid black. She had no more doubts about actual aliens kidnapping her, not one.

Scarface, Cyn had called him, strode into the cell without hesitation. He didn't spare Quin a glance. It would be his last mistake.

As he stepped closer to Cyn, Quin bolted, rising from behind him, thrusting off the wall to gain height. She hooked her right and left fists and struck his eyes at the same time, blinding him. He swung his gun around, hissing out in surprise. She lunged and kneed him in the 'balls,' which worked. As he crumpled to the floor with a guttural groan, his gun forgotten, she took a moment to catch her breath. She kicked him in the face with the heel of her sneaker before twisting and flicking the gun out of his three-fingered grip. She caught it in hers. He gave it up without a struggle. Hefting it, she shot him in the neck. No mercy. Well, she couldn't take the chance his armor might reflect the blast at her.

"It worked." Macy gaped while struggling to stand despite Cyn's assistance.

"I can't believe it," Cyn rasped.

"Great performance, you two." Quin grinned before taking a moment to study the gun in her hands. It was heavier than what she was used to. But she would manage it. Another would bring her a level of comfort she wasn't leading them to their deaths. That was next on her agenda.

She stepped over the Yithian's body and peeked through the door. The wide passage was in the same dull gray metal, and grates lined the floor. More submarine doors ran as far as she could see. Three guards, was that all? The Yithians were overly confident. *The fools.* "Cyn, I'm putting you in charge of releasing the prisoners." She gestured to the interpreter in her ear, and the woman nodded. "Mace, I'm getting you a gun. I want you to stun the shit out of these aliens. As many times as you'd like."

"Like paintball?" Mace rubbed her hands together, her smile wide.

Quin chuckled. "Give me a moment." Dropping to her haunches, she sprawled on the grated floor, taking careful aim around the opened door. She fired three short blasts, her aim true. They crumpled, making a little noise as their bodies hit the floor. She stilled and waited. No alarm sounded.

Jumping up, she raced out of the cell to grab their weapons and hand them to the women. "Hold it with two hands. They're heavy. Now help me drag the bodies into our cell."

Five minutes later, with the oily sand and soap residue mixing with their sweat, Quin gestured to Mace to shoot the four of them again. "Aim for their faces. It's the most exposed body part."

As soon as gleeful and bouncing Mace joined them in the passage, Quin pressed a button alongside the cell's door, praying it did as logic determined. Her heart leaped into her throat for the second nothing happened. She half expected the button to jettison the cell. When the door closed, relief like a summer downpour slumped her shoulders.

Chapter Five

"Get to the other cells," Quin pointed.

Cyn ran down the passage on her bare feet, peering through portholes not visible from inside the cells. She opened one door and spoke gibberish to the prisoners.

Quin waited, but when the conversation continued, she approached Cyn. "I need someone who knows this ship's design."

A midnight-blue alien stepped through the cell door and strode toward Quin. Raising her gun, she studied him, assuming he was male. He had the body of a man, muscled, wide shoulders, strong thighs, and his skin was a pretty navy blue. His bright white hair fell to his shoulders, looking soft and clean.

"This's Illan, he's a Durn. He says he knows the design," Cyn said.

Quin relaxed and studied him, poking her instincts. When they didn't rear or whimper, she lowered her gun while offering him the other weapon. He took it with one hand, which meant his muscles weren't just for show. She opened her mouth but realized he wouldn't understand her. Two more aliens were on the other side of the passage door, which, by her estimate, cordoned off each slave compartment.

She had managed to gather this information with a glance through the airlock's porthole.

"Cyn, tell him there are two guards outside the door."

Illan pressed two fingers to Quin's forehead and excruciating pain lanced through her. She squeaked and staggered, her vision blurring. He steadied her with a hand on her shoulder. "Dammit. What the hell did you do that for?" She rubbed her temple like that would erase the pain.

"My apologies. I am aware this technique is painful, but the circumstances necessitate the connection." His voice was smooth, his English impeccable.

"You can understand me?" she whispered.

Yes. His words resonated through her mind, as clear as her conscience.

Holy shit. "Did you just—?"

He harumphed. *Yes. You too may communicate with me as such. Think your words.*

She shrugged. *What the hell? Might as well try it. Aliens. Telepathy. It couldn't get more bizarre.* She met his white gaze. *Can you hear me?*

He winced. *Perhaps lower your volume.*

Sorry. She grinned. *I can't fly this ship, can you?*

No.

She sighed, throwing that scenario out the porthole. *My plan is to reach the bridge and send out a distress signal. I assume I'm moving in the right direction since the vibrations are less on this side of the passage?*

Yes.

Could he not answer with monosyllables? She scowled. *There are escape pods, right? If so, I want the prisoners to go to them in case we don't make it to the bridge.*

Those are through this door. He tapped the red button on his gun.

She opened her mouth to ask him why but kept silent. If red meant dead, she'd stay with stun. *There are two aliens on the other side. How many more can this ship carry?*

He paused and gave her question some thought. *A Yithian slave ship has the capacity for fifty males. However, Yithians only have twenty males on board. One commander, one pilot, one engineer.*

And seventeen soldiers. She finished for him. *Four down, sixteen to go.*

His gaze turned far away before he focused on her. *I estimate that is accurate.*

You know how to use that, Illan. She gestured to the weapon she'd handed him.

Stun is good. I prefer something a little more...lethal.

So she'd assumed correctly. Now wasn't the time to investigate what the other buttons did. One could very well trigger self-destruct. Drawing in a deep breath and squaring her shoulders, she pressed the button beside the airlock.

As the door opened, she knelt and fired. Her shots struck true, despite the new bruising on her knee. *Damn grates,* she winced as she stood up.

Illan had fired, as well. *Two at the other door.*

She was glad he had her back since she hadn't seen the other aliens. *Focus, Quinlan. Many lives depend on me and Illan to save them, so stay attentive. If we mess this up, it could be death for us all. I doubt these aliens tolerate rebellion.*

She gestured to the cells. *How many slave compartments?*

He scanned the cells and peered through the porthole to the next compartment. *Six in total. They like to keep these ships small.*

Undetectable the smaller the incursion. She glanced behind her where the released prisoners flooded the passage; a variety of species she couldn't take the time to examine. Instead, her focus shifted to movement behind them.

"Move," she bellowed.

Cyn yelled something, and the prisoners parted.

Quin sprinted toward the back door. She was still running when she fired two shots as soon as the door opened. Both Yithians crumpled. She dived through the opened door, landing on the grate with the gun in hand. But there were no more guards. Bounding to her feet, she winced as her knee and hip ached.

Illan joined her. *You killed the engineer.*

Studying the Yithians, she picked out one in a multi-pocketed armor, smelling mechanical. As she stood there, her ribs throbbed, a hip burned, and her elbows stung, but now wasn't the time to tend to her 'injuries.'

Good, eleven to go. Grabbing the immobile sharks' guns, she tossed them to any prisoner stepping forward to catch them. Others rushed to drag the downed Yithians into the nearest cell.

"Cyn, tell them we have four more slave compartments. We'll help take out the other guards. You must free the prisoners and lead them to the escape pods."

"I don't know where the pods are." Panic widened her eyes. Another Durn pushed through the crowd and touched Cyn's forehead. She cried out and doubled over.

Quin grimaced in sympathy.

Illan gestured to the prisoners with his gun. *They understand you.*

She faced him. *What?*

I shared my known languages with you.

You did what? She scowled. *All right. When we're done here, you're going to tell me what else your two fingers did to me.*

"What are you thinking, Quin?" Macy gripped the gun barrel in her small hand, which she leaned on. She was so short, she could use the gun as a walking stick.

Quin grinned. "Illan and I are storming the bridge. You and Cyn get everyone to the pods in case we fail."

"I'm coming with you." She hefted the gun with both hands.

Quin opened her mouth, but the steely-eyed look Macy leveled on her shut her up. She knew that expression, having seen it on her brothers' faces—stubborn and determined.

"We'll clear the guards. You focus on the other prisoners," Quin said to Cyn as they breached the next compartment.

I estimate two guards in the docking bay. Illan's serenity and self-control soothed Quin. Had he picked up on her anxiety?

I would've preferred none, but two they can handle.

After clearing the remaining four compartments, she glanced over her shoulder to ensure Cyn followed, checking each cell before opening it. With a wave in farewell, Quin, Illan, and Macy headed for the bridge. Still, no alarm had sounded, as if the Yithians had no procedure in case of such an event. *Do slaves go so meekly to the slaughter? Humans don't. If we survive this, the Yithians will realize that and change their procedures accordingly.*

My blood will take care of your female, Illan said.

He must have picked up on her concern for Cyn.

She grunted at him, whatever his 'blood' meant. *Blood?* A wiggling warmth brushed across her mind like a worm. Not creepy, just weird and uncomfortable. She shivered.

My apologies for the intrusion. Your word would be brother.

She hoped she wouldn't need to endure that again. They tiptoed down the passage leading to the bridge. Illan stopped in front of something console-like. He pressed a few holographic buttons, but his frown deepened.

My apologies again. There are twenty-five Yithians on board. My estimation was inaccurate.

She grinned. *You can't anticipate everything, Illan.*

He stared at her before giving her an arrogant huff. *I can. I am Durn.* He sighed. *In this, you are accurate. The Prince of Yithia is with the remaining Yithians. He has two royal guards with him. This is an informal excursion; the records do not show his presence.*

She shrugged. Prince or not, she would stun the hell out of him. *Five left. I assume they're on the bridge? To stand in the door would make anyone a target. Can you open it from this console?*

Yes. His white eyes crinkled with a flash of humor. *You wish to lure them out. Your human mind is cunning.*

Human? I thought aliens called us Earthians?

He smiled. *I am in your mind, Quin.*

Well, if that wasn't creepy. She grimaced. "Mace," she whispered to her friend. *Friend?* She couldn't recall when last she'd had a woman friend. *I like the idea of that.* "We're going to lure them out."

Macy raised her chin, grim determination in her clenched jaw, and hefted the gun into her hands, ready to fire.

Quin settled her gaze on Illan then ahead. *Do it.*

The door slid open. He crept down the passage until the three of them could hug the metal-paneled walls.

I programmed the door to remain open.

Quin smirked. *Good thinking.*

A Yithian stepped into the passage. He was bigger than the other sharks, and his armor had a more formal look. He died anyway. Three blasts hit him in all his vulnerable spots.

That must not have gone unnoticed. The ship swayed as if the pilot attempted to toss out the ship's contents. She took off at a run, not wanting to allow the pilot the opportunity to injure the weakened and unharnessed prisoners. He might open the cargo holds and jettison them out into space.

She forward rolled into the room, firing as she rose, taking out the pilot and the two guards. That left one shark. She stood, aiming at him. This close, she pressed the barrel of the gun to his forehead. He didn't seem frightened, not that she knew whether she could read their expressions. His gaze did shift to Illan and Macy when they entered the room.

"Sweet." Macy fist-pumped the air.

Illan scanned the room and nudged the closest Yithian with his boot. *Good. Though a little reckless.*

Quin ignored him. *Can you send out a signal?* She fired the gun, not bothering to watch the Yithian collapse. "Mace, come stand guard." She rushed to drag the commander and pilot close to the other bodies while Illan typed on the console.

"Guarding," Mace sang, her smile too wide and bright for her dirty face. She shot each shark again. "Just in case." She giggled.

He hit a button. *It is ready for your recording.*

Quin stepped over the legs of the unconscious slavers and blinked at the multi-lit console, unsure where she needed to direct her voice. She addressed the image of space in front of her.

"Mayday, Mayday. We're escaped prisoners on an alien spaceship. Requiring immediate assistance."

"Will they understand English, Quin?" Macy asked.

Quin's eyes went wide, having not considered that this might be an issue.

Illan tapped the edge of the console. *Quin, the recording is still on.*

Must she do everything? She huffed. *Well then, repeat what I said in Galactic and send it.*

"Urgent aid required. We are escaped prisoners on a Yithian slave ship. Requiring immediate assistance."

At his words, she scowled. *Sounds the same.*

He smiled, his teeth flashing white in his blue face. *Of course it does since you speak Galactic. I have sent the messages on council-approved frequencies. Pirates might monitor them. It is a chance we have to take*

She chuckled. *Did you just say chance?*

His cheeks lightened to a pale blue. *Twenty-two percent estimation pirates may answer.*

Better. She shifted her attention to the console. So many lights flickered, she didn't dare touch anything. *Can you get a message to Cyn? If so, tell her we made it.*

Illan stilled, his gaze distant. *Done. I have informed my brother.*

Thank you, Illan. He hadn't touched anything, so she had to assume he could speak to his brother as he spoke in her mind.

"Greetings, Yithian slave ship. This is the Etterian Battleship *Phoenix*. Please confirm assistance is still required." A deep voice penetrated the muted hum on the bridge and in English, as well.

Excitement and the intense warmth of hope burst through Quin's chest, snatching her breath. "Uh, hello?" She winced at her timidity, blaming her shock at such a quick response and her relief that they might be friendlies. She drew in a deep breath before answering in a firmer tone. "Yes, we still need assistance. We don't know how to operate this ship. Hell, I don't even know where we are heading or what the blasted name of it is."

The man chuckled. "We are ten minutes from your navigation point, milady. We will need to breach your vessel. Is this acceptable?"

"Hell, yes." Macy squealed, then did a little dance of joy. "Breach away." She wiggled her eyebrows at Quin.

She grinned, assuming Mace's dirty mind had gone somewhere naughty. "We have prisoners at the docking bays, ready for evacuation. I can have them launch the pods if breaching is an issue, though chasing them down might not be fun."

Macy punched Quin on the shoulder. "Gorgeous aliens," she whispered.

Quin was tempted to roll her eyes, but she hadn't done that since she was a teenager.

I have let Iddan know about the Phoenix and an impending breach.

Quin gave Illan a nod of thanks, just in time to catch movement to the right of her. Macy spun and fired another yellow blast at the Yithian commander. Then she fired on each body, as a precaution.

"Was that a blaster?" another man asked from the console, his tone dripping authority.

"Yes, the Yithian commander moved," Quin said.

"Just making sure all five stay asleep." Macy rocked on her toes.

The answering chuckle from their rescuers made Quin relax her grip on the gun, just a little. Though truth be told, she was starting to feel every second of this adventure. Her knees hurt, her ribs and hips ached from when she had hit the floor numerous times, and her elbows stung as if she'd grazed them. And she had a headache forming on her left temple. She raised a hand to feel it and grimaced at the lump forming there.

"Are any of you hurt?" She glanced at Illan and Macy.

Illan shook his head, but Macy grumbled, dipping her chin.

Ice gripped Quin. "Where, Mace?"

"A sharp something cut into me." She twisted to show her shoulder.

Quin sucked in a breath. The woman had lost a lot of blood, with the back of her pajamas stained red. "Why didn't you say anything?"

Macy shrugged, then winced—the movement must have jarred her wound. "If we were successful, help would come. If we weren't, then what injury would matter in the face of death."

Quin hugged her, careful not to touch her upper back. "That's my brave girl," she whispered into her hair.

Quin, the communications channel is still active.

She slumped as exhaustion drained her, weighing down her limbs.

"Etterian? We do have a few injuries."

"These will be taken care of, milady."

"Well, that was easy," she muttered.

Chapter Six

Xan frowned at the console, startled at the words repeating through the communications room. Though he hid his reaction well, what sliced through him was the feminine voice and its soft quality.

Oyaz gripped the back of Msar's chair. "Was the distress call in Earth English?"

Xan grunted and commanded Pilot Msar, "Respond. Offer aid."

"Partially share the comm," Oyaz said.

Xan grunted. Wise. This would allow them to communicate with each other without the other ship hearing. The female's voice came through loud and clear, her words just as surprising.

Oyaz glanced at Xan and frowned. "Human females? It seems the Yithians are capturing more humans."

Xan grunted again, still reacting to the distress call. The female had an appealing voice. "How did they escape?" Another female spoke, and the uncontrolled emotion in her voice confirmed her origin. There was humor, joy, sadness, and concern; such untamed emotions could only mean human.

"Open comms fully, Msar. Who is with you?" Xan didn't bother to hide the gruffness in his voice.

"Listen, whoever you are, I'm tired and sore, surrounded by aliens I didn't know existed. I don't know what or who they are or how they came to be here. I don't want to waste time detailing who the hell is on this piece of shit. I want off, I want a coffee, and for the love of it, a damn shower."

Silence met her outburst as the warriors in the comm room blinked at the console. Her intense response to his question increased Xan's body temperature. With a frown, he adjusted his armor to address his unprecedented reaction.

"Mace," she moaned, the sound husky and...*arousing?*

Xan scowled when his malehood responded without active stimulation.

"Hello? Is this thing on? It is? Oh, then, hi, I'm Macy. I'm so happy you guys found us. I was a little worried we might go from the fire into a volcano, y'know. Quin's a little stressed right now, so please don't take her pissy attitude personally. On the bridge, it's just us and Illan. You're a Durn, right? Oh, and my other friend Cyn's at the escape pods with the released prisoners. Is that the answer you were hoping for?"

Durn? Xan's eyebrows shot up. Durns were rare, almost extinct. "How did a Durn get on a Yithian ship?" He hadn't meant to ask aloud, but he wanted an answer. He would need as much detail as possible to communicate to King Xeus.

"I fail to see—" Quin snapped.

They waited for her to continue. When nothing happened, Xan glanced at Msar.

"The comm is still active, Supreme Commander."

"Yes, it is," the female named Macy said. "They're just talking telepathically. I find it rude, to be honest."

Xan's eyebrows shot up again.

"Mace." The original female, Quin, huffed. "Illan says he'll be happy to explain it all after we're rescued." Her words confirmed Macy's revelation.

Had a Durn fused with Quin? It was something that hadn't happened in centuries. "I don't know why you don't bloody well talk to him," she chastised the Durn.

Xan shook his head in disbelief. Only a human female would dare disrespect a Durn.

"We are two minutes away," Msar said. "You should receive a visual of our approach, milady." On their display vid, the Yithian slave ship continued its course with its fusion drives burning at full pulse.

"And which button would that be?" Quin's sarcasm brought a twitch to Xan's lips. He scowled, not liking that she seemed to have such an effect on his control. "I'd prefer my people join the others in the docking bay."

Msar glanced at Xan, who nodded. "To join the others is acceptable, milady."

"You and Illan go, I'll wait here." Her command demanded obedience; the strength in her voice was appealing as much as the tonality fascinated Xan.

"Nope, sorry, can't make me," the other female Macy bird-sang. It was the strangest thing Xan had ever heard. Oyaz too, judging by his wide-eyed expression. And she had sounded pleasant and melodic.

"Dammit, Mace," Quin gritted out. "Cyn might need you," she said in a kinder tone.

"I don't know where the bay is," Macy mumbled.

"Which is why I need Illan to go with you." There was again silence, followed by a feminine grunt of frustration. "Iddan's coming to fetch you," she said. "Stubborn Durns."

Again, Xan's lips twitched. *So, there are two Durns on board? This rarity I'll have to bring to Xeus's attention.* This encounter had interrupted his mission with the parameters altered. *I was looking forward to orbiting Earth, to perhaps finding my* Dar Eth. *Now this has delayed it. I don't know for how long.*

"Tether extended." Msar had piloted the *Phoenix* to align with the slave ship matching its current speed as well. "Breach in progress." A few blaster shots reached them. Xan assumed someone was keeping the Yithians stunned.

"You have the comm, Pilot Msar." Xan stormed out of the comm room with Oyaz close on his heels.

His strides were long, determined to reach the tether in minimal time. He must be with the boarding unit. The king would expect no less. Xan strode through the forced opening with his blaster holstered to his thigh. Judging by the strength of the female he'd spoken to, he assumed he wouldn't need it. As he stepped into the bay, he scanned the prisoners. Forty or fifty various species crowded the bay.

One human female stood on a metallic crate, calming them—her Galactic fluent yet accented. *Interpreter.* She was small and filthy, judging by her scent, but she commanded the prisoners with ease. He tilted his head to listen to her voice. She wasn't the female Quin from the comm room.

Another human female hovered behind her, trying to hold up the blaster. She was tinier, her pale legs bare. Pain glazed her eyes, but she palmed the blaster and raised it. She had a wealth of deep-brown hair around her face, and her eyes twinkled with excitement when she glanced at his males. She scented a little less dirty, so not as long on board as the other female. This one must be Macy. He blocked off all scents after smelling her since the stench of the prisoners shot colors across his vision.

"Yithians?" He focused on the Unit Captain standing alongside him.

"Imprisoned, according to the Earthian female." The male stood upright, his blue gaze not wavering from Xan's.

"Double check all rooms. Data Officer Kemt will access the data cube. As soon as we have relocated the prisoners, detonate the ship." He gripped Oyaz's shoulder. "Assist these females where needed." Xan left the cargo bay and strode down the passage underneath the slave compartments to the communications room. Something powerful drove him to reach there.

Yet, as soon as he neared the comm room's open door, he couldn't force himself to enter. A slow peek inside revealed the human female standing on the opposite side. Her small hand pointed a blaster at five slumped Yithians. Her shoulders shook, the movement bouncing the weapon. His gaze traveled to the Durn seated just to the right of her, whose shoulders trembled with laughter crinkling his eyes.

"You didn't?" the Durn gasped.

She laughed, the husky quality of it ripping through Xan, forcing him to adjust his suit's temperature control again. *Alodon's balls, does my armor have to be defective today, of all days?*

"I did." She chuckled with a wince crossing her delicate features. "Unfortunately, with my pants around my ankles, and the raccoon on my face, I tripped and fell over the railing. I landed in the thick snow with my bare ass in the air and the raccoon's claws embedded in my cheeks."

The Durn was crying he was laughing so much. Xan had never seen the like. History indicated they were a methodical species, focusing on probability and statistics, never revealing emotion.

"Do you still have the scars?" The Durn smiled at her.

"I do." She scanned the Yithians again. "Hello, Etterian." She addressed Xan without glancing in his direction.

He scowled as he ventured into the room. How could she have known he was there when he hadn't made a sound? "Greetings, Lady Quin."

She flashed him a welcoming smile, which was bright on her dirty face.

"Perhaps you will share this memory with me when we are at leisure." He closed the distance between them and held his hand out for the blaster. With a shrug, she handed it over to him. That she'd managed the weapon's weight with her thin limbs impressed him. He tapped the red button before handing the blaster back to her. "Full power kills them."

"Please, show me." She twisted the weapon to focus her gaze on the buttons.

"Yellow to stun, red to kill, blue unlocks anything electronic, and white to self-destruct." He studied her, admiring the delicacy of her features and her intense focus.

She frowned at the Durn as if he'd spoken to her. Without hesitation, she smacked the red and fired on each Yithian, killing them. "We are ready when you are." She grimaced while rubbing her hip through her dirty breeches.

The Durn must have spoken to her again. She paused to glare at him, her furious expression startling Xan, though he hid his emotions well.

"Illan, they would've tossed us into their arena and laughed as we died horrifically, so no, I don't regret killing them."

"Fair enough." Illan glanced at Xan.

Data Officer Kemt burst into the room, pressed his hand to his chest in salute, then tackled the console. Within moments, he had the data cube in hand and left. Xan trailed him, assuming his usual stride. With a small sigh, he halted, expecting to find the Durn and Quin had fallen far behind. They hadn't. They'd matched his pace with ease. Spinning on his heel, he led them to the breach. His males had escorted the prisoners into the ship and to one of their barracks.

"Are we overtaxing your resources?" She met his gaze, concern furrowing her brow.

"The *Phoenix* is a battleship with ample capacity. Their needs will be seen to."

"As long as I'm close to my friends, I'm content." She asked for too little.

He frowned, studying her dirty features and the thick yellow braid down her back.

"Human females are housed separately as decreed by my prince and his lady," Xan stated.

"You have a procedure for us?" She arched a pale eyebrow, revealing her curiosity.

"It is a tale to be told at leisure." He escorted her through the breach to where one female waited, a Durn hovering nearby. Oyaz was nowhere to be seen. Xan scowled.

"Where's Mace?" Quin demanded while hugging the pale-haired female.

"She went with an…" Cyn's gaze turned distant before she refocused on Quin. "Etterian through the breach."

Quin jerked back and faced Xan, her hands on her hips.

Grumbling about her stance, Xan tapped his O.D.I. "Pilot Msar, location of Sub-Commander Oyaz?"

"In medical, Supreme Commander."

Quin paled, pursed her lips, then gestured to the breach for Xan to lead the way.

He escorted her and Lady Cyn to the luxury quarters reserved for royalty. Every second or third battleship constructed had luxury quarters included in the design. Though in truth, the prince had never used it until he'd found his human Dar Eth. In this case, he was certain Lady Oriana would approve the use of it.

"A medic will be along to assure your good health. The replicator and rehydrator are available to you. The cleansing room is through there. The detergent is in the water. Blue button to dry." With that, he exited, drawing in a deep breath once the door closed behind him. *That had been…strange.* His body still hummed with unspent energy. He shook his head, typed commands on his O.D.I. and headed to Data Officer Kemt's office.

Chapter Seven

Etterian Battleship, Phoenix
Shared Officer's Quarters

QUIN FACED THE ROOM. Open plan with four white chairs, the walls the same color as the Yithian cells, and the kitchen but a counter with no appliances. As soon as she thought that, knowledge slammed into her about the shiny rectangles embedded in the counter—a replicator and rehydrator. The décor was in royal blues with accents of gold. One door on the right led to a shower, basin, and white box that served as the toilet. On the opposite side was a doorway to a bedroom. The bed was big enough for the three of them and long enough to take her full height. That in itself was a rare occurrence for her. Her bed at home was a special requisition. It was why she hated to travel—an odd emotion for someone who was a travel photographer.

"Cyn, you get first dibs on the shower." Quin pointed at the bathroom. "You've been the longest without hygiene."

Cyn grinned. "I smell that bad?" She sniffed her armpit, then wrinkled her nose. "Yup, skunk deodorant, get your free sample." She laughed as the door closed her in.

Quin swallowed a bark of laughter, unable to endure her ribs crushing her if she coughed or chuckled. On the bridge, Illan had asked about the scar on her cheek, had said he knew the memory, but would love for her to tell the story. After the tense situation, just that walk down memory lane had her close to tears.

She sat where she stood, too tired to stand, too scared to touch anything. Her skin crawled with how dirty she was. Every muscle in her body burned, and her nostrils stung with each breath, making her eyes water. She tried not to think about it, her mind still reeling at how successful her idiotic plan had been. So many things could've gone wrong, and she'd forged ahead regardless of how this could have killed her new friends. As it was, Macy had been injured.

Worse, Quin didn't know these Etterians. Could she trust them?

She closed her eyes for a moment, then jerked awake when Cyn stepped out of the bathroom in a white bathrobe. She looked stunning. Sandy blonde hair cascaded around her, the color of pale beach sand. Her blue eyes were wide in her face, her nose tiny, lips pink and full. She wore a white terry cloth robe. Yet it draped around her five-foot-eight lithe figure like a kimono.

The door behind Quin opened. Groaning, she clambered to her feet. Everything ached, stiff, throbbing, and at one point, she thought she would never be able to bend her knees again. For someone who had put her body through so much training, she suffered more than she should have.

Macy danced around her, trailing two men with exact coloring and in full military gear. "Cyn, Quin, meet Oyaz and Rior." She waved her arms as she laughed. She too had a white robe over her pajamas.

Quin expected her to do jazz hands at any moment. Cyn had sunk into one of the white chairs, her shoulders slumping, but she wore a wide smile for Macy. *Oh, to sit.* Quin's gym leggings and tank stuck to her, the foam's gritty stickiness layered her skin, her braid lay heavy over her shoulder, and her face itched. She didn't want her backside to ruin the *white* fabric. *White's impossible to keep clean.* She settled on Oyaz and Rior's spotless uniforms.

"Miladies." Oyaz stood to the side, clasping his hands behind his back.

"Rior's a medic, and he did an amazing job on my shoulder. I'm all good, right, Rior?"

The poor man blinked at Macy then a genuine smile lit his face. "I am happy to assist. I am to attend to miladies, as well."

"Good. I'll use the shower." Macy's gaze narrowed on the bathroom before she skipped across to it.

"Is she always this...joyful?" Rior asked while he scanned Quin, hovering his arm over her. His bronze skin flickered with multi-colored holographics.

"Yes, although, I've only known her a few days." Quin swayed then straightened, tightening her muscles. Taking command of her limbs, focus, and thoughts meant she could endure all manner of discomfort...and not fall flat on her face.

He removed a black box from a pocket in his military pants, and as he held it a few inches away from her body, her exhaustion faded. The constant twang and burn of strained muscles or grazed skin also eased. Just like that, her ribs no longer hurt.

"Any residual pain I need to attend to?"

"Thanks, Rior, I feel amazing." Quin grinned, bouncing on her toes to test her healed body.

"Good." He weaved around her and approached Cyn. "Milady, may I attend to you?"

"There's nothing wrong with me a long sleep won't cure, Rior." Cyn hesitated. "Although, the Yithians did put a device in my ear. I'd be grateful if you check it out, maybe remove it?"

He scanned her anyway. Quin shook her head as she paced, waiting for Macy to finish in the shower. Oyaz watched her but said nothing.

An excited squeal came from the bathroom. Oyaz pushed off the wall, ready to storm to Macy's aid.

"The air-dryer," Cyn leaned around to meet Quin's gaze. "Blue button."

Quin fell into a pace again.

"The device cannot be removed, milady, but it cannot harm you further. I have healed any bruising its insertion caused."

Cyn paled. "Thank you anyway, Rior."

The older Etterian bowed, and with Oyaz, they left them alone.

"Aren't they hot? I'd let Rior be my sugar daddy any day." Macy strolled out in a white wrap that fell past her feet, dragging on the floor behind her. She was much shorter than the two of them, five-foot-fourish if Quin had to guess. Her figure was curvaceous, and with her brown curls swirling around her head and tumbling down her back, she was downright adorable. Her brown eyes sparkled, and she beamed. "Best damn shower, in like, ever." She flopped into a chair. "Can you believe we're on an Etterian battleship?"

"Maybe you'll find a sexy alien lover." Cyn wiggled her eyebrows. She dazed out, and her smile brightened. Iddan must've spoken to her. Her cheeks flushed before she giggled. It looked odd like Cyn had consumed a leisure drug of some sort and chatted to an imaginary friend. Quin hoped she didn't appear as deranged when Illan spoke to her.

What she wanted was to sleep for days despite being healed. Just the thought of lying on a bed eased the residual tension tightening her shoulders. Sure the ordeal was over, but their future was still in the air. A glance at her stained tank had her grimacing.

"Let me hop in the shower. Then we can organize food and clothing. That damn tree of a commander assumed we would walk around naked and starve to death." She drew in a calming breath, too emotionally drained to maintain her indignation.

"Those damn trees are gorgeous." Macy tugged Cyn out of the chair for a quick dance.

Quin frowned. All she could remember was their bronze skin and dark hair. She hadn't taken the time to focus on the details. "I didn't look. Next time I see an Etterian…"

First, she needed clothes. No way would she parade around in a robe. What if the Etterians weren't honorable? She couldn't attempt another takeover barely clothed. Leaning on the kitchen counter, she stroked the black glass, searching for the switch. It flickered to life, streaming available options. Like loading a rifle using muscle memory, her fingers flew across the surface like she'd done this a thousand times before. Her understanding of the curved letters, perhaps cuneiform, meant one thing.

She raised her face to the ceiling, then grimaced, lowering her chin. Illan wasn't God and didn't inhabit the heavens. *Illan? Can I work the rehydrator because of you?*

Of course. His arrogance curled her fingers into fists, and she thumped the glass, choosing...'Hats' in the process.

"Thanks," she muttered. *Are the Etterians taking care of you?*

We are Durn.

She gritted her teeth and focused on the 'Garments' section to save her sanity. She stabbed 'leggings' and her size. A glance to the side showed Macy spinning the holographic images of food on the rehydrator as if she played an old-school one-arm bandit at a casino. Quin grinned, tapped icons, and changed the language to English. Another tip thanks to Illan.

Macy squealed, then browsed in earnest.

One day soon, you'll explain what the hell being a Durn means. Quin brushed the created leggings aside like its appearance wasn't an amazing feat.

You know my history and that of my people.

Quin stopped herself from eye-rolling. The act was lost on Illan. *Knowing and accessing it are different things, Illan.* She huffed and chose a T-shirt in lemon yellow. As it materialized on the glass, that wiggly worm squirmed across her psyche. In a whoosh, images flicked across her mind like a movie: his life, his culture, their drive for perfection, she even understood a few of his studies. Then the terrible disease that killed his people, with just a few hundred surviving. The images and emotions flashing by were so intense, a sharp pain pierced her temple, similar to when Illan pressed his fingers to that exact spot. Overwhelming grief consumed her like a smoke cloud preceding a firestorm. His sorrow swelled like a crescendo, slamming into her, along with Iddan's shared pain and now hers. Her knees gave in, and she crumpled to the floor.

I'm so sorry, Illan. Your people. Your home. Tears flowed unheeded. Crippling grief saturated every cell until what was his became hers. She didn't know where he ended and she began. Nor could she cut off the connection.

"Quin?" Macy hugged Quin. "What's wrong?" Her voice warbled, pitching with fear. She ran her hand up and down Quin's back, trying to soothe her.

"The Durn...all gone." Quin struggled to form words, then succumbed, opening her heart and soul to let the grief flow through her.

With her fingers buried in Macy's sopping bathrobe, time slowed. Her clogged nose, rattled breathing, and mutterings dwindled into hiccups and sniffles.

"What's going on?" Cyn crouched beside them.

"I think Illan showed her something sad," Macy said as she rocked Quin with them sprawled on the cold metal floor.

Sad? Quin tightened her hold on Macy, tempted to shake her. Losing a planet wasn't sad, it was devastating. *Illan, can I show her? Is there a way?*

Silence met her request.

What the hell? Now he shuts up?

She released Macy and pulled back, nudging her head at the chairs.

Macy jumped up and tried to help Quin. She shook her head as she staggered to her feet, using the counter as leverage.

Cyn crowded her, cupping Quin's elbows. No way could the petite blonde stop Quin from hitting the floor. "You okay?" Her eyes widened, and she pursed her lips, concern in her gentle tone.

Quin offered a weak smile and grabbed her new clothing, clutching them to her chest. "I'm good."

"You sure?"

"Cyn, I'm fine." Quin huffed. "You?"

"Starving. So how do we order food on this ship?" Her gaze turned distant. She frowned, then faced the glass. "It does what?" She tapped the rehydrator and gasped.

Quin grinned.

"What the hell?" Cyn slid her fingers across the glass, spinning the selection. "Damn." She whistled. "They even have coffee. Pizza. Hamburgers. Fries. Death by chocolate ice cream? Quick, pinch me."

"I'd like a bottle of water."

Cyn requested three. "Pepperoni pizza, extra cheese." She ordered three of those too. With the food replicated and the aromas filling the room, she carried the feast to the table in the middle of the white chairs.

Hunger gurgled Quin's stomach, but instead of scooping a slice of pizza, she grabbed a bottle and downed it. Water had never tasted this sweet. She leaned against the bathroom's wall, slapping the new clothes on her thigh while Cyn collapsed into one of the chairs.

Macy snatched a slice of pizza. "Go, shower, Quin."

"I'll tackle the replicator and get Mace and me some clothes." Cyn licked a finger.

Quin rushed into the bathroom and peeled off her clothing the moment the door swished closed. She stepped into the shower, stroking the white paneled walls looking for a tap or a button. The spray switched on and at a lovely temperature too. She washed, frowning at having to rub her body without soap, wincing as she touched certain spots. She glanced down and grimaced at the faded scratches and yellow-green bruises. *Yup, sexy, Quin, as usual*. She snorted. *Just a normal day for me then.* She'd had cracked ribs for sure, a bruised knee, a grazed hip, bleeding elbows, and a nice egg on her forehead. All healed with a black box?

Once she'd wiped every accessible inch of her body, making sure that horrible foam was gone, she pressed the blue button and fell into an attack stance when wind blasted her from all angles. She giggled, now seeing why Mace had yelped. With a shake of her head, she raised her arms and waited for the air-dryer to do its thing. But when she grabbed her leggings and tank, she scowled. She'd forgotten underwear. Right, bathrobe it would have to be. The gray button revealed a compartment that held a stack of robes. As soon as she pulled one on, it slithered and tightened around her. She broke out in goosebumps. *Well, that was the true meaning of one size fits all.* Why hadn't Macy's conformed to her shape? Maybe she was too small?

Quin left the bathroom and eased her body into the chair, smiling as it adjusted to cup her backside for maximum comfort. She let herself relax at the realization the nightmarish ordeal was over. While tearing off a slice of pizza, she smiled at her friends. That was the best part, she had friends. It almost made the kidnapping and escape worth it.

They blinked at her.

"What?" Quin asked around a bite of pizza.

"You have beautiful eyes," Macy said, her pizza slice halfway to her mouth.

"I've never seen anything like it," Cyn said.

Quin blushed and lowered her gaze. *Shit, I forgot about my eyes.* "It's just heterochromia iridum, one eye's gray, the other hazel."

"That's so freakin' awesome." Macy grabbed Quin's pizza-filled hand as she bounced in her seat.

"They're stunning." Cyn winked and took pity on Quin by suggesting to Macy that they 'figure' out how the replicator worked.

Quin flashed her a grateful smile. The heat on her cheeks subsided while she watched Macy squeal over the clothing options. Their happiness and well-being made this day Quin's best ever.

Chapter Eight

"It is complete, Supreme Commander. The archival vid is set to start from the first strike the females made against the Yithians."

Xan gestured to Data Officer Kemt to proceed. The data recovery room was smallish, so the presence of three Etterian males made it restrictive. But as soon as the image appeared of Lady Quin leaping and punching the Yithian in both eyes simultaneously, his focus was unwavering.

"Alodon's balls, I've never seen such an attack." Oyaz's awe mirrored Xan's with each subsequent reveal.

Her fusing with the Durn, her charging down the passage to dive through the air-door... *She tackled this as a true warrior.* Xan grumbled. *I couldn't have planned a better escape.*

"Not good," Oyaz said when the vid switched to black.

"The human females I have met do not possess such skills. She is well trained," Xan said with grudging respect.

"She cannot be a spy." Oyaz shook his head at such a possibility. "That is illogical."

"I agree," Xan frowned, displeased with this conundrum. "Too many factors would have to be in place for this to be a ruse."

"The humans would have to contact the Yithians to organize this," Oyaz said.

"An impossibility in truth," Xan said. "The Yithians would also not have allowed the destruction of their ship without extensive gains. I do not see any in the findings so far."

"Neither are the Yithians aware of our routes, so her rescue by an Etterian ship was not guaranteed," Oyaz said.

"And how would the Durns have played a part? We do not know where and when the Yithians captured them. The data cube does not have those specifics," Kemt said.

"Yet they were, and one chose to fuse with a human female." Xan scowled, a spike of pain striking his temple. Something about this bothered him, as if taking this rescue at face value seemed too simple.

"Perhaps it was to communicate? Judging by the timing of the mind fuse, Lady Warrior needed to instruct and inform," Kemt said.

Lady Warrior? I like the sound of that. Xan remembered the vid showing that specific interaction with the Durn. At how Lady Quin had whimpered, the procedure had looked painful, and something within him had rebelled at the female harmed.

Kemt blinked at him, expectant.

"It is as we suspected." Xan squared his shoulders. "Good work, Kemt."

"Supreme Commander, one more thing." Kemt halted their departure.

Xan paused. Even though Kemt was new to his unit, he'd shown his insightfulness both in the rescuing of Lady Ava and in this situation.

"Prince Yada was on that ship."

Xan scowled, not liking this development. His mind flashed to the richly-adorned Yithian she'd blasted. The kill shot *had* come from Quin. If Yithia discovered this, their retribution would be swift and extreme. "Is Yithia aware?"

"No, Supreme Commander. All transmissions leaving the ship prior to the seizure were standard comms, indicating nothing defective with the ship, its crew, or its cargo."

"Having destroyed it was the best recourse." Xan exhaled a long breath.

"The Yithians will have a mystery on their hands and nothing else." Oyaz offered a small smile.

Xan strode down the grated passage to where they housed the Durn blood-bonds in one of his unallocated officer's quarters, suitable for such a rare find. The door chimed his request to enter, and while they waited, Xan rocked on his heels, unable to rein in an unprecedented flush of energy.

"Supreme Commander, do enter," a Durn blood-bond called out when the door slid open. He indicated for Xan and Oyaz to make themselves comfortable.

They did, though Xan chose to sit on the edge of the comfy with his elbows on his bent knees.

"I know why you have come, Supreme Commander," said the older blood-bond. He faced Xan, his white eyes startling against his midnight-blue skin. "You wish to understand the human known as Quinlan Walsh? Whether she is a spy?"

Xan's scowl deepened, as he chastised himself for not expecting the unexpected.

The Durn laughed.

"I thought Durns do not have a sense of humor?" Oyaz asked, buying Xan a little time to process his thoughts.

Xan appreciated that about him, which was why he made such a good sub-commander and his closest battle-bond. The many battles they had fought together had forged a bond stronger than those he had with his blood-bonds.

"It is something we have taught ourselves," the other Durn said. "I am Iddan il Tur-Lekbez, and this is my older blood-bond, Illan. He fused with Quin and I with Cyndi Stanford, the human female with the interpreter."

"I am Supreme Commander Xan et Assan, and this is Sub-Commander Oyaz et Boaz. Why did you fuse with Lady Cyndi? She had the interpreter so to communicate wasn't the motive."

"I recognized something in her that I had thought never to find, a kindred soul."

Illan leveled his gaze on Xan. "Your fascination with Quin is appropriate, Supreme Commander. She led the capture of the Yithian slave ship. By the time Cyn released us, Quin had stunned four guards. For this reason, it was safe to fuse with her. It was also essential. We needed to communicate."

"You have been in her mind, is there anything that might indicate deviousness on her part, or required vigilance on ours?" Xan didn't want this male to betray any confidences, merely to assuage the strange prickliness he was experiencing. It took his battle-honed control to not rub his forearms.

"She is no danger to the Etterians. Her actions, though precise, efficient, and effective, stemmed out of desperation. I cannot fault her strategic analysis in crisis, nor her ability to be cunning and ingenious. I do, however, have an issue with her recklessness."

"The dive into the comm room," Xan said.

Illan arched his white eyebrows. "Yes. Using the opened door to lure the Yithians out was her strategic plan. But after having killed only one, she stormed the room." He held up his hand in case Xan wished to speak. "I was in her mind. She didn't do it for vainglory. Her concern was for the passengers." He chuckled. "I have to admit, entering the comm room and seeing her standing there, one hand holding the blaster to the prince's forehead...what a pleasure."

"That *was* a good image." Oyaz grinned, surprising a lip twitch from Xan.

"She is who she says she is," Xan said matter-of-factly. *Durns do not deceive.* "For how long will you remain fused?" he asked both Durns.

"It is permanent, Supreme Commander. We have lost the skill to break such a connection once it has formed."

"Do you fuse often?" Oyaz leaned forward, clasping his hands between his knees.

"No, it is a violation of privacy and exhausting to shield one's thoughts continuously," Iddan said with a neutral expression. "Cyndi has yet to learn the skill."

"Quin, as well. These females are entertaining. I cannot remember when last I enjoyed such intense, fluctuating emotions."

"Yes, when she mourned for our people, Illan the depth of her sorrow crossed our connection. It was...overwhelming. Grief to such a degree is an emotion I cannot endure."

"She...?" Xan was almost afraid to ask.

"Quin asked about our people. I showed her. The intensity of her grief was unparalleled. I can assure you, Supreme Commander, it is an emotion I do not wish to experience again."

"I have not shown this to Cyn. She is a far gentler creature. Such horror would harm her." The Durn blood-bonds' gazes glazed over as if they communicated with each other.

"Will that be all, Supreme Commander?" Iddan glanced at Xan.

"Of course, we would be pleased to answer any further concerns you may have," Illan said, his stoicism irritating.

Xan stood and left with Oyaz close on his heels. He drew to a halt once the door closed behind them.

"Alodon's balls, Oyaz. How can a female be that skilled? They are so tiny, so soft, their physiology easily damaged." He held his wrist to his lips. "Medic Rior, have you seen to the human females?"

"Yes, Supreme Commander."

Good. Maybe Rior's findings would reveal what bothered Xan. "What is your location?"

"Medical, Supreme Commander."

Xan hurried down the passage toward medical situated in the common. Etterian males tended to cause more injuries when sparring. The placement of medical in the common was, therefore, an expedient one.

"What concerns you, Xan?" Oyaz omitting his title told him how disturbed he was at Xan's anxious behavior.

"I cannot clarify it. Irritability or an inability to find calm? I may require your presence when we comm the king."

Oyaz clenched his jaw but followed him. They entered the common, ignoring the males in the other spaces—eating, reading, exercising, or sparring on the mat in the center of the room. He ignored the mixture of other species from the prisoners, as well, despite the strangeness of it.

"Report," Xan said to Medic Rior.

"Dehydration and malnutrition in the ladies Macera and Cyndi. I repaired Lady Cyndi's ear. The interpreter cannot be removed; her ear has merged with it." Rior flicked his fingers across his O.D.I. An image appeared on his display vid, showing a scan of Lady Cyndi's skull. "The language section of her brain remains healthy, though a little larger than the same section in ladies Macera and Quinlan. It is as per Medic Der's findings with Lady Ava. I could attempt the use of the nano-meds but if the interpreter is not harming her and there is no signal transmitting from it..."

He gestured to a piece of twisted metal the size of Xan's small finger. "Lady Macera had a serious wound on her shoulder with this metal embedded. I removed it and repaired the wound with synthetic skin, as is protocol."

The display vid altered to show various images of the bruising on Quin's body, all of them self-inflicted. Xan's breath stilled at the sight of her pale skin marred with blues and purples. His irritability increased a level, twitching his fingers. Fury pulsed along his veins, driving him to seek retribution. Had they not destroyed the Yithian ship, he would demand they do so now.

"Lady Quinlan had extensive bruising on her hips, knees, ribs, arms, and elbows, with minor lacerations on her elbows. She had a swelling on her temple. There is no impaired vision or extensive damage. The cleanser is set to meet their needs, with anesthetic for the three ladies for one day only."

"Thank you, Medic Rior." With a frustrated sigh, Xan ran his hand over his face. "It is time I spoke to Lady Quinlan. Anything to have this irritation cease."

"May I suggest the viewing deck?" Oyaz said.

"A more casual environment; she will not feel I am interrogating her," Xan offered a weak smile—it was all he could muster. "Good suggestion, Oyaz. My thanks."

"You *do* seem to be a little...unfocused, Xan." He nudged his head in the direction of Lady Quinlan's quarters. "I'll escort her to you. Perhaps a few minutes to gather your thoughts would quiet your unease."

"You are a good sub-commander, Oyaz."

"Of course I am," He strolled away, his arrogant response calling forth a chuckle.

Xan strode to the viewing deck, finding the seating carved into the bulkhead. It was the only area that allowed display vids to reflect the passing stars. Windows on a spacecraft were a weakness. The compromise of an area with large display vids to replicate any environment had appeased the royal bonds. He had to admit; it was beautiful. It wasn't something he often took the time to admire, though.

Closing his eyes, he focused on his breathing despite his senses writhing like he was on the edge of a battlefield teeming with gika. His reactions were too intense and unexpected for such a situation. Admiration for Lady Quin's skillset was a given, but this oversensitivity gritted his teeth. He couldn't control himself, his heartbeat, his riotous emotions.

With a long exhale, he opened his eyes and studied the passing stars and planets. Time was endless, and from this, he drew a level of peace. He only had to be patient.

CHAPTER NINE

Etterian Battleship, Phoenix
The Viewing Deck

QUIN GREETED THE ETTERIAN man from earlier who stepped through their door. She took the time to study him since Macy had raved about these men. He was tall, dark, and handsome, giving Wyatt a run for his money. His chest was massive, carved and emphasized by his black sleeveless chest armor that looked police-issued. His bare arms were bulky, even his hands were large, his fingers long. His chest tapered into a tight waist with his narrow hips encased in military, cargo pants. His huge, thick-soled biker-like boots were military and black. *Damn.* Quin understood Macy's attraction. *Even Garrett doesn't look this good.*

"Lady Quinlan, I am Sub-Commander Oyaz. Allow me to escort you to Supreme Commander Xan." His voice was deep, sexy

Quin flashed a smile at Macy and Cyn, wriggling her eyebrows. "Certainly, Sub-Commander. I assume this is an interrogation of sorts?" She gestured for him to lead the way, and he did so. Her eyebrows shot up at the sight of his fine backside encased by the thick black fabric. *Nice.*

"This is not an interrogation. The supreme commander has a few questions," Oyaz said, striding in front of her.

She kept pace with ease. "Does he have questions for Macy and Cyn? If so, he *will* ask me. I don't want them traumatized any further."

Oyaz flashed her a look, humor sparking his eyes, but he said no more.

Entering the viewing deck, Quin strode toward the supreme commander standing alone. She slowed her approach, taking the time to study him, as she'd promised the girls. Her breath hitched at the sight of this unyielding man who waited for her. He was tall. She'd estimate six-feet-five, maybe six? Taller than Oyaz and dressed in the same armor, she wondered what marked him as the superior officer. He'd crossed his bare, muscled arms behind him and spread his long legs in a universal military stance. Everything about his posture said strength and authority. She lingered on the curve of his backside as it flowed into his thick thighs to his booted and large feet.

Her heart fluttered. *Can I call a man's ass delicious?* She didn't care whether she could, to her it was. His chest was wide, barreled and emphasized by his black military armor. With his bronzed skin, his muscles looked like carved granite. His strong arms promised to hold her close, keep her safe and carry her weight if needed. His broad shoulders would be too thick for her fingers to curl over. His collarbone flowed along the curve of his shoulders. His thick neck led her gaze to a solid jaw, firm and drawn tight as if the weight of the world was his to carry. He was in excellent shape, his chest was better than Garrett's, his shoulders wider than Wyatt's, proportionally speaking.

His hands had wide palms and long fingers; capable looking. *Holy shit, now this is a fine specimen.*

Her heart rate increased, and her palms dampened. Excited and nervous, she struggled with an unexpected wash of shyness, as well. Her fingers twitched with a rush of heat and adrenaline.

He faced her, and for a moment, she caught his features—defined edges, a square jawline, and a wide forehead. A long, narrow nose softened his angles with his wide oversized bottom lip begging her to nibble on it. Dark-blue round eyes under ebony slashing eyebrows palpitated her heart. *Tall, dark, and stunningly handsome.*

He dropped to a knee with one hand slamming down on the floor to stop a total descent. She gasped, lunging forward.

On his knee, he gripped the bulkhead. His knuckles whitened with the force he used. Pain tensed his posture, trembling his massive body. Instead of assisting him as her heart demanded, she bolted down the passage. Her slippered feet pounded the metal flooring. She accosted the first man she saw.

"Get me Oyaz, now," she said.

His eyebrows arched and, with hesitation, he punched into that glowing thing on his arm. Cybernetics wasn't new tech since her guardians had often discussed upgrades. A few had considered something similar to the holographic images flittering above the man's wrist.

"He is on his way, milady."

"Thank you." She paced the corridor, torn between returning to the supreme commander or waiting for Oyaz. If something happened to their commander, would these aliens blame her? She pursed her lips. It was wiser to wait here. Slicing glances between the door of the viewing deck and the end of the passage, she gritted her teeth. Oyaz was taking his sweet time. The man she'd detained had abandoned her. No doubt she'd offended him in some way. Damn, she hoped not.

"What is it?" Oyaz jogged toward her.

"It's your commander. He's kneeling and in pain." She grabbed Oyaz's forearm and tugged him toward the deck.

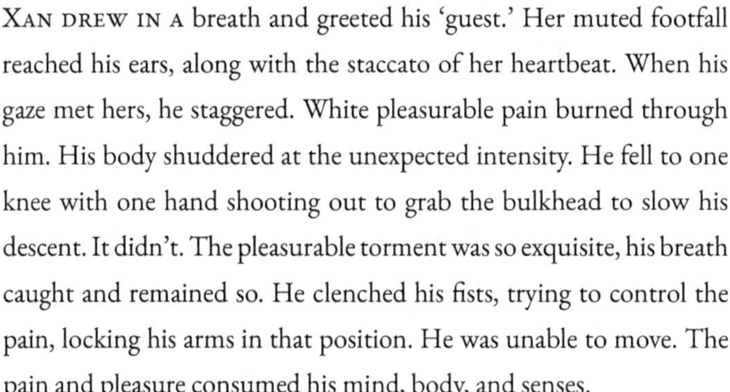

XAN DREW IN A breath and greeted his 'guest.' Her muted footfall reached his ears, along with the staccato of her heartbeat. When his gaze met hers, he staggered. White pleasurable pain burned through him. His body shuddered at the unexpected intensity. He fell to one knee with one hand shooting out to grab the bulkhead to slow his descent. It didn't. The pleasurable torment was so exquisite, his breath caught and remained so. He clenched his fists, trying to control the pain, locking his arms in that position. He was unable to move. The pain and pleasure consumed his mind, body, and senses.

He drew in ragged breaths, calling forth a level of control yet untested only to inhale her scent—sweet, rich, intoxicating. He moaned, shuddering in reaction.

A vision of her formed like a memory. Water flowed over her wet hair, clinging to her eyelashes as he held her against the cleansing room wall. She'd hooked her legs around his waist as he feasted on her breathtaking breasts. They were pliant against his lips, even better than her backside filling his hand. She made the most amazing gasps and whimpers as he teased her and tormented himself. In the vision, his eyes closed against the sensations rolling through him with a tingling heated pleasure stroking his skin. He could *feel* the strength of her thighs, her softness, the heat of her skin, the water flowing over their entwined bodies. He could *taste* the sweetness of her nipple.

"Xan." Oyaz's voice, as if from a great distance.

Xan grumbled something, not quite ready to leave the vision, to cease *experiencing* her.

"Is he all right?"

He groaned. Her melodic voice rubbed over his hypersensitive nerves, tightened his nipples, and made him harder than the mined rock in the Fuyra caves.

"I am well," he growled. With a deep breath, inhaling her scent in the process, he forced his fingers to splay out before pushing off the bulkhead to rise. His limbs were weak and trembled, his other hand still clenched into a fist to hold back the sweet agony.

Oyaz mumbled about summoning a medic, but at least he wasn't touching Xan anymore. For that, he was grateful. He wanted to strip until *nothing* touched his skin. He opened his eyes and leveled them on his battle-bond.

"Alodon's balls," Oyaz whispered.

Xan closed his eyes again, knowing what stunned Oyaz. The dark-blue eyes of an Etterian male reverted to ice-blue when he met his Dar Eth.

And Quin was his. His. The joy was indescribable and set his chest on fire with its intensity.

"Should I fetch Rior?" She studied Xan, running her gaze over him.

The ache in his chest increased at her concern. He drew in another deep breath before facing her. He groaned again. *She is exquisite. Why did I not see her so when we first met? Had her filth hidden her so well from me?*

His gaze raked over her, taking in the dark-blue breeches she wore that clung to every muscled curve of her. She had thighs he could grab hold of, and the vision of said thighs, naked and contoured, flashed in his mind. Her tight yellow tunic emphasized her flat stomach and the swell of her breasts. Her nipples pebbled under his admiring gaze, and the sweet fruity scent of her arousal reached him.

"He is well, milady." Oyaz grinned and, with a final glance, left them alone.

Xan stepped toward her, closing the distance between them. She fidgeted under his stare, then buried her hands in the front pockets of her breeches, dragging them down to expose a little of her bare stomach. He growled, his focus snagged by the sway and curl of her yellow-gold hair. His gaze traveled her face, noting her determined chin, pointy and small, the high cheekbones, parted lips, pert nose, and... *Alodon's balls, her eyes.*

"Your eyes are beautiful." She stole his words from him.

"So are yours." He peered into one gray and one pale green. Individually they were pretty, combined, they were... "Mesmerizing."

A perske-colored blush spread across her cheeks and down her throat. He wanted to follow its path with his lips and tongue but had to settle for his gaze tracing the color to linger on a brown dot on her collarbone.

"Shall we begin the interrogation?" She was a little breathless—the rapid rise and fall of her chest confirmed she was aware of the attraction between them.

"This is not an interrogation. I wanted to know your history, blood-bonds, how the Yithians abducted you." He inhaled her scent, struggling to hold onto it and needing to memorize it.

"Is that all? How about a dental exam?" she teased, her eyes crinkling with humor as she peeked at him.

He smiled in return, liking this warmer side of her. The curl of his lips felt...unnatural. "Medic Rior has seen to that." He attempted to rein in his joy and just managed to.

"Let's get this over with." She sat, pressing a hand against the vid as if to catch a passing star.

His focus rested on her fingers, their short nails, wishing she touched him instead. His breath hitched at that sharp need.

"I grew up with three brothers and their four male friends. From an early age, I had to learn to protect myself from their endless pranks. They didn't see me as a girl until I grew these." She indicated her breasts with a dismissive flick of a wrist.

He took a second to admire them before settling on her face again. *She had an issue with her breasts. As do I. I'm not nuzzling them.* For a moment, he closed his eyes to gain a little of his legendary control.

"Not that it stopped them from training me. They protected me—chased away boys and later men. Well, to be honest, my height did that too, among other things."

"Your height?" He frowned. Her height was perfect, although shorter than an Etterian female's average height. He longed to gather her in his arms, to press her daintiness against him.

She rose to show him her height. He stood, as well, looking *down* at her. A glorious smile spread across her face, the beauty of it affecting the steady rhythm of his heart. He scowled and adjusted his suit, appreciating its assistance.

She gestured to all of him, her breasts bouncing in her enthusiasm, drawing his gaze with ease. "Men who are taller than me are rare," she said by way of explanation. "I think my height intimidates them."

"And *my* height makes you joyful?" He frowned again.

"It's refreshing to be among men taller than me." She sat, still smiling, forcing him to resume his seat too, though he was careful to adjust his uniform to accommodate his arousal.

"What other things?" he asked. "Your words indicated your height was one of many deterrents."

"Oh, yes...my strength, my seven guardians, my ability to kill. Many things." Her tense shoulders said how she felt even when she delivered her words in a casual manner.

"If a male wants you, none of these should matter," he said with an intensity he didn't understand. It pleased him that no male had claimed her. The thought of a male touching her shot red heat through him, blurring the edges of his vision. He drew in a slow, calming breath, reminding himself she was his now.

"And if I get angry and accidentally break his arm? No man wants to worry about that on top of everything else."

"You could not harm me." He studied her thin yet toned arms. She ran her gaze over him, touching his face and torso. What she thought, she didn't reveal.

"No, I don't think I could hurt you. Are all Etterians like you?" With a twirl of her finger, she gestured to the *Phoenix*.

"Yes." He waited, curious as to how she might respond.

Her mouth parted. "All muscled and battle-honed?" Her eyes widened in delight.

He grumbled and shifted in his seat, attempting to alleviate the pressure and heat building in his loins. "We train our whole lives to protect Etteria, our females, and our honor." His chest swelled. She was his to protect, please, and care for.

"My guardians made sure I could fight and defend myself so, in a way, I trained my whole life too. They're in the military, you see." She dipped her chin. Her unbound hair fell over a shoulder to brush her forearm like coils of molten gold. "Every time one of them comes home, they teach me something new." And she'd hated that, revealing her unhappiness in her 'casual' shrug. "Combat with or without a hand weapon, sniper skills, war games, endurance training, survival skills..." She ticked off against her fingers but froze when she realized he stared at her hands. She formed a fist. In the vision, she'd gripped his biceps with her hands.

"Are your guardians your only blood-bonds?" He dragged his gaze to her eyes and fought the sigh that vibrated up his throat.

"If by blood-bonds you mean family, then I only have the three brothers. Mom and Dad died when I was fourteen, but by then, Lucas was old enough to become my legal guardian. My four other guardians are like blood-bonds. I'm their sister, in a way."

She bit her lip as she fell silent. The tiny white teeth pressing the soft hahyt petal of her lip tempted him more than was logical. Her breathing altered, and she dropped her gaze. The change in her demeanor alarmed Xan. Humans were an emotional and unpredictable species.

"Will I ever see them again?" At her whisper, he lunged before he knew he was going to. He sat behind her, slipped his arms around her waist, and pulled her against his chest, rumbling at how good it was to hold her.

"Yes, you will see them again." He nuzzled her hair, breathing in her scent. "I need to inform my king, but I anticipate that each prisoner will return to their world, technology willing." He shivered at the negligent weight of her in his arms. The experience *felt*...right. The way she rested against him with her body relaxed was exquisite as if she trusted him not to harm her.

"Technology willing?" The silky tips of her fingers brushing along his forearm drew the focus of his thoughts and senses. It was a long moment before he realized she'd asked him a question.

"The Global Council has forbidden all interference with low to mid-grade civilizations. If the Yithians have abducted people from a planet unaware that alien life exists, we cannot risk returning them to their homes."

"Returning to Earth isn't necessary, but I do need to let them know not to worry." She twisted within his arms to glance at him, bringing her mouth close to his.

A tremor rippled through him as he stared at her parted lips, fighting the temptation. *If she'd been Etterian, they would have consummated their pairing by now.*

"That's possible, right?" She chewed on her bottom lip again.

He zeroed in on her dented flesh, enticing him to nibble there.

She frowned. "To find a place for me that's not on Earth?"

"You do not want to return home?" He raised his gaze to meet hers, only to experience the sensation of falling, drowning in their captivating depths. He tightened his arms, her softness filling his hands, pressing against his chest, surrounding him with her scent.

"To a life spent waiting for my brothers to visit? No, thank you." She tugged on his forearms, asking him to release her. He didn't budge. "I'm not sad anymore. You can release me."

"I do not want to." He buried his face into her cool curls and drew in a deep breath, again. There was something addictive about her scent.

"That's very supreme commander of you to say," she teased.

He chuckled, joy engulfing him. Only battle lust called forth mirth from him, which was why Oyaz insisted on sparring when he was irritable. Now, a lust, a yearning of a different kind summoned his sense of humor.

"How in Alodon's hell were they able to abduct you?" He attempted to distract her, not wanting her to pull away from him. *I am incapable of releasing her. Just a few more minutes.* Then he would have the strength to let her go.

"I'd just finished my kickboxing class later than usual. I was restless and dissatisfied, which is why I put in extra time. Training to make my body so tired I'd be able to sleep." She drew in a breath before continuing, "I'd just left the building, paused to admire the stars, and saw only darkness seconds later. They must have stunned me."

"Worst mistake they ever made." He tightened his arms, gathering her closer to his chest. When her spine stiffened, he glanced at her. Her dazed expression confirmed Illan spoke to her. Uncontrollable anger raged through him, bright, hot, inciting. *My Dar Eth is mine and mine alone. The* Ethera *cannot expect me to share her.* He struggled with this unknown, forceful, and unpleasant emotion.

But she'd taken to caressing his arm again; her fingertips made the anger ebb away. It was but a respite. He'd have to deal with his reaction since she was his as she was Illan's.

"Tell me about yourself, Xan," she said into the comfortable silence that had descended.

He glanced at her. She'd closed her eyes. The dark circles under them showed her exhaustion. He grumbled at his selfishness. *My Dar Eth comes first, always.* He gathered her body to his, his arm around her back and under her knees. In one smooth motion, he stood, taking her with him. She didn't complain or chastise him. Instead, she snuggled against him trustingly.

Alodon's balls, it is incredible to hold her such.

He nuzzled her hair again, carrying her with ease to her quarters. His males cast curious glances, but he ignored them. His long legs made short work of the distance and soon found himself outside her quarters, awaiting a response to his entrance request.

"Did something happen?" Cyn's gaze settled on Quin draped across his arms, her trust beautiful to him.

He tightened his arms, not looking forward to releasing her. "Be at ease, milady. Quin but sleeps."

Cyn gaped. "She fell asleep in your arms?"

He strode forward, as if to say, 'step aside.' She did, and he rushed through, lowering his Dar Eth onto the bed. He took a moment to draw a blanket over her and watched as she snuggled under it.

A footstep behind him snagged his attention. *How long have I been staring?* Judging by the females' smiles, a while.

"My apologies, miladies." He left their quarters, ignoring his heated face. Dazed at the change in his life, he marched to his quarters for a moment alone. Reclining on his bed, he relived each second since meeting her—from the moment her voice had rasped across the comm, demanding a rescue, to her sprawled in bed, her hair flowing over the pillow like a molten wave. He was unable to sleep for a different reason this time...exhilaration.

Chapter Ten

IN HER QUARTERS, WITH a distracted Illan, Quin dragged her thoughts from the interrogation. What an odd experience. So many strange things occurred, and she wasn't sure how she felt about them. She'd admit she had reacted like a blushing virgin when she'd seen him...the supreme commander. Just thinking of his title made her grin. Someone who outranked Lucas and her guardians would be more than acceptable. She snorted. What, now she was planning on finding herself an alien lover? Mace must be rubbing off on her.

But to be fair... His broad shoulders, those thick arms, tree trunk thighs, and his barrel chest? He spoke of his honor with such conviction and in a deep raspy voice. Quin was spellbound, gawking at him like a debutant. The sting of embarrassment lingered. His intense gaze had locked onto hers, pleading with her to understand. In a way, she did. He protected what was his and their way of life. But he had continued to watch her with his beautiful ice-blue eyes hooded, his expression intense. It had made her squirm as if butterflies infested her stomach. With his forceful gaze, he had admired her. He seemed interested in her and not at all intimidated by her abilities. It was a unique situation. Liking the look of him made it harder for her to focus, to not stare at the most beautiful man she'd ever seen.

She struggled to stay in the moment and listen to Illan's groans of appreciation. The urge to overanalyze the short afternoon spent with Xan was overwhelming and embarrassing at the same time. She had more control than this.

She melted into the comfy as she had in his arms. The heat of him at her back, the sheer size of his chest as he cocooned her? She'd been right. He felt safe, strong, and he smelled like no cologne she'd ever come across. She could bottle it and make a fortune, but then again, she didn't want to share him, which was a silly compulsion. She'd just met the man. She had no claim over him. But dammit, she'd never met a man she desired this much and this quickly either. To say he knocked her socks off was an understatement. His embrace was like Garrett's, although Garrett hadn't inspired all these other emotions that Xan called forth.

She recalled Illan talking to her and how Xan's hold had stiffened. As an Etterian, could he sense telepathy? Her heart whispered he was jealous, but she huffed. Her mind argued he couldn't know Illan had spoken to her, nor would he care either way. She scowled, hating how right her mind often was.

And the conversation had been nothing but a check-in to make sure she was fine. Like she wasn't on a battleship surrounded by warriors? Still, it was sweet despite being a little smothering. Now she was stuck with a man in her head, knowing her deepest secrets and desires. She should be pissed, but under the circumstances, what Illan had done, what he had sacrificed had made the take-over possible.

Quin, are you well?

Oh, yes, she was more than well. Healed, fed, and being held by a gorgeous man? *Getting to know the supreme commander.*

She wondered how she'd found herself held in one man's arms while talking to another. Although, given a choice, she'd take Xan's arms above Illan's conversational skills any day. The Durn chuckled, and she winced, having forgotten she would never be alone with her thoughts again.

No offense, Illan, but I'm enjoying being in his arms.

Warmth crossed their link. *I can feel that. I will visit tomorrow. Sleep well, Quin.*

With that, Illan was gone judging by the silence of their connection. She wished she knew how to do that. And when he'd said, 'sleep well,' he hadn't meant right there and then. Fresh heat stained her cheeks. She'd fallen asleep on the supreme commander. Oh, will the mortification never end?

Illan's moan brought her back to the conversation.

"Okay, so I speak and understand Galactic, read it too. What else?" She smirked.

He sat in a comfy, sampling his first hot chocolate. She wasn't sure whether his paler-than-usual skin tone was something of concern. Him not spasming on the floor was a good sign.

"Languages, history, and knowledge of other species, but also the ability to telepathically communicate," he mumbled between sips. "Chocolate...remarkable."

"That's it? I endure excruciating pain for that?"

"Excruciating?" His white brows arched over his pale eyes.

"Just checking if you're paying attention," she teased as she shifted in the comfy that hugged her as snugly as Xan had. "What's your plan now that you're free?"

"A ninety-eight percent estimation Iddan and I will spend a great deal of time in Issneen, Etteria's Royal City." He shrugged, more relaxed than his usual tense self.

"I don't know what I'll be doing. Xan says I don't have to return to Earth, but I don't want to be a burden either. Have any ideas what I can do?"

Illan had a full understanding of what she did as a profession. In a way, his mental intrusion was comfortable like a best friend or sister. He knew everything about her, and there was nothing she could do or say that would surprise him.

"Travel the universe and photograph it?" he said.

"Yes, I could...but how expensive are spaceships? I don't suppose there's a tourist tour ship?" She pictured a spaceship looking like an ancient, bright-red, double-decker bus from Earth's history.

"No, not much tourism happens between planets, but there are exploration cruisers and transport junkets. You would, however, have to travel to the places on their roster." He jumped up to dispose of his empty cup and order another hot chocolate.

She considered warning him about the effects of too much sugar, then dismissed her concerns. Like a child, he would have to learn the hard way, and besides, he was in her mind. Any warning was a given.

"The universe is not a safe place. Some planets are not hospitable. Some of the inhabitants, humanoid or beasts, would kill you before you step onto their soil." He settled into his comfy again, cupping the hot chocolate in his long-fingered hands. "Also, you would need to remember the technology-willing clause of the Global Council when dealing with any inhabited planet. It is fortunate you now have knowledge of the planets, their location within the systems, their environments, dangers, and cultures."

"I do? Should I take your word for it?" She snorted. So far, all he'd helped her with was the mastering of the replicator and rehydrator. Great knowledge to have in the vastness of space.

"What is a sogair?" He raised the cup to his lips and took a reverent sip.

How the hell would she know what—? *Sogair.* Images and information flashed in her mind, and she answered without thought. "A sogair is a dirty blood-red panther-like creature with sharp claws, razor-sharp teeth, and a supernatural sense of smell. It is a predator with extreme speed, determination, and a focus that only death can sever. Long-range weaponry is best."

He smirked, and, had he been human, she half expected an "I told you so."

"Nice. I approve." She bounded up to order from the rehydrator. "But I sense I don't know everything," she said as she handed him a slab of chocolate.

He took it with tentative fingers, lowered the cup to the table, then sniffed the brown rectangle. "Yes, I didn't want to overwhelm your primitive mind." He flashed a grin before he popped a brown square into his mouth. He mumbled his approval, the half-consumed hot chocolate forsaken.

"Gee, thanks." She grabbed a piece of chocolate from his hand.

He glared at her for the audacity.

"So, what don't I get to know?" she asked as she nibbled on the block.

"Languages you can load onto an O.D.I. Let's see, some of my studies—they would bore you—and memories of my life before the destruction," he said, his gaze still focused on the half-eaten slab of chocolate. His skin fluctuated between pale and dark, like mottled marble stone.

"All valid exclusions." She reached for another block. He slapped her hand away and glared at her again, warning her that it would be safer to get her own.

It's not as if you'll eat the whole slab. She pouted.

"Getting to know the supreme commander?"

Her head shot up to study Illan's expressions. Was he amused or was his curiosity genuine? She saw nothing to alarm her, so she tried to assess his mood through their connection. Still, no amusement.

"He hugged me, that's all," She chose to believe Illan was curious. "As do all my guardians." She forced a shrug, trying to convey indifference.

"What came through our mind-fuse is strong. You liked his hug." Illan sucked on a block of chocolate.

She thought over that strange interrogation. Xan was authoritative, well-mannered, and confident. His presence overwhelmed, and the chemistry between them was off the charts. Then again, she could be wrong.

"I did, Illan." She shifted in the comfy, staring at her chocolate-coated fingertips. "Not that it matters."

"Why not?" He pushed his chocolate aside, having had enough. *At last.* The marble effect of his skin worsened, and she wondered if Medic Rior understood Durn biology. "What do you fear?"

"Dammit, Illan, I don't even know how to handle guys at home, never mind how to deal with alien men."

"Males. Your use of man is derived from hu*man*." He pressed a hand to his chest and paled further. "I did not pass on the Etterian information. I believe it is better if Xan shares his culture with you."

Typical alien, thinking data was the solution to her problems. "And this information would've helped me with this strange shyness? With this attraction? Nothing I could've learned about Etterian males would give me confidence, Illan."

"Quinlan, you are beautiful and capable. Why do you doubt yourself now?"

She huffed. *Do I have to explain this? Can't you just look inside me and see?*

His smile was gentle. *I could but admitting it will force you to realize you are being silly.*

"Silly?" she squeaked, her cheeks burning. "I have no experience with men other than to be hurt, disappointed, angry, and frustrated."

"Being unreasonably frightened is not silly?" He met her gaze, challenging her to see reason.

"Blasted alien…," she grumbled, hating that he was correct. It did sound silly when she spoke her fears aloud.

Chapter Eleven

King Xeus had stared at Xan's eyes with absolute wonder for what had felt like eons. "Congratulations, Xan."

"Thank you, my king."

"Now, what makes this so urgent? And why the extra security protocols for this comm?"

"This is regarding three human females, my king."

"And one of those is your Dar Eth?"

Xan attempted to identify *the* emotions crushing his chest. They were so unfamiliar; he knew not where to begin. His Dar Eth? That alone bombarded him with emotion. He felt...unstable. *Felt*...there was the crux of it. Gone was his usual stoicism.

"They seized a Yithian slave ship with the help of two Durn," Xan said. *Was that just a few days ago?*

"Two Durn?" The king pinched his lips. "My males do have more fun these days."

"They saved forty-seven prisoners—a variety of species. I am sending you the sec vids." Xan pressed a button and waited.

King Xeus gaped as he watched the seizure of the slave ship. Xan had seen it several times, not only to observe his Dar Eth but also in an attempt to understand her.

"Is she yours?" the king asked. Xan nodded. "You are truly blessed."

"Thank you, my king." He rubbed his chest where the new ache resided, one that made his breathing difficult.

"I assume you destroyed the slave ship? Would this be the one that transported Prince Yada?"

"My Dar Eth killed the prince," Xan said.

Xeus stilled, his eyes widened, narrowed, then he pursed his lips. "Return the prisoners to their home worlds, technology willing, and offer asylum to those without worlds. With special care for the Durns and the human *women*, bring them to Etteria. If they wish to, of course. Human *women* can be tricky to deal with."

The king pronounced *women* with such pride. Under the influence of Lady Oriana, no doubt. She was the first human Dar Eth and now the king's daughter.

"I will take these abductions to the council. In the meantime, I am dispatching an additional fleet of battleships to guard Earth. I will insist the council grant Etteria the right to search each Yithian ship for human prisoners, no matter how small the craft."

"A wise decision, my king."

Xeus offered a small smile. "I am proud of you, Xan. You have never let me down."

Xan closed his eyes at the influx of unexpected joy at Xeus's praise. "At your service, my king."

"One day, I will get you to call me Xeus." He sighed before the image went black.

"Always exhausting." Oyaz grinned. "It is widely known you share blood with the royal bonds, Xan, and even more well known that you earned this position. When will you let this go?"

"Will never do?" Xan smiled, the forming of it easier than he'd thought possible. Already the Ethera was changing him. "My mother was Xeus's aunt. The connection to royalty is thin."

"It still exists. I am pleased for you, Xan. The Maker's timing is perfect," Oyaz stood there relaxed, his shoulders not tensed, no frown of concern. For once, he was free to just be a battle-bond.

"I am grateful, Oyaz." Xan gripped Oyaz's forearm, hoping to convey how much he valued their friendship.

"I cannot see you claiming her soon, though. I understand their emotions guide them."

"I agree. To force her would not be honorable." Xan released a long exhale. But he thought of nothing else. The constant bombardment on his control, thoughts, and senses crippled him. "She must choose to be with me." *As per the vision, she must give herself to me and me alone.*

A vibration intruded, and Oyaz glanced at his O.D.I. "The prisoners are demanding to see the human females."

"Women not females." Xan strode out of the comm room toward the women's quarters. Oyaz fell in behind him. The narrow passages didn't allow for side-by-side thoroughfare. "We have not harmed them. To suggest otherwise is unacceptable." He reached their door and made his request.

With a swish, it opened to reveal his Dar Eth. His eyes narrowed at the sight of her. He clenched his hands as he fought the urge to reach for her.

"Hello." She smiled, stepping back to let him in.

Oyaz nudged him when Xan hesitated. He stumbled forward but flashed his battle-bond a warning. Oyaz's grin widened.

"No respect," Xan whispered, expecting only his sub-commander to hear him. He received a chuckle from Oyaz for his efforts.

"The prisoners are asking for you," Oyaz said to the room. "All of you."

"Shit, Oyaz. I'm not dressed," Macy said, darting into the bedroom.

Cyn tossed black shoes at Quin, who caught one, but the other went wild. Xan snatched it out of the air and offered it to Quin. She gave him a smile of thanks then rushed to the comfy and sat to slip them on.

He stood behind her to fish-tail braid her hair. And she let him. His chest swelled. *She let me care for her. Alodon's balls; I am a youngin where this female is concerned.*

"Thank you." She held out a hair tie, and when he took it, his fingertips brushed her palm. She shivered and darted her focus everywhere but on him, "Mace? Ready?"

"I guess."

"You guess? You look good in those jeans." At Cyn's compliment, Macy dipped her chin, hiding her face behind a waterfall of hair.

Xan didn't understand the female...woman's reaction.

"Enough of this nonsense." Macy squared her shoulders and headed for the door.

Quin jumped up to follow. With him still holding her braid, she didn't go far. She squeaked when she realized this. Not that he'd hurt her. He chuckled before releasing her hair. She glanced to the side as if to hide her cheeks. The orange-pink or perske flush on her skin must denote embarrassment or shyness.

"Why do they need to see us?" she rasped.

He studied the curve of her neck and the delicate shell of her ear as he stilled his breathing to listen to her heartbeat. Its rhythm was erratic, as was her breathing. Her scent reached him then, and he shuddered.

"If you keep scenting aroused, we will never know." He didn't recognize his hoarse voice, nor would he investigate the change. He snaked out his hand to grab hers. The Ethera calmed. Touching her in any way eased the irrational need enough to bolster his control.

Her blush deepened, the color traveling down the delicate column of her neck.

"You can smell...?" She gaped.

He groaned at the dark pink depths of her mouth, tempting him to taste her.

"Quin?" Macy popped through the door. "Are you coming?"

"Not yet," she grumbled.

Xan tugged her behind him. "Your scent grows stronger, female," he growled. His words or rough voice increased her heartbeat. Her breath hitched.

"I won't apologize," she said.

Xan spun and crushed her to the passage bulkhead, pressing his body against hers. He trembled at the sensation of her softness beneath him. Her scent intensified. She moaned—a husky sound from the back of her throat—and her fingers on his chest spasmed. "I shouldn't apologize more often." She grinned as she met his gaze.

"Um, Supreme Commander, could you please release my friend?" Macy stared at the two of them.

Quin's eyes closed at the intrusion, even as she slid her hands up his chest to cup his neck. His breath lodged in his throat. His fingers on her hips convulsed.

"Besides, you'll want somewhere private." Macy chuckled. "Well, as private with Illan snooping." She danced, bouncing on her toes. "Once you kiss, Quin, you'll want to finish what you started."

Quin's eyes flew open to meet Xan's gaze. She chuckled and leaned forward to press a kiss to his chin. "She's right," she whispered. "I'd want you to finish."

He growled again and ran his hands from her hips to her waist, pushing her garment up, desperate to touch her skin. He shivered at the silkiness under his fingertips but stepped back. If he touched her a second longer, the delay would validate the prisoners' concern.

She walked away from him, following Macy to the common where the prisoners waited. He used the time to gain control and focus on the tasks at hand. It took all his strength for his hands to stop trembling and his breathing to return to normal. When he entered the common, the prisoners had surrounded the women, eagerly touching them, conveying their gratitude. Quin's lingering glance and clenched jaw had him smiling. She was hating this.

Until she met the Lysarans. Xan straightened as he pushed off the bulkhead. Iddan introduced her to the two Lysaran prisoners, and the smile she gave them was genuine, even as she threw back her head and laughed. Xan circled the room and her, unashamed that he eavesdropped.

"You're Lysaran? Am I pronouncing that correctly?" she asked with perfect diplomacy.

He frowned. The way her gaze traveled over the Lysarans told him she found them attractive. He growled loud enough to warn males off. But when she searched the room and found him, her eyes lit up and a bright smile formed on her kissable lips. "Xan, come meet Bry-dar and Myn-ras. I hear their planet is beautiful."

He obeyed without hesitation, not only because he couldn't help himself but also to indicate she belonged to him. He cupped her hip as he tugged her against his body. "Lysara is a paradise." He gazed at her upturned face. "You may come with when we deliver them home."

"I'd love to." Her easy delight drew a sigh from him. "Tell me, Bry-dar, do you drink blood?"

Silence descended on their group. Macy giggled, dipping to peer at Bry-dar's teeth. "They do look like vampire teeth," she squealed, bursting with excitement. The Lysarans gaped at her moments before awe merged into pure delight. They drew in deep and thorough breaths, their bodies turning toward her.

"Vampire?" Xan asked, waiting for his O.D.I. to inform him. The images and descriptions filling his mind had him chuckling. "I agree with your assessment, miladies."

"They're not pale though, so that's a plus." Macy bounced, clapping her hands before darting around Cyndi to pull her away from Iddan. "Show her, Myn-ras," she said to the Lysaran male. Cyndi squeaked when she saw their teeth, then burst into laughter at her reaction. She took the time to study them, pinching their chins to do so.

"What is so fascinating about Lysarans?" Xan asked Quin, his lips brushing her ear as he whispered the question.

"They are caramel-skinned, lean-muscled, broad-shouldered, with brown hair to their midbacks, and amber-gold eyes—exquisite eyes on gorgeous men."

Frowning, Xan ran his gaze over the Lysarans. "You said my eyes are beautiful, am I a gorgeous male?"

Quin chuckled. "Your eyes are breath-taking." She glanced away.

"Kaiha, are they always this emotional?" Bry-dar asked Oyaz.

"Yes." Oyaz grinned. "And as a male, it is challenging to maintain control on their behalf."

"You wish to control them?" Bry-dar jerked back, alarmed. "On Lysara, they would be goddesses." The male's gaze adored Macy, his wonder raising the hairs on the back of Xan's neck. "You know our situation, Etterians. They may be the salvation we have been searching for."

"As they are ours," Xan said to Myn-ras, who studied his ice-blue eyes.

Xan grasped his Dar Eth's soft wrist. He gave her a gentle tug toward the outside of the gathering. She arched a brow as he slipped an arm around her to hold her close. "Once your presence has appeased them, would you like to comm your guardians?"

The smile she bestowed upon him—as beautiful as the rising suns of Etteria—made his chest ache.

"Just a few more minutes." She faced the Maloidian male who wad-dled toward her. He was the oldest of the prisoners, his skin a mustard yellow, his markings all but faded. His tentacles swayed casually as he grabbed her forearm for a squeeze before releasing it.

"Thank you, I cannot express how much my freedom means to me," he said in Galactic, his voice rasping.

"It was a concerted effort. I couldn't have done it without everyone's cooperation." Quin repeated the words she'd said to each person. Her stiff posture and forced smile showed how uncomfortable she was receiving this attention.

"Apologies, lommia, she struggles to accept gratitude," Xan said to the elderly Maloidian.

"Lommia?" She laced her fingers through Xan's, as natural as if they'd always been together. Her ease and acceptance revealed how open-hearted and generous humans were.

"A title of respect awarded to an elderly Maloidian," he said into her hair, then pressed a kiss there because he couldn't resist the temptation.

"Have all your needs been seen to? Were you able to notify your family?" she asked the Maloidian.

He beamed. "Yes, thank you. I hope to see them soon."

"We were lucky the Etterians received our distress signal. Illan said there was a twenty-two percent chance pirates may answer." She shivered with furrows marring her temple. "I will admit, I don't know how we would've handled that."

"I am certain you would have found a solution. Earthians are resourceful," the Maloidian said.

"Thank you for your kind words, lommia." She patted his hand. "I'm contacting my family now. Would you excuse me?"

Xan led her away, grateful to have her to himself.

Chapter Twelve

Etterian Battleship, Phoenix
Communications Room

"AIDEN?" QUIN SPOKE INTO the display vid.

Xan had brought her to the communications room. He said it made for a clearer connection. She didn't care where the call happened as long as it did. The need to speak to her brothers drove her like the necessity to breathe. That Lucas and Mason hadn't answered her calls infuriated her. She vibrated with pent-up anger, her fingers clenching and unfurling under Xan's vigilant gaze. Added to this was embarrassment. Her brothers cared so little, they didn't bother to answer. It wasn't as if she contacted them often. She stamped her foot, but the action didn't ease her frustration. "Dammit, Aiden, stop being an ass."

"Hello, squirt. You know this is for emergencies only," her brother said.

She studied his dirty T-shirt and disheveled hair. He'd pulled an all-nighter again. She wasn't going to chastise him, not this time. It didn't matter anymore.

"This *is* an emergency, idiot. Not that Lucas or Mase give a shit," she muttered.

"You look well…" Aiden met her gaze to make a point. In this case, she had no injuries, therefore, this wasn't a *medical* emergency. If he was in the room, she'd have smacked him by now.

"Aiden, just listen. I've been kidnapped."

"That's not a joking matter." He scowled, his gray eyes hooded with anger.

"That would be my penchant for practical jokes?" *Idiot. How can I be related to that?*

His eyes widened. "Is this a ransom call?"

At last, he was taking her seriously. His focus shifted to something on the side, his fingers tapping away at a keyboard. Typical. Even kidnapped didn't garner his undivided attention.

"No, I sort of escaped and am now en route to another planet."

His head shot up, his brow furrowing. "Are you saying space pirates kidnapped you? That shit is real?"

"No, and don't ask if they've probed me."

He stared at her for the longest moment. It was the most attention she'd received from him in years. "You're not returning to Earth, are you?"

He'd never visited her, so what difference did it make if she was off-world.

"No." A weight lifted from her shoulders, and she sliced a glance at Xan leaning against a bulkhead, watching her with heavy-lidded eyes.

"I don't like this, Quinlan. Lucas is going to—"

"Then he should've answered my call," she snapped. Interrupting irritated him. *Tit for tat, big brother.*

"Do you promise you're all right? No one is making you speak to me at gunpoint?"

"If they were, I couldn't answer that, now could I?" She threw him a huge smile. "I'm happy, brother. I *chose* not to return."

"You had the option? Are you insane?" His voice rose, his anger climbed, then he drew in a deep breath to begin his tirade.

She wasn't going to endure one of those if she didn't have to. He saw her as the annoying addition to their family, one he had to generate some emotion for. But she was an adult woman, capable of making her decisions, and in this case, she chose to run.

"Aiden? The signal's...breaking...up. We're going through a tunnel... Bye, brother." She disconnected the communication with a huff.

"He is an unpleasant male," Xan said. "I do not like his treatment of you."

That he came to her defense warmed her. But then it was verbal defense, wasn't it, with Aiden light years away. Her gaze lingered on Xan's bulging biceps, and her smile spread. Aiden wouldn't stand a chance face to face.

"He's always been like that, barely tolerates me, hates it when I disrupt his life..." *Among other things.*

"Is there anyone else you wish to comm?" Xan's offer, despite what must be an expensive service, made her squeeze his hand.

She shook her head, not wishing to impose. "By now, all my guardians will know. I suspect they have a secret code word for me. Or phrase." She shrugged. Xan blinked at her. "Like one word that encapsulates the problem. For example, if Aiden communicates this code, like firebrand, then all the guardians would know I'm in danger. I don't know what it is, though."

"Supreme Commander Xan, I have an irate human male demanding to speak to Lady Quinlan," Pilot Msar said.

"See, that would be Lucas, the eldest," she said to Xan.

"Do you wish to speak to him?" he asked her, no doubt concerned after Aiden's behavior.

"Yes, please."

Lucas's worried face appeared on the display vid. "What do you mean kidnapped? And what's this nonsense about you not coming home?"

"Yup, all of that. You're welcome to visit me." She arched a brow at Xan. "Is that possible, and if so, how long is the journey?"

"It is possible for you, *ensa*. Two weeks to reach Etteria on any of our returning battleships."

"What language is that? And who are you speaking to?" Lucas's voice vibrated with fury, his pinched lips confirming it. What had Aiden said to have Lucas believe she was in trouble? So typical.

"I'm speaking Galactic to the Supreme Commander of this battleship." She wished she could record her brother's reaction.

He gaped, his mouth opening and closing like a fish. "*Holy shit*, squirt. What have you gotten yourself into?"

"Nothing that requires a rescue." She folded her arms across her chest. "I tested out the skills you taught me and made two friends. I'm traveling to another planet and enjoying every moment of it. Can't you be happy for me?"

His sigh was long and forlorn. "It's just so sudden, and you know, this's breaking Wyatt's heart."

Her breath caught. *This will kill Wyatt.* "I'm sorry, Lucas. For once, I'm doing what I want. And you guys can still visit me, it just requires a longer furlough than usual."

"We can visit Earth if you wish it, *ensa.*"

At Xan's words, she beamed at him. She hadn't missed the *we* in his offer. He would travel with her, she hoped. "Xan says I can visit you too. So, you see, it's not goodbye."

Lucas grumbled, but that meant she was winning him over.

"All right, I'll let the family know. Garrett's not going to like this either."

"He made his choice." She recalled the decisive moment when she'd left them at dinner.

"That he did, but he's still a guardian *and* your friend." Lucas studied her for a moment. "You've grown up, squirt. Not that I like where it's taken you, though." He ran a frustrated hand over his shaved head. "I pictured you married with kids, not out there chasing the stars."

"Married? To whom? Victor? Is that even legal?" she teased, receiving a smirk from Lucas for her trouble.

Xan growled beside her, and a glance had her frowning. *What did I say to displease him?*

"Point made. I love you, Quinny. Please, look after yourself." Lucas waited for her nod.

"You too, big brother. Love you." She ended the communication, hopefully for the last time that day.

"I prefer his treatment of you," Xan said before announcing with a clenched jaw, "You will not mate Victor."

She grinned at his command. "No, I won't marry Victor. He's a toy Lucas bought me. Shows you how lonely I was to treat a toy as a companion."

Her revelation arched his eyebrow. "A female as beautiful as you should not be lonely." He rubbed his chest as if he had indigestion.

What thrilled her was his compliment. *He said I'm beautiful.*

"Our males form attachments to their greatswords." He lowered his hand to rest on her hip, the gesture possessive.

Wow, he's moving fast. Torn between excitement and trepidation, she wasn't lying when she'd told Illan she didn't know how to handle men. She hoped it was hunger that coiled within her lower belly. Butterflies exploded with the pixie dust from their wings settling in her chest like champagne bubbles. That had to be lust, right?

"We also do, though not for greatswords," she said.

When he tugged her closer, she pressed her hand to his chest and dipped her nose to breathe in his warm and spicy cologne.

"Tell me about Wyatt," Xan said. "How can you break his heart? I do not know this attack."

She chuckled. "It's not an offensive move. Breaking someone's heart means they will be so miserable their heart cannot bear the strain. Wyatt is one of my guardians who loves having me to come home to. They're too lazy to find wives, to be honest." She patted Xan's chest, loving the firmness of his muscles beneath her fingers.

"Quinlan," his voice lowered to a rasp, drawing her attention with ease. "Your expression changed when you spoke to Lucas. It was intense, exquisite."

She stared, trying to assess whether he was messing with her. "Love?" she asked, testing his reaction. Why didn't he know what that was?

"Love." He frowned. "Thank you for answering me in truth."

"A pleasure. I promised to meet Macy for lunch. Do you wish to join us?"

"I am on shift. I shall see you this evening, *ensa*." He pressed a lingering kiss to her forehead.

She smiled, wishing she could freeze this moment. Her guardians had often kissed her temple, but it had never been like this. Goosebumps traveled back and forth, taking trips from her scalp to her toes. And her heart reacted to his touch like it was on a free-for-all roller-coaster ride. She forced herself to step away from him, but trailing her fingers down his armored chest was beyond her control. Considering starting her lunch with a shot of tequila, she left him in the comm room.

Chapter Thirteen

Etterian Battleship, Phoenix
Communications Room

Xan resisted the urge to shuffle his feet. He'd wanted to see Quin. The Ethera had demanded he see her. Here he stood outside their door requesting access. It opened to Cyndi, and he nodded a greeting, not quite trusting his voice.

"Quin?" Cyndi gestured for him to enter.

"What is it, Cyn?"

His hearts somersaulted when she appeared in the doorway to their bedroom. Her long tunic ended at mid-thigh with her legs bare. He ogled her for a moment before focusing on her hair. She'd tilted her head to the side and was running a brush through the golden locks. The shimmering waterfall fascinated him.

"Morning, Supreme Commander." She arched a pale brow, a silent inquiry as to his presence.

"Good morning, Quinlan," he said, grateful his voice sounded normal. "Should I return when you are clothed?" He would have preferred to see her unclothed.

Macera tossed Quin a garment, which she caught in mid-air before disappearing into her room. Moments later, she reappeared in blue breeches and a similar tunic, this time in pink. She chose a comfy and slipped on blue footwear.

"Ready." She approached him. "Are we going somewhere specific?"

The urge to slide his arm around her waist and yank her against him bombarded him. He longed to bury his nose in her neck and inhale her scent, perhaps press a kiss to her silky skin. Instead, he grumbled under his breath at his dissolving self-control and opened the door. He gestured to her to proceed him. As soon as she stepped into the passage, he glanced at the other females who gawked at him as if his behavior was extraordinary.

"I would prefer to explain the situation," he said the moment the door closed, granting them privacy.

"I'd appreciate that." Quin waited, but he had no intention of leading her away.

She'd left her hair down to swirl around her with each move she made. And the narrow confines of the passage had them almost touching. He gazed at her upturned face, his fingers curling into fists at his sides.

"Xan?" she asked, her brow crinkling with what he hoped was concern.

"Are you leaving your hair unbound?"

"Yes."

He grumbled at the Ethera's ability to choose a temptress and marched down the passages toward the unmanned comm room. Spinning to face her, he leaned his hips against the console and folded his arms across his chest.

"We destroyed the Yithian slave ship with the prince on it. Should their King Urio discover this, it would mean war."

She stilled with her gaze turning internal. "Xan, Illan says the prince was too unprotected to have been there in an official capacity."

Xan scowled at the intrusion, hating the reminder that even in an empty comm room, he wasn't alone with her. "Please inform Illan that if he wishes to participate in this conversation—"

"I am here." Illan entered the room.

Fury was swift and blinding, and for a moment, Xan ceased to breathe. He growled a warning, one he assumed the Durn would understand. "Did you teach her Etterian?" he asked in his language, his tone clipped.

"No, your culture is yours alone to convey," Illan answered in Etterian as he threw a glance at Quin. Her face had darkened, perhaps angry at the exclusion from the conversation.

"Good. She is my Dar Eth, so your presence here is unnecessary. You go too far, Durn," Xan said.

"I apologize for the intrusion, Supreme Commander," Illan said in Galactic, including Quin in their discussion.

With a longsuffering sigh, Xan reverted to Galactic as well. "Yithians kidnap females...women from Earth. They must not discover the same species destroyed their slave ship *and* killed their prince."

"How would they find out it was me? You could've killed the prince." Her gaze traveled his form, implying he could kill. She blessed him with a wink.

His lips twitched, but he kept the smile from forming. "I hope they believe you incapable and place the blame on our shoulders. Earth will not fare well against Yithia."

She gasped with horror darkening her now pale features. "We wouldn't survive," she said, raising a hand to cover her gaping mouth. "What have I done?"

"Etterians train for war. But with Yithia, we can only battle them on the surface or in space. We cannot penetrate the oceans to reach their cities. A war with Yithia will be long and frustrating."

"They have underwater cities," she squeaked, bounced on her toes before spinning to grip Illan's forearm. "They're beautiful, Illan. Although, how they could use glass-like material and mold it into those strange shapes, I've no idea. Why didn't you share the construction with me?"

"You act as if I know everything, Quin." He chuckled.

"Oh," she said with perske glowing on her cheeks and her eyes sparkling.

Xan admired her delight as he considered their words. The mind-fuse must be bi-directional with memories and learned skills, but more revealing than this was that the Durn had chosen what not to share. So, Illan's words earlier meant that he'd, at least, granted Xan the opportunity to teach Quin about Etterians.

"Yithia is seventy percent water. Yithians prefer to live underwater due to the temperature control it offers on their three-sun planet. Unfortunately, it is difficult to target the cities. Our weaponry is powerless," Xan said.

"You don't have submarines?" Her eyes widened. "A technologically advanced civilization such as Etteria must have mastered deep sea warfare?"

Xan's eyelids fluttered as his O.D.I. instructed him on her English word 'submarine,' but as the images and schematics flickered across his mind, his smile broadened. Excitement uncoiled in his stomach to consume him, his fingers trembling as he typed into his O.D.I. Adviser Cales and King Xeus needed to know this. He copied Kemt in the message, instructing him to investigate further. This must take priority.

"I'll take that smile as a no?" Her voice lowered until it rasped along his senses, drawing his attention. *She likes my smile?* "So why tell me this?" She didn't meet his gaze. Her eyes darted everywhere but on him, and her heart pounded loud enough to reach his advanced hearing.

She stilled, and her mouth dropped open. She glared at Illan before shooting a glance at Xan. Her cheeks brightened. Her body stiffened, and she shifted away from him, but it wasn't far enough to diminish the strength of her scent. She was aroused.

He drew in a deep breath, his fingers tightening on the console as a shiver raced down his spine. "I wish…" He cleared his throat. "…to keep you informed since you have shown specific abilities. I would also prefer to prepare for any outcome."

She pinched her lips. "Forewarned is forearmed."

"If that is all?" Illan asked as he inched closer to the door.

Xan scowled. He wanted to roar at the male's needless intrusion. The Durn paused, glanced at Quin, and smiled before leaving them alone.

"Why couldn't you tell me this in my quarters?" She closed the distance between them, her posture aggressive.

"Here we are private," he said. Engulfed by her scent, his nostrils flared.

Despite the lustful intensity in her eyes, she didn't back down. "Privacy is important, why? Cyn and Mace are trustworthy."

Xan didn't know how to respond. *I need her, need to be with her. Does she not feel what is between us? An Etterian female would have.* He scowled. *Not that I would exchange Quin for anyone else.*

"You fascinate me," he said, his voice hoarse. He chose honesty, and it pleased him when his words widened her eyes.

"I do?"

He released his held breath at her astonished delight. *My attention isn't unwanted.* This was good. It gave him hope he could claim her soon.

"Yes." He pushed off the console and stopped an inch from touching her.

She slid her hand from his forearm to his clenched fist before cupping his knuckles. He shuddered at the texture of her skin on his.

"Your strategists must've considered the impact a war with Yithia might have on the galaxy." She dipped to meet his gaze. "So, what has you tense?"

He flipped his hand to capture her fingers. Connected, he used it to draw her closer to him. Her warmth surrounded him, and a muffled moan tore from him. He raised his gaze to the ceiling, fighting for calm. "A war does not matter to me. I am tense because I fight the need to touch you."

She stared at their joined hands, his bronzed skin striking against her pale hand, but at his words, her gaze shot up to meet his. Her mouth parted, and he grumbled at the additional temptation. His control was legendary, yet it had forsaken him.

"You *are* touching me." She squeezed his hand.

He smiled as he grasped her hip to pull her closer until a Maloidian dagger couldn't slip between them. "I crave your touch yet when I receive it, it does not satisfy. The craving only deepens." The revelation bewildered him as his gaze darted between her eyes and her parted lips.

"I assume this is sexual," she said, arching her eyebrow as she raised her left hand to rest on his chest. That she touched him without hesitation hitched his breath.

"It is infinitely more."

"More?" She stilled, her gaze turning inward. She scowled and pressed her forehead to his chest.

He glided his hand from her hip, up her back, to bury his fingers in her curls. He relished the length of her against him, her thighs rubbing his.

"Illan needs us urgently," she said to his chest. "He waits in my quarters." She glanced up to meet Xan's gaze, her lips twisting in displeasure.

That the Durn would again interrupt their interaction infuriated Xan. He clenched his jaw as he crushed her against him, not willing to release her. "He dares command me?" he said, his voice strained with anger.

"He's a Durn." She smiled while brushing her fingertips over his pinched lips.

He shuddered before grabbing her hand to press a kiss on her palm.

"He isn't prone to melodramatics, so it *must* be urgent. Let's, at least, hear him out." She raised her face to the ceiling, a frown marring her temple. "Then quit listening in." She huffed. "You haven't taught me how to yet, idiot." She threw an apologetic look at Xan.

He broke away from her and tugged her behind him, as pleased with this as she was and as frustrated with this mind fuse. As soon as they entered her quarters, a grinning Illan stepped forward.

Iddan stood to one side with a smile curling his blue lips. "Idiot? I have often thought him such," he chuckled.

"Only a human would dare to call me that." Illan gestured to Oyaz, who leaned against the bulkhead.

Oyaz appeared unconcerned, but Xan knew him well. His battle-bond radiated tension. *This was serious. Why hadn't he messaged? Why use Illan to reach them?*

"We are incapacitated, and we suspect the offender is a prisoner, perhaps more than one," Oyaz said to no one in particular.

"Sabotage?" Quin frowned.

Xan glanced at her and stiffened. Sabotage meant she was in danger, and endangering Dar Eths, claimed or unclaimed, was unacceptable.

"I have received strange comms from various sources. Twice in the last few days, the engineers replaced the cylinders for the fusion drives. With no documented defects, they have inexplicably fractured. Pilot Msar deactivated the drives to perform the repairs," Oyaz said, his voice ringing with frustration.

"The sec vids confirm the destruction?" Xan asked.

"No, there is nothing, no suspicious activity, almost as if someone tampered with the data. Kemt is investigating this since only a select few on this ship have the skills and the access to do so." Oyaz scowled and unfolded his arms only to refold them across his chest, his body remaining tense.

"There's more," Xan said since he knew Oyaz, his mannerisms, expressions, and how his mind operated.

"Yes, life support malfunctioned, powering up the backup tanks. Doing these repairs has cost us four hours. They tampered with the acceptable oxygen levels, and the emergency failsafe kicked in. As malfunctions go, this was minor but still critical."

"So they had to know the ship's design well." Xan studied Oyaz, waiting for his battle-bond's stance to relax. But when it stiffened further, he scowled, clenching his jaw against such a blatant attack. Worse, it was from an unknown enemy. "What else?"

"We are transmitting an encrypted signal to an unknown receiver. Kemt has disabled it, but it has compromised our location. The usual comms masked the low-frequency signal. We still do not know what it communicated nor what awaits us en route." He lowered his arms to his side now that he had delivered the information.

"It is a prisoner, that is the logical conclusion." Xan glanced at Quin, who'd yet to comment. He frowned at Lady Cyndi. "Milady, you were with the prisoners the longest. Did anyone act out of the ordinary, any behavior that could raise suspicion?"

She laced her fingers through Iddan's. "They were happy we rescued them. A few were a little cold toward us, distrustful. I can't say it's unexpected. We're an unknown species."

"Have we documented these prisoners, their origins, the people they contacted?" Quin asked. "I mean, we can't assume they spoke to their families."

"Kemt is investigating this," Oyaz said, "but perhaps he should do a more detailed assessment."

Xan grunted. "See to it, Oyaz. Someone gains by this delay."

"It would mean waiting for something en route to us. That makes the most sense," Quin said. "Here, we can control the battleground. Who knows what they're preparing for our arrival."

"Alter our course, Oyaz. The Yithians would gain the most, and perhaps news has reached them of their prince's death." Xan weighed his options. "Have Kemt delve into any Yithian connections to the prisoners and their blood-bonds."

"Acknowledged, Supreme Commander."

"Are you sure it's them?" Quin's face paled. The sharp scent of her sadness hit him, and he grimaced, hating that she felt so. "Did I bring this upon us by killing the prince?"

"Your actions were justified, *ensa*." Xan looped an arm around her waist to gather her closer.

She rested her hands on his forearms, but her sadness didn't fade. "That doesn't mean I made wise choices."

While lost in thought, she rubbed circles across his skin, drawing shivers from him. He stepped back to lace his fingers through hers, then escorted her to stand in front of the display vid. He activated it and requested all sec vids from the common when the prisoners had demanded to see the human females. Everyone gathered around the vid to observe the interactions.

Quin couldn't focus past Xan, his expressions and mannerisms. On the sec vid, the way he watched her, how his gaze trailed her around the common, how he positioned his body as if he guarded her told anyone who paid attention that she belonged to him. She drew in a slow, deep breath, trying to hide the gasp pushing at her lungs. She knew he was interested in her but not at this level of intensity. His dedication was something she'd never experienced. He was so interested in her that nothing else in the room mattered.

She snuck a glance at him and sighed. If he didn't kiss her soon, she might have to take matters into her hands. Heat unfolded in her core, and she hurried to clench her thighs together. Her efforts were in vain. His nostrils flared, and his gaze dropped to hers. He drew in a deep inhale, paused with his chest puffed out, then released his breath with a whoosh. His ice-blue eyes swirled. He used their clasped hands to gather her flush against him before crushing her hand to his chest. He rested his other hand on her hip, stroking the fabric of her leggings. Her nerve endings and senses narrowed on his touch.

"No, it cannot be." Oyaz pointed at the familiar Maloidian and scowled. "He seemed so docile, so grateful."

"That sweet old man?" Macy gasped. "He has a son he hasn't seen in a while and hoped he could bring him home."

"Msar, locate Pannos, the Maloidian," Xan snapped into his wrist.

"Last known location was in engine room three." The surprise in Msar's voice came through the device. "That cannot be accurate; it is an access secure area."

"I will investigate." Xan strode to the door, tugging Quin with him. "I will return for you," he whispered, gazing into her eyes.

"I'm going with you, Xan, and if you say no, I'll go by myself," she said. He scowled, not liking her threat. Well, tough. This was her fault, and dammit, she would fix this. "I'm guilty of bringing this upon us. Please, let me help."

He studied her features, and when he spoke, his deep baritone was serious. "I understand the guilt you feel, your need to rectify what is not your fault. But I fight the need to safeguard you." He scooped her into his arms and buried his face in her neck. "You may search with me. I am better able to protect you then."

Giving him a grateful smile even though he wouldn't see it, she tightened her arms around his neck, marveling at his ability to hold her like this. Wasn't she heavy? But she wasn't going to complain. It was damn good to be in his arms. Leaning back, she pressed a quick kiss on his cheek like the chaste ones she gave her guardians.

His gaze lingered on her lips, then he lowered her to pull her behind him, all the while grumbling something under his breath.

Chapter Fourteen

Etterian Battleship, Phoenix
On the hunt

THEY HAD SEARCHED THROUGH all five engine rooms and found no loitering Maloidian saboteur. The way Xan slipped in and out of spaces without making a sound would impress Carter, for sure. It seemed as if Xan wanted to observe Pannos first before capturing him. They were now striding toward the gravity generators. Xan's tense shoulders revealed he hoped they didn't locate Pannos there. She couldn't imagine what damage the old male could do. What could he do to a gravity generator that would impact a battleship of this size? This information was not part of Illan's two-finger touch.

"Alodon's balls." Xan ripped off a maintenance grill and gestured to Quin.

She sliced glances both ways down the passage, then slid in feet first. The duct was large enough for an Etterian male to crawl through. She made to shuffle down further, but Xan whispered, "Stay."

She shifted to the side, allowing him space next to her. He pulled the panel shut, clipping it. She inched upward to peek through the grill. Silence pressed in as she struggled to listen for footsteps.

The moment the Maloidian approached, Xan pressed his hand over her mouth as a precaution, in case she made a sound their advanced hearing could pick up. She tilted her head to peer at his outline in the dark tunnel. She released a slow breath as quietly as she could. A minute or two later, he lowered his hand.

He activated his O.D.I. and sent forth instructions. The holographic keys splashed their colors across his chest and chin. Parts of him illuminated—the bold angle of his chin, the incredible gentleness of his lips, the curve of a cheekbone—before the darkness returned.

Lying there blind, she strained her ears to listen for any movement. She couldn't hear Xan breathe let alone anything outside the tunnel. If he wasn't touching her, she would've thought she was alone. In the quiet, her heartbeat thumped in her ears.

The first thing she realized was that Xan crowded her within the crawl space. The length of her pressed against his hard edges, and where they touched, tingles sparked to life.

The second thing was that he smelled good, like heated spice and something earthy. She inhaled, slow, quiet, and thorough, savoring the scent of him, wishing she could bury her nose in his chest or his neck like a drug addict.

The third thing was that she had somehow rested her hand against his chest. His rapid heartbeat thrummed under her palm. His heat kept the chill in the crawl space at bay.

He shifted, pressing her back until she touched the metallic duct wall. He clasped her hip in a possessive grip.

This close, her pebbled nipples rubbed his chest, sending tingles from there to her core. It spasmed in reaction, intensifying the insistent ache. Embarrassment fired her cheeks. He'd smell her. There was no way to hide her reaction. She glanced to where his face should be and parted her mouth to speak, then remembered she had to remain quiet.

His lips brushed hers.

They were hot yet soft. Her ears rung. Her heart catapulted. She was startled enough for a gasp to escape. He crushed his mouth over hers, capturing the sound, silencing her. The heated taste of him made her want to moan, but she held it back. Instead, she welcomed his searching tongue, so bold and forceful in its entry. She shivered at his intrusion.

Having never been kissed, this was an incredible experience for her. Her hands fluttered over his chest, up his neck to clasp his cheeks, holding him still so her tongue could meet his. She pushed his with her tentative one, not certain what she was doing but needing to taste him, to duel with him. He rumbled, the vibration flowing through her nipples where she pressed against his chest. He nipped at her lips, sipping on her before crushing her to him, his mouth possessing her.

She stopped breathing, stopped caring about remaining silent, about anything for that matter. She feathered her fingers down to his chest, clawing at the muscles there as she looped her leg around his hip—struggling to get as close to him as possible. He groaned and lowered his hand from her hip to clasp her backside, his fingers embedding in the pliant flesh he found. He ground his arousal into the juncture at her thighs, snatching her ability to breathe. The sensations shooting through her were pleasurable and aching.

He broke the kiss but didn't move away, his fingers still flexed, squeezing her backside and drawing forth another throbbing ache in her core.

"Quin." He drew in a sharp breath.

"Xan," she rasped. "I enjoyed that."

"You did," he said.

She blushed, glad he couldn't see her flushed face. "Yes." She grinned at his confidence.

"I will be kissing you more often." He squeezed her backside still in his firm grasp.

"You will," she said, giving him back a little of his arrogance.

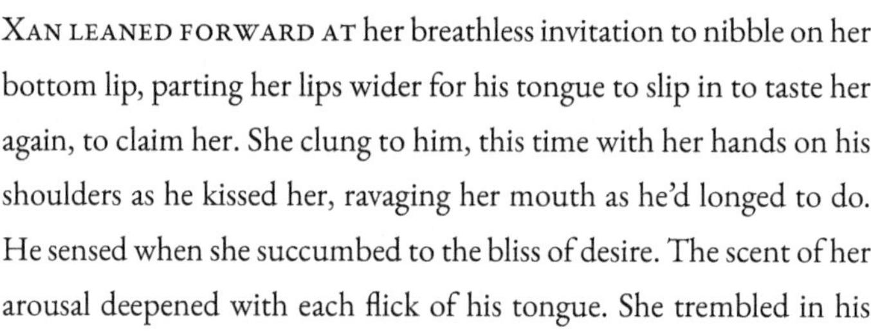

XAN LEANED FORWARD AT her breathless invitation to nibble on her bottom lip, parting her lips wider for his tongue to slip in to taste her again, to claim her. She clung to him, this time with her hands on his shoulders as he kissed her, ravaging her mouth as he'd longed to do. He sensed when she succumbed to the bliss of desire. The scent of her arousal deepened with each flick of his tongue. She trembled in his arms. If he didn't slow down, he would claim her in this tunnel.

Despite his mental instruction, he released her backside to slip his hand under her garment, to touch her silky warm skin. He growled. Sliding his hand further up, he took the fabric of her tunic with it until he reached her undergarment. There, he splayed out his fingers, holding her tighter against his chest. He couldn't get her close enough. He needed her skin against his and her silky hands caressing his body.

He kissed a heated path to her earlobe, sucking on it. Her gasping and arching pleased him and made his hard arousal burn with need.

"Quin." He breathed her name into her ear.

"I know, Xan," she said. "But I don't want you to stop."

"I need to *see* your responses, to *feel* your soft skin... We must stop." He caught her nod since Etterian vision was superior, even in the shadows. He memorized every detail—her flushed face and kiss-swollen lips. Drawing in a shaky breath, he pressed his forehead to hers.

"Is he gone?" she asked.

"Yes." With trembling fingers, he unclipped the maintenance grill and pushed it out. He pulled himself out before leaning in to tug her free. As soon as her feet cleared the tunnel, he crushed her to his chest, keeping her there, her toes dangling high off the floor. "You tempt me to be uncivilized." He met her beautiful gaze. "I want to throw you over my shoulder, keep you captive, and inflict pleasure upon you until you cannot speak."

"I would let you take me captive." She meant it, that she would *let him*. She wrapped her legs around his waist and captured his mouth with hers.

He groaned, content to consume her like this for an eternity.

"Do I want to know?" Oyaz smirked.

They broke apart, breathless. Xan allowed her to slide down his body until her feet touched the floor.

"We found the saboteur," she whispered. "I'll let you and Oyaz hunt him down while I take a cold shower." She squeeze Xan's hand before jogging off.

"A cold shower?" Oyaz asked as they watched her disappear through the door.

Xan offered his sub-commander a tight smile. "I might have to try one."

"It sounds effective if the O.D.I. is correct in its explanation."

Xan grunted as he rubbed his face, frustratingly aroused with no guarantee of easing the ache soon.

"We apprehended him while you tended to more important matters," Oyaz teased as he steered Xan to the sec center where the Maloidian male awaited them.

"Indeed," Xan grinned. At last, he'd tasted her. And the memory of it made him realize two things...

One taste hadn't appeased the craving.

And, he had every intention of kissing her again, repeatedly.

Chapter Fifteen

Macy thumped Illan on the arm when he grumbled for the thousandth time.

He yelped and glared at her. "How did you convince me to do this?" He rubbed his arm while slicing glances down the passage.

"What?" she gaped. "I asked you for directions, yet here you are. This isn't on me."

"Oyaz would expect me to dissuade you from this madness, not be complicit in it."

She squeaked and raised her fist.

Illan threw out his hand and leaped away from her. "I am curious." He harumphed.

She schooled her features, folded her arms across her chest, and tapped her foot as if impatient. Damn toes spasmed from this morning's workout, ruining her pissed-off-Gran stance. She twisted and turned to uncramp her toes while trying not to giggle.

Illan blinked at her, watching her do the marionette-dance, his eyes twitching.

"By all means, please do elaborate," she snapped while bouncing on her feet, working free the cramp.

"I cannot fathom why you need to see Pannos."

She tilted her head, implying he was being an idiot. "Oh, well, it's simple. I want to know his motives."

Illan slumped, leaned against the bulkhead, and grinned. "Ah, I see." He straightened. "Then we best have done with this. The security center is down the next passage."

She jerked back and scowled. "So close? I swear, Illan, next time we spar, I'll make sure to knee you where it hurts."

He frowned, not from anger but in puzzlement. She couldn't be sure he wasn't calculating the statistics of her successfully kneeing him in the groin.

"I fail to understand this threat, Macy. Would it not hurt everywhere on my body if you knee me?"

She threw up her hands, grabbed his forearm, and dragged him around the corner. And stilled. At the end of the passage stood a circular room, glowing bright white. In the center of that was a desk with an Etterian warrior on duty. She shoved Illan against the metallic wall and plastered herself beside him.

"Shit. I hadn't thought about guards," she whispered while Illan peered around her. "Now what?"

"If Quin was here—"

"He'd be on the floor, groaning, stunned, or dead. Yeah, I get I'm not Quin." Macy huffed. She pushed off the bulkhead, straightened her baggy shirt stained from her earlier ice cream binge, and squared her shoulders. "But I am adorable me, and sweet-talking is my superpower."

"Macy," Illan hissed, but she ignored him and flounced down the passage.

She smiled at the guard and rested her elbows on the counter. "Hi."

"Good day, milady. How can I be of assistance?" The Etterian's gaze traveled her face.

She fluttered her eyelashes in all innocence. "I'd like to visit my friend."

She twirled to study the cells. Seamless metallic panels lined the walls. Dull lighting illuminated the one cell housing Pannos. Why have a jail if honor was everything? Was there such a thing as a dishonorable Etterian? She doubted it but supposed it was possible. There were good and bad people in all cultures.

"I have received no notification of your visit. Is Supreme Commander Xan or Sub-Commander Oyaz aware of your request?"

"Xan's too busy with Quin to care about me. And I'm not talking to Oyaz after he slammed me into the mat this morning and knocked the ever-loving breath out of me." She pressed a hand to her chest. "I thought I was dying."

The Etterian's eyes twitched. She frowned. Was she having this effect on everyone now?

"My apologies, milady. Visits must be authorized."

Shit, were all Etterians this stubborn? She gritted her teeth, about to demand he contact Oyaz.

"An exception can be made, I am certain." Illan strode into the lit circle.

Now he helps? She huffed and damned if the guard didn't salute Illan as if he was effing royalty.

Illan grinned and dipped his head to whisper, "Superpower, huh?"

She shrugged. "Every heroine has off days." She nudged Illan shoulder to shoulder. "Thank you."

With a skip, she crossed to Pannos's cell, wary of the humming. The front was open, though she guessed she needed to avoid the pulsing white line running the length of it. She'd seen enough illegal vids to know to be suspicious of anything unusual. She snorted. Here she was, sneaking into a security center. Nothing odd about that.

"Pannos?"

The old Maloidian male sat on his bed, and at her greeting, his sad gaze rose to meet hers.

"Lady Macy," he said, though his usual enthusiasm was absent as expected under the circumstances.

She sank to the floor to sit Indian style, and in her blue jeans, it was easy. Thankfully, her padded backside softened the hard floor.

"Tell me what's going on, lommia? Why couldn't you come to us...to me? You know I would've done everything to help." She studied his downcast head, his slumped shoulders, and sorrow lanced through her. Under the bright lighting, the shadows under his eyes revealed how he'd worried, lost sleep, and allowed this to affect his health. Yet his tentacles swayed like they were caught in a gentle breeze.

"My son..." His voice cracked. "The Yithians have my son, milady. When I commed my blood-bond to let him know I was safe and that you had rescued me from the Yithians, he informed me they'd captured Mannx." His head drooped in despair. "Because of me, they know you took their ship. I did not think beyond my selfish need. For this, I have jeopardized your planet. I cannot ask your forgiveness... I truly cannot."

"I have hope and faith, Iommia, that everything will work out for the better. And I can't fault you for wanting to save your son. I would've moved heaven and hell to save my child."

"You are not angry with me?" Pannos's solid-black eyes widened.

"Of course not. You were desperate. The Etterians won't understand, though. You did violate their trust." She winced.

"I know. Thank you for speaking to me, Lady Macy." He graced her with a small smile, but it didn't reach his eyes. Not that she could tell in his black murky depths. Expressions were different and yet similar across species.

"Would you mind if I visited again?" She scanned the cell, devoid of anything interesting. As far as she was concerned, if anyone could fix this situation, it would be the Etterians. Did she have an absurd faith in them? Yes, but dammit, who else could sort this out? "Or is this goodbye, Pannos?" Tears stung her eyes, and she blinked them away. Desperation was all too familiar. It contorted your thoughts and led you down the wrong path.

Pannos sighed. "You are an emotive species, mitkaari. I will never regret meeting you." He rose to his feet and shuffled toward the shimmering light. "I would appreciate it if you did visit." He smiled at her, and this time, it crinkled the edges of his eyes like laugh lines. The devil was in the details, her gran used to say.

"Don't give up yet. Xan and Oyaz will do what they can for all parties. They're the good guys, Pannos, and everyone knows good always kicks evil's ass."

"Your faith is that of a child, mitkaari, but I thank you for sharing it with me."

She jumped to her feet, threw a beaming smile at the security guard, looped an arm through Illan's, and ushered him the hell out of there. "I could do with apple pie. My treat."

"Do I have a say?" Illan smiled, patting her hand resting on his forearm.

"Nope, and you'll thank me later."

XAN STOOD ALONGSIDE OYAZ, staring at the display vid in the comm room. His kiss-swollen lips now formed the scowl reflected in the display vid. His thoughts rested on another human. Msar had informed him of Lady Macy's presence in the security center. They'd observed the interaction on the vid. Xan's discussion with Pannos had revealed none of what the old Maloidian had shared with the human woman.

"Her faith in us is breathtaking," Xan said.

"Alodon's balls," Oyaz said, anger hardening his voice. "He opened to her like blossoming hahyts. Is it her softness? Her sweet voice?"

"Regardless, we now know why." Xan drew in a deep breath while running his forefinger along his bottom lip.

"So, it is not just humans Yithia has targeted. I shudder to think how long these abductions have been happening. They need to cease, Xan."

"I agree. We must find a way to monitor their activities. No one knows why and what they are doing. That is for our strategists to resolve. The current dilemma remains. Do we rescue his son and pardon the lommia? Do we leave his son to his fate and punish his father?"

"That is why you are the supreme commander, and I am not." Oyaz offered a small smile.

Xan grumbled, having needed his battle-bond's guidance in this. That Pannos had endangered his Dar Eth clouded his judgment. "If you were the supreme commander?" he asked.

"You know my answer to this, Xan," Oyaz said.

Xan grunted. "Free the son, punish the father. However, we are on the precipice of war. Should we mount a rescue, it may trigger the first battle."

"There is more than one way to mount a rescue. Force is not always the best approach." Oyaz arched a pointed brow.

"I know, yet it is the most enjoyable." Xan grinned. "Regardless, a decision has been made."

"So it has." Oyaz tapped the vid, freezing it on Macy's upturned face. "Time to take my charge to task for her reckless behavior."

Xan chuckled. "And the Durn? May the Maker bless your efforts."

"Supreme Commander." Msar glanced over his shoulder before facing the console. "The Maloidian Pannos has requested your presence."

"Why?" Oyaz tapped the console, zooming in on the old Maloidian where he sat in his cell. His back was rigid, his jaw set. He radiated determination despite the gentle sway of his tentacles.

"He did not say, Sub-Commander."

Without another word, Oyaz straightened and trailed Xan to the security center.

"I half expect the two *damu* to be lurking in the passages," Xan said. "Truly, Oyaz, Lady Macy should be in espionage."

"I doubt Malo would agree. She's stubborn and might not obey his commands." Oyaz chuckled. "I suspect the only male able to tame her would be her Eth."

"We shall see." Xan almost pitied whoever her Eth was. He strode passed the sec warrior to stand before Pannos. "How can I assist, lommia?"

The Maloidian pushed off the bed to shuffle across to the energy barrier. His tentacles swayed like seaweed at the bottom of the oceans. "Thank you for coming, Supreme Commander. I have one request. Please...please, save my son."

"Your son?" Xan went for ignorance while hiding the fury tightening his muscles. Why hadn't the old fool mentioned his *damu* in their earlier discussion? Etterians were a trustworthy people, for the most part. He discounted the recent deception played by Medic Teric in an attempt to save his daughter. Xan gritted his teeth. Also at the Yithians' doing. This was becoming absurd.

"Take me in his stead. Leave me in your infamous mines, I do not care, but please, save my Mannx." Pannos crumpled to his knees, narrowly missing the lethal barrier.

Xan gestured to the sec warrior to shut it off. He knelt beside the older male and lifted him to his feet, careful not to harm him. Sadness poured off Pannos, his markings fluctuating between dark and faded.

"Why did the Yithians take him?" Xan asked, setting the male onto the bed, lest his legs fail him again.

"You know?" Pannos raised his gaze to the ceiling. "Do not be angry with Lady Macy, please, Supreme Commander Xan. Her heart—"

"She is kindness personified." Oyaz leaned against the bulkhead. "She is in no danger, lommia."

Pannos dipped his chin. "She made me realize I should have revealed all to you from the start. I am truly sorry."

"Why was Mannx taken, Pannos?" Xan ground out.

"He farms surface caverns on Yithia and serves as a messenger between Maloid and the Yithian Kbal."

Oyaz pushed off the bulkhead.

Xan straightened, the hair at the back of his neck rising. "King Urio is aware of Kbal's plans?"

Pannos bobbed his head. "I suspect so. Why else target a farmer?" He rubbed his eyes, temple, and over his tentacles, agitating them. "He is a messenger for Kbal on his frequent trips to the market. Kbal is building a significant following."

Xan pursed his lips. He'd chosen to free the son, and this added information reinforced the decision as honorable. Now, he would comm King Xeus and inform him of Urio's possible awareness of Kbal's actions. The so-called alliance with the Yithian rebels might fall away. Still, a nation divided couldn't stand united. And Maloid's knowledge of this didn't bode well.

"I thank you for revealing the truth, Pannos. And Lady Macy is correct." Xan smiled. "We're the 'good guys.'" He faced the sec warrior. "Relocate Pannos to the barracks but have Pilot Msar monitor his movements."

"One foot in a forbidden area and your son will remain in Yithian custody." Oyaz frowned. "Tell me, lommia, what did the signal transmit?"

Pannos hesitated. "Your location, destination, and images of the human females."

Xan froze, spun on his heel, and roared, "Of my Dar Eth?" He curled his hands into fists and punched the bulkhead, buckling it. "You would endanger—?"

"I know. I am sorry. It was them or my son and my grand spawn." Pannos folded in on himself. "It sent only images. The Yithians would still have to battle their way through you to reach the females. I assumed they would be safe in your hands." He raised his gaze to Xan's. "They are protected?"

"Yes, but their planet is not as guarded."

Pannos nodded at Oyaz. "It is as I feared."

Xan strode away, ready to kill the selfish male. He stabbed the holographic letters on his O.D.I. to request a comm with Adviser Cales. The order to double the number of battleships deployed had to come from the king, and if need be, Xan would call Xeus uncle if it brought Earth's salvation.

Chapter Sixteen

Planet Lysara

A Kuta Shuttle

"It's beautiful." Quin stood behind the shuttle pilot, Nuos, *if* she was pronouncing it correctly. She was probably butchering it, and he was too polite to tell her. *What was wrong with John or Bob?*

The kuta dipped and swerved toward Lysara, a jungle world. She had mental images and all the knowledge about this red and green planet, thanks to Illan. Yet to see it for herself made those images her own. She would have new memories to add to Illan's knowledge.

Tall, gigantic trees looked thousands of years old. Skimming over the red vegetation, the wide and dense canopies hid the ground beneath it. And from their approaching angle, decaying areas glowed pale gray where the trees had died. The devastation made the planet look freckled. That had happened to Earth until the government had panicked and banned all manufacturing utilizing wood. Too many products had required wood as a component.

In Lysara's case, external forces hadn't killed the trees; they'd simply died. A drought, a disease, maybe even a change in weather patterns could've caused such destruction. Illan estimated it was due to the Lysarans and the decline of their people. She gasped. No, that couldn't be right. She pressed a hand to her mouth to hide her chuckle. Illan believed the lack of sex had done this to the planet, that sex influenced the weather and, therefore, the environment. She peeked at Bry-dar and Myn-ras buckled in across from her and itched to ask them if Illan was telling the truth.

They were an interesting species. They had vampiric teeth. The sight of them still made her smile. And their sense of smell was so advanced they could pick up emotions, which is why they adored *Earthian females,* so they'd said.

She had hugged them goodbye before boarding the shuttle. Well, before Xan had entered the shuttle bay. He tended to growl when people touched her. She kind of liked his overprotective vibes, for now.

Nuos landed the shuttle on a specified docking platform the Lysarans kept clear of the jungle. And it was for authorized vessels only. No visitors could step foot on Lysaran soil without express permission from their king, Sy'mar Lok-soto. All visitors had to undergo quarantine to ensure the Lysaran ecosystem remained untainted. En route, they implemented the quarantine, and it would last for a few more days if they disembarked. According to her Illan-knowledge, the quarantine was shorter for returning Lysarans.

After waving at them from the shuttle door, she strapped herself into her seat and studied Xan's handsome face as he checked she'd fastened the belt properly. Sometimes, he could be a pain in the backside about her safety. Like she hadn't survived years without him? Like she hadn't taken a Yithian ship, saved people? She snorted as he dropped into a seat next to her. He couldn't help himself. His gaze rested on her, his focus intense, even as the ice-blue of his eyes swirled. Their one kiss had been spicy hot and sizzling, everything she'd longed for. The point was that a kiss didn't a boyfriend make. She would have to speak to him, just to find out what was going on in that gorgeous head of his.

Illan huffed. *You know I can read your thoughts, Quin.*

She frowned, and here she'd been hoping for a little personal time with her thoughts. *How are you able to talk to me?*

She sensed his shrug. *Distance is of no importance with a Durn mind fuse.* The silence continued for a few minutes. *You knock his socks off, isn't that what you'd say?*

Her breath caught as her eyes darted to Xan, finding his gaze still on her. *Do I knock his socks off? Shit, I'll need to ask him.*

Sifting through my memories again, Illan? She smirked as Illan bristled.

Humans are fascinating. I am particularly fond of your interactions with Garrett Winters. He appears to be more than a guardian to you.

Garrett? Sure, she may have had a little hero worship, but that ship had burned. *Lost opportunity, I guess, since neither of us pursued those feelings, Illan.*

And yet, Quinny, you still have them if you dig deep enough. Fascinating. These feelings should have dissipated now that you have the supreme commander. Yet they've remained.

Did she still have a thing for Garrett? No, Illan had to be wrong. *But do I? Have the supreme commander, I mean. I don't know anything about him or his culture. Nor does he know me. Sure, he's gorgeous. But just because I want to do things to him or with him doesn't mean anything. Want is not the same as need is not the same as have. I want him, but need and have him? I don't know, Illan. He might not feel the same way. Maybe he's overprotective because we're human?*

You may be correct. Iddan guards Cyn, Oyaz and I see to Macy, and she does need the two of us. I don't know from where her endless source of enthusiasm originates.

Xan laced Quin's fingers through his. She released a long breath, liking that he touched her as often as he could. She hadn't realized she was a demonstrative person. Sure, her guardians received their fair share of hugs when they visited, but nothing to this degree.

Not that she minded his touch or presence. Both brought comfort and stimulation, if that made any sense.

She studied his face, the softness of his bottom lip, and glanced away, hoping to calm her erratic heartbeat. *I could be developing a crush on the poor man.*

Male, Illan said in a bored tone, doubting she would never grasp the difference. *Crush? My O.D.I. informs me it means infatuation?*

A violent jerk shuddered the shuttle, almost jarring her teeth from her jaw. *What the hell?*

Illan, I think we've been hit. Track our shuttle. Let Oyaz know. This thing's going down.

His voice was crisp as he demanded, *Confirm your location.*

She growled. *How the hell should I know? We just dropped off the Lysarans and are on our way back.*

Stay safe. And the connection went silent.

Beside her, Xan tensed as he rattled instructions in his lyrical language. Nuos tapped away at the console, and the three other men...*males* were fastening themselves into their seats. Yet through it all, Xan held her hand as if they were on a picnic. It took all her effort not to panic, to keep her shoulders relaxed, her breathing regular despite the adrenaline pumping through her body and pounding her heart a mile a minute.

This wasn't worse than throwing herself out of a helicopter. Yes, she'd had a parachute strapped on. And no, *that* hadn't made it easier. Wyatt had planned that excursion for weeks. She hadn't had the heart to tell him she didn't want to go. His face had shone with excitement, his need to share this with her more than evident. So, like the woman they'd raised her to be, she'd tamped down her fears and dislikes and had thrown herself out of the helicopter hovering over the Kali Gandaki valley near Kagbeni. She'd squealed the first few meters, then as she'd splayed out her limbs, the roar of the wind isolated her with her thoughts and the beauty of the fast-approaching landscape.

The ride down had been exhilarating and peaceful. The *landing* had been the worst experience of her life. Spraining her ankle was par for the course but having to hike almost a full day to the nearest village? Wyatt had been a darling, though, carrying her as much as he could, up the pathways, over streams, even attempting to catch a ride from passing vehicles.

The shuttle jerked again. A high-pitched whine screamed from the rear. Overhead lights flickered between blue and red. *Burn and die*, she chuckled. The urge to squeal like a little girl almost overwhelmed her. What kept her gripping the flimsy strings of sanity was her imagining their facial expressions if she ran around the compartment like a headless chicken alternating between shrieking and crying. She laughed, wishing she could do it anyway—the memory would've been priceless.

"Are you enjoying yourself, Quin?" Xan's husky voice had her gaze flying to meet his startled one.

His question made her realize she *was* having fun. The rush of adrenaline punching through her was the same as when Garrett took her up in an antiquated fighter jet. He'd borrowed the plane from his friend, a retired aviator mechanic. She'd laughed then as they broke the sound barrier.

"Yes." She smiled. "Garrett would love this."

"Garrett?"

"One of my guardians. He's a pilot." She grabbed the top of Xan's hand, giving it a firm squeeze. He studied her for a long moment before he drew in a deep breath.

"When we are at leisure," he said, "but for now, the shuttle is losing altitude. Nuos is targeting a beach to ensure a smoother landing."

"Wise, it's the only bare strip of land on this planet, right?"

Xan lingered on her lips. He wanted to kiss her so desperately that he couldn't string two thoughts together. Her excitement washed over him, spiking his senses. He hadn't expected his emotions and reactions to be so closely tied to hers.

"Brace," Nuos yelled.

Xan threw his arms around her, crushing her against his chest. They hit the beach with a force that threatened to pull them out of their seats. Quin laughed as the shuttle hurtled along the sand—her enjoyment was sensual and infectious. He hid his smile in the caressing silken strands of her hair.

As soon as the shuttle slid to a stop, he undid their straps, tugged her into his arms, and brushed his lips across her mouth as he inhaled the essence that was her. Her untamed soul called to his in a way he couldn't explain. She blinked at him, then caressed him from his temple, along his cheek to his jaw. The sensation was indescribable like the variety of emotions she evoked within him.

"Did you notify the *Phoenix*?" he asked Nuos, his gaze not straying from her face while he memorized her expressions.

"Still unable to reach the sub-commander, nor Msar." Nuos strode across to them.

Xan flicked Nuos a glance. "Are the sludge tanks damaged, the replicator or rehydrator functional?"

"They are operational. The blasts were precise, disabling shuttle only."

Xan's males checked their armor and weaponry. He glanced at Quin, at her dark blue breeches, her flowery tunic, and her bare toes in her footwear. He scowled. Lysara was an inhospitable planet to those unprepared. "Come, Quin, you need armor."

"I do?" Her eyes sparkled.

He released her and led her to the replicator. Using her stored measurements, he called forth a mini-Etterian armor—chest, pants, and magnetic boots. Then the true dilemma hit him. She needed to change, but where? A kuta shuttle was a lightweight yet durable single compartment personnel carrier. It was utilized for short journeys with maximum seating and minimal features. In truth, a box.

He stormed to the door and opened it, driving his males out before standing guard at its entrance. He ached to steal a glance when the fabric whispered. Only when she stamped her feet, testing out the new footwear, did he glance at her. Alodon's balls, the chest armor fitted her like a second skin. And her scent was incredible. It had altered, intensified as if she was fertile. But that was an impossibility. It wasn't the Oley month.

"Quin." He sucked in another deep breath. "Why is your scent changing?"

Her head shot up. Perske stained her cheeks and traveled down her throat. "What can you smell? Is it blood?" she squeaked.

He inhaled again and shook his head. "I scent no blood, just rich, intoxicating...you." His voice was guttural and no longer under his control.

"No blood's good. I hope I make it back to the *Phoenix* before..." She didn't meet his gaze.

"Are you saying you *are* fertile?" He groaned before running a hand over his face. He wasn't certain he wanted to hear her response.

"It's just my monthly cycle, Xan." She shrugged as if it mattered not.

"Monthly?" he whispered, his hands shaking. "You will scent like this every month?"

"Is now the time to discuss this, Xan?"

"Yes," he roared, anger and fear shooting through him. "Lysara is home to the wilanegy. They are invincible beasts with foot-long blue spikes. They are feared for their bloodlust and incredible strength. The more they scent fear or *blood*, the crazier they attack. And if you bleed, they will come for you, *ensa*."

Her eyes widened, and she nodded, indicating she understood the danger she placed them in. "I don't know what you're expecting from me, Xan. I can't stop it from happening."

"Very well, Quin. We will deal with it *if* it happens."

"I wish I could compel my period to wait. Shit, millions of women have wished for that at some point. But even in a life or death situation, I don't have that ability."

He blinked at her, understanding half of what she said. "Explain later what this all entails."

"How much time do we have before the attackers can find us?" She rushed over to the replicator to punch at the keys.

"A few minutes, why?" He stood alongside her.

She ordered a black bag to put in an array of gadgets he couldn't name. She stuffed in a rope, foodstuffs, and sachets of water. Then shoved many items into the pockets of her pants until they deformed the shape of her thighs. She glanced out the open door and winced. After ordering viz-wear and sliding them on top of her head, she requested a few weapons.

"What are you doing, *ensa*?" He studied the items appearing on the replicator's surface. Though they were strange, their purpose was clear. Anger solidified his shoulders, and he picked up a lightweight dagger to gesture with it. These implied he couldn't protect her. That none of his males could.

"Always prepare, Xan. If something happens and we're separated, would you want me defenseless?"

He grumbled, hating that she had the right of it. When he said nothing more, she darted to the locker to pull out a blaster.

"Please, help me with this." She handed it to him.

Since he'd shown her how to fire it, he couldn't deny her the use of it. He kneeled to strap it to her leg, his fingers lingering on her inner thigh.

"Thank you." She curled her hand halfway over his shoulder for stability. Releasing him, she trailed her fingertips from his ear, along his jaw to his chin. Then she dipped to press a sweet kiss to his lips.

He froze.

"Do you have explosives?" she said into his parted mouth.

"What now, Quin?" He smiled. So like her to seduce him for more weapons and ammunition.

"We might have to destroy the shuttle..." She slipped the backpack on with her gaze not leaving his.

"It will self-destruct in two minutes." He rose to his full height.

She grinned, marched to the open door of the downed shuttle, and jumped the three-meter distance to the beach with an ease that implied practice. Landing smoothly, she spun to analyze her surroundings, wincing again at the bright sunlight before flipping the viz-wear over her eyes.

Lysara was a paradise. The oceans were a deep emerald green. The trees had light gray bark and bold red canopies. Dark purple foliage lined the floor of the jungle. The glossy leaves were large and twisted and appeared succulent. He landed next to her and strode toward his males, who'd formed a perimeter fifty meters out.

"Illan's information is accurate," she said, drawing his gaze. "But what isn't in his Durn knowledge is the warmth of the sun on my armor, the brightness of the pale-yellow sky, the scent of the cream beaches. It smells like Earth's sea and sand without the coconut tanning lotion." Images flashed in his mind, of Earth's oceans and this coconut lotion. "What's the plan?" she asked.

"Find the nearest settlement and contact the *Phoenix*," he said. "The shuttle cannot comm Pilot Msar. None of our O.D.I.s link with the *Phoenix*. We are stranded."

"There is no way for Oyaz to trace us if the O.D.I.s aren't connecting?" She arched a pale brow.

"We are transmitting our locations. They are just not penetrating whatever is dampening us." Xan frowned at her need for clarification. What wasn't clear in his words?

"If the search shuttles were low enough, perhaps then?"

"Quin, they do not know we have crashed. There will be no immediate rescue," he growled out, losing patience with her.

"Xan, they *do* know we have crashed. Illan, remember?" She snorted and strode to where Nuos waited.

Xan scowled. Her golden braid swayed as she crossed the sand, yet that didn't distract him from the realization he was redundant and powerless. As an Etterian male, he trained for situations like this and was more than capable of protecting his Dar Eth and his unit. But the Maker had decided to bless Xan with a female who didn't need his skills or strength. Regardless, he was *still* the supreme commander. His males relied on him, even if she didn't appear to need him.

"Nuos, gather the males. We head for higher ground. Lady Quin has spoken to Illan, and assistance is on course." *Watch me take command, female.*

"She has? This is good news, milady." Nuos joined Medic Eira, Warriors Lurz and Jokta, and they marched to where the jungle wall met the cream-colored sands of the beach.

They breached the dense foliage lining the jungle floor to forge a path. Thick vines connected the trees, sturdy enough for someone to swing from tree to tree as was the Lysaran custom.

"How is this possible?" Quin trailed Xan. "The sun can't penetrate the trees to reach the floor. How do these plants flourish without sunlight?"

"The tree canopies retract throughout the day. This is how the Lysarans tell time."

Illan must not have known this. Her mouth fell open, and her eyes sparkled with delight. Xan shook his head, attempting to stay on point. His Dar Eth was a walking distraction.

He continued down the path each warrior took turns to forge. When it was his turn, he stepped forward, swinging his Maloidi-an-serrated dagger, his long strides covering distances with ease. Upon entering a small clearing, five meters in diameter, he scanned the area, then raised his gaze to the pale-yellow sky. On his last trip to Lysara many years before, he hadn't encountered the signal dampening or such a clearing. It was as if a tree had never grown here. There was no evidence of one having been removed either. And no purple plants grew on the floor, despite the soil appearing fertile.

Quin weaved among his males, giving them a brown block and a packet of water. She offered him the same. He stared at the small square, dark against her pale hand. Sheathing his dagger, he accepted her offering. He picked up the block between forefinger and thumb and stared at it. She popped her piece into her mouth. The way her eyes stuttered closed hitched his breath. Her expression was identical to the one in his vision. He placed the block on his tongue and moaned at the sweet and intense flavor that coated his tongue.

"What...what is this?" He rolled his tongue in his mouth, trying to savor every drop.

"Chocolate. It's a high energy source and tastes divine." She smiled before ripping the packet open with her tiny teeth. The action was animalistic...and arousing.

He held his packet in front of her, pressed together the two circles marked on the corner, and it opened. She flashed an unrepentant smile, closed the backpack, and swung it on again while fisting the packet to squeeze water into her mouth. She sucked on the packet, making annoying and suggestive sounds that shouldn't have made his malehood twitch.

"Do you think we'll reach safety before semi-darkness?" She fell into step behind him.

Night-time on Lysara was a relative term since there wasn't complete darkness with two suns. Illan would know this.

"The arrival of the evening will not hinder us. Though the sky is beautiful in various shades of purple."

"I look forward to seeing it for myself. So, it's safe to sleep under the stars? No huge snakes, creepy spiders, blood-sucking mosquitoes?"

"Your planet sounds hazardous." Xan chuckled a few moments later after his O.D.I. flashed images detailing these Earthian creatures.

"I'm sure most planets are. It depends on the dominant species, I suppose," she said.

He froze.

Nuos waved at him to back up. Xan sniffed the air and faced Quin. The urge to protect her drove him to stride across to her. He moved quicker and quieter than she could. She'd responded to Nuos, taking careful steps backward. When Xan swept her into his arms and threw her over his shoulder, her smothered squeak said he'd taken her by surprise. Now wasn't the time to fill her in, but she was silent, implying she understood the necessity of speed and stealth.

They had backtracked about a mile when he halted and lowered her feet to the ground.

"A troop of wilanegy; we will go around them." He veered right and hacked a new path.

She trailed him without saying a word.

Chapter Seventeen

QUIN WAS A LITTLE light-headed at the higher oxygen content in the air. Inhaling fresh unrecycled air gave her a buzz. She whipped out the compass she'd requested from the replicator and scowled when the needle went haywire. *Typical. What a waste of sludge. What did I expect? That every planet had a true north?* She shrugged. It had made sense, though. With a sigh, she shoved the compass into its pocket.

They'd hiked for hours, and despite training her body, the steady exercise had her muscles burning. But as they continued at a fast pace, an agony of another sort rested in her pelvis. She grimaced. With each step she took, it worsened, and without her trusty painkillers, this month's cycle promised to be hell. She glanced at the males in the unit and pinched her lips, drawing in slow controlled breaths. They'd thrust out their chins, determined, not bothered by the walking yet still on guard, slicing glances from side-to-side or checking behind them.

A spike of pain shot through her, and she gripped a tree, leaning her backside against it as she doubled over, clutching her pelvis. She drew in silent breaths, releasing them as calmly as she could manage. Controlling pain was possible with breathing techniques, but she was in two minds about that. Knife and bullet wounds meant she'd experienced enough pain to test out the theory. Sometimes it worked, sometimes it didn't.

Medic Eira spoke to Xan in their language, but she was mid-technique. Until she could control the pain, what they discussed or what was on the path ahead would have to wait. But when silence descended, she sensed their gazes. She groaned, finding all five males staring at her.

"Just give me a moment." She sucked in sharp breaths, hoping to speed up the process. Surely the rich oxygen air would allow that.

"Why did you not tell me?" Xan's pursed lips said he wasn't pleased with her.

"I can do this." She lifted her chin before forcing herself to straighten.

With a muted growl, he indicated to his males to set up a base. He gripped her shoulders, the heat of his palms made her somehow feel better. "It is a richer air quality, a heavier gravity, a softer terrain. You cannot expect your body to handle all three."

She shook her head. He thought she was too weak to keep up. *Typical.* "Xan, it's near. We need to get to high ground, and I mean now." She gave him a pointed look.

His gaze narrowed, then flew wide with his cheeks darkening.

Ah, at last, he understands.

"How…do you know?" He focused on her hands clutching her stomach.

"Painful cramps like someone is kicking you in your balls every few minutes." Wincing, she pressed on her lower abdomen.

"You are in pain? Medic Eira!" Xan summoned the medic.

She huffed, almost sorry for him. She could imagine what these males would be like when their wives fell pregnant. Shaking her head, she fought back an exhausted smile.

"Base canceled," Xan said to his males, halting them mid-task. "Lady Quinlan is in pain, Medic Eira. See to it. We need to reach the clearing with due urgency."

Eira shuffled closer to scan her with his O.D.I.

"Can you slow the cramps, Eira?" she asked. "They bring the bleeding." She refused to blush. It was silly to be embarrassed when each damn male could *scent* her *fertility*.

"I cannot. I can only dull the pain." Eira offered a small smile. "My apologies, milady."

"Please don't, Eira. I need to know when the cramping stops." She forced her body to unbend again, despite the agony wrenching her insides. No alien should ever say an Earthian female couldn't endure.

Eira stilled, studied her face, then shook his head. "Supreme Commander Xan has stated that I—"

"Xan, dammit, it's my body." She glared at him with her hands on her hips, her posture aggressive, but she didn't care.

A pulse ticked at the base of his jaw. He scanned her with his ice-blue gaze before settling on her face. "Then unpack all your gear and hand over the bag. Perhaps with you less burdened, we will travel faster."

Her breath hitched, and she fought the familiar ache in her chest caused by her disappointing a guardian. It was why she'd allowed them to drag her through hell because she couldn't bear failing them.

"Are you saying I slow you down?" Her words came out in a whisper.

"Of course not. You move well. It is I who forgets you are human." His honest response and backhanded compliment had her mumbling as she unpacked her pockets and unstrapped the blaster to shove into the bag.

Quin?

She froze with her hand outstretched, the bag dangling from her fingers. *Oh, thank the Lord, Illan, where are you?*

I do not bare good news. We are struggling to locate you. Our scanners cannot connect to a single O.D.I.

"Shit." She stomped her foot and winced. *Are you at least on this cursed planet?*

Cursed? Lysara is a paradise.

She crossed to Xan, handing him the backpack. *It isn't when you're about to be* fertile *surrounded by blood-crazed wilanegy.*

Truth?

She threw her hands into the air. *No, I'm making this shit story up because I feel like it.* Silence met her response, and she frowned. *Sorry, Illan, I'm pissy when I'm in pain.*

"Is Illan talking to you? Are they near?" Xan gazed at the sky, no doubt searching for a shuttle.

She shook her head.

We located your destroyed shuttle. Illan projected an image of the self-destructed shuttle—its mangled metallic pieces littered the beach. *But we're unable to penetrate the foliage to virtually track your path.*

Xan crowded her, peering at her with one brow arched. She placed her hand on his chest and stared at her fingers splayed wide, denting the glorious muscle beneath her touch. He was so warm, the urge to lean against him, to siphon a little of his heat, had her tilting toward him.

Have you encountered any other shuttles? We still don't know who shot us down. "I asked Illan if he knows who fired at us."

Xan covered her hand with his, keeping her in place. "Is he coming? How many shuttles are en route?"

No other vessels. Illan scanned the sky, clear of flying objects. *Data Officer Tius has a theory on the attack, though.*

Good. So, if we returned to the shuttle, we'd find you there? Not that she knew how far they'd hiked. The dense jungle gave no indication of distance.

Yes.

"Illan says they can meet us back at our shuttle. They haven't seen any other spaceships."

Xan clenched and released his jaw even as he stroked her knuckles with his thumb. "No, we are closer to our destination than to the shuttle. To return would be illogical."

He said no. She scowled, wishing she'd thought to order a flare gun from the replicator. She had night vision goggles and daggers for various purposes but no flare gun.

"Inform him to search for the highest point and land there."

She huffed. What high point? She couldn't see past the blasted trees. *Xan says we're heading for the highest visual point. He asked that you wait for us there.*

Illan smirked. *Asked?*

Quin chuckled, the sound loud in the quiet of the jungle. *Commanded. He is who he is.*

She closed the distance between her and Xan and tugged her hand free after patting his chest. He faced ahead to forge a new path, swinging his dagger with efficient force, rippling his back muscles in the process with his long braid swaying hypnotically across his greatsword.

"How do you know where you're going?" she asked since he didn't appear to have a navigation tool of some sort. She knew damn well compasses were useless. They probably used their O.D.I. under normal circumstances, but here on Lysara, those didn't work either.

"Scent," he said as if that explained it.

Chapter Eighteen

Xan froze and held out a hand to stop her. She did. Her guardians had trained her to respond without hesitation. His gaze softened with sadness as if he was saying farewell. He gave her such a sweet smile, incongruent with his usual reserved expressions. She frowned and scanned their surroundings. *Is he in mortal danger?* She took a step toward him and met solid muscle. Jokta held her. She glanced at him, then at Xan as he sank a foot into the sand. *Quicksand?*

She lunged for him, but Jokta yanked her back. No matter what she threw at him, kicks, punches, the male held firm. "Please." She panted, clinging to his arms.

"Do not come closer, my Quin." Xan's intense gaze traveled over her as if he memorized her, believing he would never see her again. He withdrew his greatsword, his gaze lowering to his feet.

"It is a rare Gracc. Their large bodies lie under the ground surface awaiting a victim," Eira said in a matter-of-fact tone.

She stared at him for the longest of moments, accessing the information Illan had shared with her. Graccs had no known weaknesses, and their bodies went meters under the surface. *Shit.*

"How much time does he have?" She struggled to breathe. Her heart thumped, banging against her ribcage. She lunged, gripped with the need to save him, to kiss him, to do something, anything, but Jokta didn't budge.

"Not long," he mumbled, his arms clamped around her.

"Are you telling me you're just going to stand here and watch him...*die*?" Anger warred with desperation, and she shuddered before renewing the struggle for freedom.

"There is nothing we can do," Jokta growled. "If you go to him, you will die too."

What? She blinked. "But I have a rope. Xan, can't we pull you out?"

"Its teeth are directed inward, you pull, and it will shred me." Gripping the hilt of his greatsword with one hand, Xan unhooked her bag and tossed it aside. He spun his sword and held it like he planned to plunge it into the ground.

Biological diagrams flashed in her mind showing the direction of a Gracc's teeth with a bite force quotient somewhere in the four digits. It would paralyze him before digesting him over ten days. It had a flexible jaw, able to expand to a wider diameter to accommodate larger prey.

"But what if we make it think you're bigger than you are? Would it release you then?" She scanned the clearing, searching for any markings, something to show her where its sensors hid.

"Yes. That may work," Nuos said with a calculating smile. "If we position ourselves and stimulate along its sensors it may just open its mouth wider..."

"And I am swallowed sooner?" Xan snapped. "I do not like this plan."

"Dying's a bad plan no matter what. Standing there and doing nothing to stop it is the dumbest idea." She threw out a hand. "Let me try, Xan. I...I can't bear to just stand by and...lose you."

He gave her a small nod, muttering something. Jokta released her, and she scrambled for her bag, ignoring Mr. Pessimist, to yank out the rope. She searched the layered ground and picked up a hefty rock to tie on the end. With careful aim, she tried to throw it over the lowest tree branch above her.

By her third attempt, she realized she didn't have the strength and handed it to Jokta, who was by far the biggest Etterian in the unit. "We need to hoist him straight up, or else the teeth will tear through him." She threw Jokta an expectant look.

He grunted, but with one throw, the rope and rock flew over the branch. It landed on the ground with a muffled thump. She untied it, then tossed the other end of the rope to Xan, who had sunk another two feet, the sands falling away in an ever-growing whirlpool. Darkness peeked through with white tusks the size of her arm rising out of the hole.

"How do you know where the sensors are?" she asked Nuos, ignoring any comments from Xan, who'd at least sheathed his sword and grabbed the rope.

"Approximately within a two-meter perimeter from the supreme commander." Nuos gestured with his fingers, and they formed a circle around Xan.

When she wanted to do the same, each male shook his head. She fumed and stood by the bag to watch, tapping her feet as she paced on the spot. Eira, Nuos, and Lurz stamped their feet with enough force for the vibrations to travel through her boots. She folded her arms across her chest and gritted her teeth. So what she couldn't stamp as hard? They could have let her try. Still, she shared with Illan about the perimeter and method of calling the creature. *The blue bastard didn't know everything.*

She stood rooted to the spot as the ground rippled like liquid sand, and a massive hole opened around Xan. Jokta grunted as the rope tightened now that he supported Xan's weight. He tugged at the same time Xan climbed up until his boots cleared the gaping mouth. He glanced at Jokta and nodded, swinging his legs to gain momentum. Lurz lunged behind Jokta to grab the rope for added leverage. Within moments, Xan launched himself and landed on his feet, inches to the right of Lurz.

"Well done," he roared with a dimpled grin, grabbing the forearms of each of his males before facing her. His males beamed, not that he'd noticed. His sole focus was on her. Her stomach flip-flopped at the sight of his incredible smile. *Hot damn. Two dimples?*

"And you call my planet hazardous?" she teased, struggling to breathe under his admiring gaze. Her attention rested for a long moment on his slime-coated pants, almost in disbelief at how things had played out.

"That was an unbelievable plan, Quin." He strode toward her, his body tense again, his fists clenched at his sides.

"War games, remember." She willed herself not to blush under his intense scrutiny. Needing to do something, she closed the bag and handed it to him.

"Do you have such a creature on Earth?" His gaze traveled her face as intensely as before.

She worked a loose strand of hair behind her ear, looking any-where but at him. "No, although I saw something Gracc-like in a movie. It had rows and rows of teeth circling its mouth." She twirled a finger, indicating the jungle. "It was in a desert, and it digested its prey over a thousand years."

He winced. "An entertainment vid? I would like to see it." He wrapped his fingers around her arm, just above the elbow, and pulled her toward him. "Thank you, and when I am not covered in saliva, I will show you my gratitude as is my right." He pressed a lingering kiss to the crown of her head. "The clearings make sense now. They are where the Gracc lurks," he said to the unit before circling along the circumference to forge a path.

She hurried to catch up, her gaze ensnared by the huge hole still in the center of the clearing. Spearhead-shaped tusks pointed inward. They had the look of elephant tusks but with serrated edges. The stench of decaying plant matter and meat made her gag. She shivered at how close Xan had come to dying.

"We need to dodge wilanegy and clearings?" She accepted the coiled rope from Jokta, offering him a smile of thanks. When she opened the bag and shoved the rope in, the chocolate caught her eye. She broke off two pieces before passing the rest back, then tapped Xan on the shoulder to offer him his block. He took it without hesitation.

A rustle and creaking wood came from above. Blinding sun-light streamed down to the ground, and the purple succulents bloomed with bright white flowers. She gasped and spun, dazzled by the beautiful blossoms. A heady scent rose to greet her, and she inhaled its sweetness.

"Two hours to evening," Xan said while sucking on his chocolate. "Another hour and we should reach the high point."

"If there are no further delays," she said.

He grinned. The appearance of a dimple caught her breath. *Damn, even one dimple is lethal.*

"I scent water," he said as Nuos marched ahead to hack the purple plants.

She frowned at the destroyed flowers just before she crushed them under her boots. Sadness dampened her eagerness to be done with this adventure, and for a moment, she mourned their destruction.

Half an hour later, they encountered a pool of tranquil green water. Xan dropped the bag on the muddy bank and waded into the pool to rinse off his waterproof-but-not-Gracc-saliva-proof pants. He emerged dripping water and collected the bag to follow Nuos.

"We cannot remain here. This is a wilanegy watering spot." He gestured to the large paths on the opposite side of the pool. The plants had grown around the used paths forming organic tunnels. "Come, Quin, the high-point is just over there."

She trailed him without a word.

"Are you still in pain?" he asked without glancing at her.

"No," she said, "the cramping is gone. But adrenaline might have numbed the pain... I hope not."

He stopped to study her, then drew in a deep breath. His nostrils flared. He grumbled something in his language before cupping her cheek. "Your scent is delicious but muted. Water affects our ability to smell and hear. We cannot remain here."

Did he just say...delicious? She grinned. *Well, that can't be too bad, right?*

"And not being able to smell means..." She tapped her chin. "No forewarning?" She narrowed in on the high organic tunnels the wilanegy had formed. "Leaving you blindsided."

He circled his arm around her waist and swung her, placing her ahead of him on the path. But he didn't release her. Instead, he drew her against his chest and pressed a kiss to her neck. She shivered, sparks trickling down to her nipples. Wow.

With a nudge of his pelvis, she stumbled forward and fell into an easy pace. She dared not peek at him, but she swore her backside tingled under his admiring gaze.

Chapter Nineteen

Something shifted the plants around a tunnel. Quin froze, blinked, and threw out a hand, catching Lurz across the chest. The trio of wilanegy bore down on them without warning. What they had feared might happen, came to pass. Lurz thrust her behind him, his body forming a futile barrier. She gawked at the stampeding beasts. They looked like gorillas—large, blue, and spiked as per Illan's information.

What he couldn't share was how it was to see them, to smell their dried-blood and fetid odor. Or how their gurgling roars made her heart leap into her throat. Her knees trembled. Her guardians had never trained her for such a scenario, and playing dead like with a bear wouldn't work. Xan was right. These creatures seemed invincible. The only weak spot was perhaps their eyes, but to reach there, she would have to risk their spikes and meaty paws. Yet Illan's data said to aim for the neck. No spikes grew there. Swords were the only effective weapons since blasters couldn't penetrate their thick fur. And she'd left her sword on the battleship. Silly her.

"Are you bleeding?" Lurz kept his gaze on the advancing troop.

"No," she huffed while pulling out a dagger. The rest of her *armory* was in the bag with... She sought out Xan.

A wilanegy had him up against a tree trunk. With greatsword in hand, he slashed at its spikes, barely keeping it back. Nuos tried to lure it away from Xan by slicing at its hindquarters. Eira and Jokta were dealing with their own and were faring better. They had at least injured its eye. The third one approached Lurz and her.

With each step it took, Lurz forced her back until there was nowhere to go. The ground fell away, then a meter's drop to the steep rocky bank into the pool. If she jumped down, the movement would make it charge. Lurz glanced over his shoulder and scowled at their predicament.

"Go." As determination settled on his features, he pinched his lips. He was prepared to sacrifice his life for hers. *The idiot.* She studied the pool as a plan formed. If they swam across it, maybe the beast couldn't follow or it would slow it down, buying them time. It was better than choosing to die.

"Can they swim?" she asked.

"Milady,...go." He glared at her before turning away, believing the matter settled.

The idiot has never dealt with a stubborn woman before. He's about to receive his first lesson.

She launched herself onto his back, hooked her legs around his torso and her arms around his head, protecting him but making him top heavy. She flung herself backward, dragging him over the edge. She hit the ground shoulder first, gritting her teeth at the pop. Ignoring the excruciating pain setting her back on fire, she allowed the momentum to roll them down the bank until they stilled. His weight pinned her into the mud, sinking her inches deep. Having a two-hundred-pound Etterian male land on her was something she never wanted to repeat. And judging by the wilanegy's roar, they weren't safe yet. Slapping at his shoulders, she yelled at him to get off her. When he did, she sucked in a deep breath, relishing the air filling her lungs. Her vision cleared, and she jumped up, skidding across the mud. Fiery numbness traveled down her arm from the dislocated shoulder, but she couldn't spare it time.

"Get in the water," she said and waded into the pool. Her shoulder and back screamed at her as she dove one-armed into the water to paddle like a two-year-old. Damaging her shoulder hadn't been part of the plan. Lurz had listened to her and splashed behind her while *three* wilanegy clambered to the water's edge.

Crippling pain of another sort pierced her chest, snatching her breath and blurring her vision with unshed tears. If all the beasts were free, that meant Xan and his males hadn't made it.

"Xan," she whimpered as she searched the embankment.

As Lurz swam past her, he looped an arm around her to drag her with him. He trudged out of the pool and dumped her in the mud with little finesse.

"Your antics bought us time. Death is inevitable," he thundered, pointing at the wilanegy sliding into the pool

She ignored him as she one-handedly staggered to her feet and gestured to his blaster still strapped to his thigh.

"As soon as all three are in the water, stun them."

Lurz jerked back as if he'd been hit. He turned as the beasts charged into the water, their roaring angry and frantic.

"Blast the water…" he repeated and unclipped his blaster. He inched closer to the edge just as Xan and Nuos appeared on the ledge.

At the sight of Xan, a sweet joy burst through her chest. She flashed him a wide smile. They grabbed their blasters as well and aimed for the water seeing Lurz raise his blaster. With a nod to each other, they fired at the pool's surface.

Squeals and roars followed as the beasts writhed and died. Silence settled with strange fishlike creatures surfacing, bobbing in the waves. The stench of charred wilanegy burned her nostrils. She shuddered to think what the males were experiencing with their heightened sense of smell. But then again, she didn't care. As long as they were no longer in danger, then suffering under the stench was acceptable.

"Are you bleeding?" Xan stormed toward her, his long strides bringing him around the pool.

"I. Am. Not. Bleeding," she growled, crumpling to her knees, exhausted now the adrenaline had left her. She cradled her arm, trying not to jar the dislocation.

"You, Lurz?" Nuos asked.

"No, just wet," the ungrateful male muttered.

She snuck a glance at him, wondering if he was still angry with her.

"They scented the air and charged after you." Nuos grabbed Lurz on his shoulder. "That was good thinking, blasting the water."

Lurz scowled.

Yup, still super pissed. She slumped. The throbbing in her shoulder grew stronger with each second that passed.

"It was milady's id—"

"Where is Eira? Jokta?" She gave Lurz a pointed look.

"Eira is wounded." Xan dropped to his haunches in front of her.

Lurz and Nuos turned their backs on them, granting them privacy. She almost rolled her eyes. With their preternatural hearing, nothing was private.

"How are you, *ensa*?" Xan studied her face before assessing her wet body. He drew in a deep breath and froze. "I scent blood that even the water cannot mask."

"Oh, for the love of..." She clambered to her feet to glare at him, then at Nuos and Lurz. "The next male to ask me if I have my monthly will have his balls shot off with his own blaster." She spun on her heel and stomped to the embankment. The heat on her cheeks rivaled the agony in her shoulder. Furious with males in general, she stamped her feet despite the pain ricocheting through her with each step.

"Quin," Xan boomed and in his most authoritative voice too. She froze and glared at him.

"You have a wound on your back," he said in a calm tone that didn't hide how furious he was with her.

She flashed him an apologetic smile. "Having an Etterian male land on you is always fun." She marched back to where the drama had begun.

Jokta knelt beside Eira but there was no blood, just a large broken body. By the droop of Jokta's shoulders, she had to assume it was bad. She gasped and scrambled to the other side of Eira's body to hold his hand.

"How bad is it?" she asked as she studied Eira's mud and blood-splattered face.

He opened his eyes to look at her, so she pressed a hand to his cheek.

"He needs the med-E.D. He is bleeding internally in too many places for the med-gun to handle. If we do not get him to medical…" Jokta sighed, leaving the details unsaid. "He has a few hours at most."

She blinked, ice drenching her from scalp to her knees, tingling as it traveled. No. This couldn't be happening. These were aliens. They were supposed to have conquered death. Her eyes burned, and she squeezed them shut, fighting for air. Something crushed her chest, and the urge to wail at the universe, at the injustice of it all, consumed her.

She didn't know Eira that well, had just met him. But he had hopes and dreams and a family who loved him, no doubt. And if she had been in his shoes, she'd want someone to try their best to save her.

She raised her face to the yellow sky while tightening her grip on Eira's hand. *Illan!*

What is it?

His immediate response was like a deep breath on a crisp winter morning. *I need you now. We have a badly wounded warrior. He's dying.*

Silence reigned, and for a moment, she thought he hadn't heard her. *Death is inevitable, Quinlan.*

She settled her gaze on Eira—his face paling to a gray under his bronze skin tone. *Not on my watch. Leave no soldier behind.* A tear slipped down her cheek unheeded. *Please, Illan.* Silence met her plea as a solid wall of sorrow gripped her. Why Eira mattered, she didn't know. She just couldn't bear to see him die. And, as she imagined Lucas on a battleground, she prayed that when his time came, someone would be there for him in his final moments. She choked back a sob. For all her guardians, even her irritating youngest brother. They all deserved to experience the fullest of life. Now, Eira wouldn't.

There is nothing I can do, Quin.

Illan's tone settled on her like a massive blanket, too thick to breathe.

Eira's breathing rasped, a gurgle trailed each breath, and spots of blue blood dewed his lips. She squared her shoulders and bit her lip against the agony of her wound. It coated the pain in her heart. She shoved aside her helplessness and stroked his hand, trying to will him better.

All she could do was offer comfort.

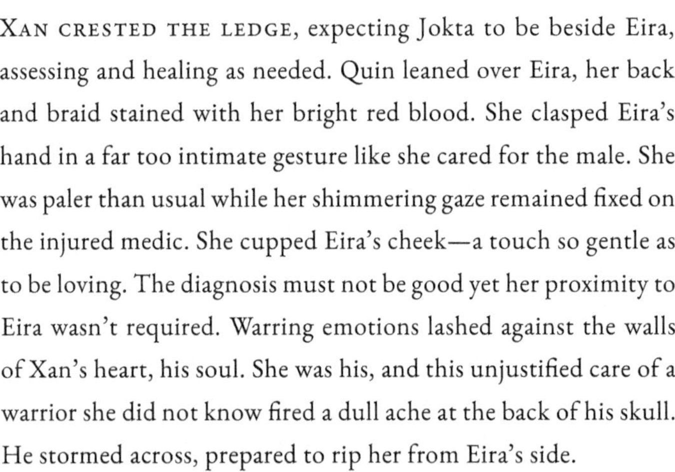

XAN CRESTED THE LEDGE, expecting Jokta to be beside Eira, assessing and healing as needed. Quin leaned over Eira, her back and braid stained with her bright red blood. She clasped Eira's hand in a far too intimate gesture like she cared for the male. She was paler than usual while her shimmering gaze remained fixed on the injured medic. She cupped Eira's cheek—a touch so gentle as to be loving. The diagnosis must not be good yet her proximity to Eira wasn't required. Warring emotions lashed against the walls of Xan's heart, his soul. She was his, and this unjustified care of a warrior she did not know fired a dull ache at the back of his skull. He stormed across, prepared to rip her from Eira's side.

"What in Alodon's hell is going on, Jokta?" he asked. The warrior bounded up to hold him back. Xan's vision clouded. Anger swelled within him. He tensed his body to strike. No male came between him and his Dar Eth.

"Supreme Commander, she mourns for him." Jokta grabbed Xan's fists and lowered them.

Xan's gaze shifted to her face again, now at a loss on how to proceed. "Why?"

"When I informed her Eira would die, sorrow poured off her." Jokta inhaled, forcing Xan to do the same. Earthy bitterness soaked the air. "Her focus went internal as it does when she speaks to the Durn." Jokta sliced a glance at Eira. "The med-gun cannot stimulate the body to heal with so many serious wounds. We need the Med-E.D. Even if we used all our med-guns, it would not be sufficient. His death is soon. He does not wish to live." Jokta grumbled to himself before slumping. "I owe him a life debt, Supreme Commander."

An unfulfilled one if he dies. Eira's eyes stuttered open to gaze at Xan's Dar Eth. A smile cracked his bloodstained lips. Xan's chest tightened as he recalled how joyful the male had been not too long ago. That had dwindled. The loss of emotion occurred when a male was close to the void. Eira must have been battling the final stages. Since dying while killing a Gika was no longer possible, that left aging Etterians with no alternative.

"Thank you, milady," Eira rasped. In slow motion, he sought out Jokta, giving him a slight nod, and whispered too low for Quin to hear, "In death, my debt is canceled. In life, Lady Quinlan will honor your sacrifice."

He closed his eyes. His head tilted to the side, and his body sagged. He had gone. Xan pressed his hand to his chest in a final salute for a great male who'd served Etteria without fault.

Quin cried out and tapped Eira's cheek. "No, no, no... Eira, please." Tears streamed down her cheeks and dripped off her chin. "Please, Lord, don't take him. Eira." She glared at the yellow sky. "What's the damned point of having you, Illan?" she snapped. "You're useless, you blue bastard. Never here when I need you." She dipped her chin, her body trembled, and she sprawled across Eira's chest, sobbing like a youngin.

Xan stilled. Volatile emotions lambasted him. Anger was familiar and the strongest. He marched to the other side of the clearing, needing distance and air to clear his thoughts. "Alodon's balls. These humans are too passionate, like *damu*. She mourns a male she has known a day. Why do I have to have the most complicated, stubborn, frustrating Dar Eth on this side of the galaxy? Why could the Maker not gift me with a docile female?" Xan punched the closest trunk before handing his bruised and bleeding hand to Nuos to scan. He relished the sting for the second it lasted. "One who does not recklessly endanger herself." He grimaced. Her pain tainted the air with sharp acidic notes.

"She did take Lurz over the edge." Nuos stared at Eira's body, sadness in his eyes.

"It was a good plan," Lurz muttered.

"Which part?" Xan growled. "Dropping you over the edge or killing the wilanegy? Truth. When we return to the battleship, I *will* confine her to her quarters." His body trembled with rage and...*fear*. Neither emotion was acceptable to an Etterian male, to him.

"Supreme Commander." Lurz gestured to Quin.

Xan spun as she slumped over Eira's body. His anger, frustration, and helplessness dissipated. She needed him. He yanked his hand away from Nuos mid-med-gun scan and raced to her side, falling to his knees. He scooped her into his arms, shuddering at her body so close to his. She curled against him, moaning in pain but not rousing.

"She sleeps," he said to his unit as he admired her beauty. "Jokta, tend to her wounds. I cannot bear to scent her blood, to know she suffers."

"The *kuna* will see you now." A Lysaran landed soundlessly among the males.

Xan tightened his arms around Quin and blinked at the male. He hadn't scented nor heard them. Three more Lysarans dropped to the ground around them. Xan sighed. He'd been wondering whether this might turn into a diplomatic issue. After all, they had crash landed without permission and the full environmental synchronization treatment.

"The lady must be healed first," Jokta positioned himself between the males and Xan.

"The *kuna* awaits," the male said, his tone brooking no argument.

Xan growled, staggering to his feet. "My Dar Eth is injured," he bellowed.

"The injured *kashi* will be seen too," the Lysaran said.

With a glare, Xan trailed the Lysarans with one certainty, Adviser Cales would shave his head for this. He lowered his gaze to Quin as peace claimed his soul. He would sacrifice more for her. The loss of his hair, of his honor, they mattered not, not anymore.

Jokta grunted as he hoisted Eira's body over his shoulder before following. The male's body would be returned to his remaining blood or battle-bonds, as was their custom.

Xan gathered Quin against his chest. Despite what he'd said, he wouldn't exchange her for any other female.

Chapter Twenty

AN HOUR LATER, THROUGH various twists and turns, Xan arrived at the bottom of wide, hand-carved stone steps that led up to an imposing ancient stone building. He clasped a still-sleeping Quin to his chest. That she had slept for so long concerned him. He wanted her awake, but not if she suffered. The unbearable need to care for her warred with the drive to protect her from all danger.

Humans were weaker than Etterians, something he tended to forget in the face of her courage and stubbornness. She had been through much since the Yithians kidnapped her. At least her heartbeat was steady, her breathing even. Her body required that she rest, and he would allow it. She weighed nothing and didn't hinder him as he climbed the steps. As soon as he reached the last few, a blue male stepped toward him. Iddan.

"Greetings, Supreme Commander," the Durn said. "Illan rests. He was unable to shield himself from her unexpected grief." Iddan gestured to the uncovered terrace. "If you will allow me, I will escort you and your Dar Eth to the guest chambers. Jokta, please follow Kym-tar. Quarters have been arranged for you and your unit."

"I must follow Lady Quin, Iddan. She remains unhealed." Jokta fell into line behind Xan.

Wanting a moment alone with Quin, Xan said to the warrior, "I will tend to her."

"I owe her a life debt, Supreme Commander."

Xan grunted. Eira *had* transferred the debt. Without another word, Iddan set off along the terrace while Lurz and Nuos trailed the Lysaran named Kym-tar.

"Do we stay long to justify the allocation of chambers?" Xan scowled at the further delay.

"You remain until such a time as the *kuna* grants your release," Iddan said.

"We are prisoners?" That hadn't occurred to Xan as a possibility. All the cognizant species in the known universe knew not to imprison an Etterian male.

"No, Supreme Commander. The *kuna* wishes for you to heal and rest. *And* he has decided to meet your human."

Alodon's balls. Xan lowered his gaze to Quin's face as he had been doing since he gathered her in his arms.

The chamber assigned to them was luxurious and spacious. One corner had counters and shelves holding cooking utensils and equipment he didn't know. A replicator and rehydrator were set to the side. Four massive chairs in muted blues dominated the room. The fur coat of a wilanegy sprawled across the floor. Under other circumstances, he might have taken the time to admire the flickering boxes giving off a warm light. Or the scenery from the private balcony running the length of the room through folding doors.

Instead, he lowered Quin into a chair. Despite being able to heal her, doing so would ease the burden Jokta now carried. Xan stepped back to allow him access.

He winced when Jokta popped her shoulder into place. She moaned in her sleep but didn't rouse. This was good, granting her oblivion from the pain.

The warrior hesitated, raising and dropping his hands from where they'd hovered above her shoulder. "Supreme Commander, I must tend to her back. Her armor..."

Xan glanced at Iddan, who excused himself to wait outside for Jokta. Xan lifted Quin into a sitting position, holding her against his chest with her face resting just below his collarbone. He reached between their bodies and pressed the amour's release mechanism. It loosened for him to work it off her arms while keeping her covered. Once he tossed the armor onto the wooden flooring, Jokta scanned the wound.

"The healing is complete, Supreme Commander. Their physiology is remarkably susceptible to our healing technology. The med-patch should soothe her until we can administer synthetic skin. I suggest it remains in place." He slipped his med-gun into his pocket and left.

Alone, at last, Xan draped her more on the chair before shrugging off his armor, leaving it where it fell, his boots alongside it. He grunted at the sight of his ever-present arousal. His malehood throbbed, making demands as only the Ethera could. And though his hands itched to touch her, now wasn't the time. The scent of her dried blood burned his nostrils and kept tension in his body, serving as a constant reminder of how he had failed to protect her even against her recklessness.

He removed her boots and pants, allowing his hands to caress her tiny toes, her smooth legs—all to appease the Ethera. He tried not to stare at the thin fabric coverings over her breasts and feminine folds, deciding to leave them on for his sanity. When he gathered her into his arms, he shivered as skin touched skin. Carrying her into the cleansing room, he stepped into the cubicle. The water activated, and he turned within the square for maximum coverage. With one arm, he balanced her against his body to slide his fingers over her med-patch and around it. It would remain dry. That didn't concern him. As long as the blood washed away, he would be able to breathe easier. While at it, he ensured the water drenched and cleansed her braid.

She moaned, her limbs twitching. He crooned to her in Etterian, hoping she would awaken and wishing she wouldn't. If she did, then he could kiss her as he had yearned to do this day. But if he kissed her, he wouldn't stop there. He *craved* her. He wasn't certain she wanted to belong to him yet. Humans were different. Etterian females were raised to anticipate a pairing and would experience the same intensity and need. He had to be patient, had to pray his control and strength were sufficient.

Gathering her once more into his arms, he deactivated the water. Barefoot and dripping wet, he waited the required time for the air-dryer, then crossed the chambers to the bed and lowered her onto it, ensuring she was comfortable. He drew a blanket over her and sat on the edge, watching her sleep, inhaling her scent as he listened to her steady heartbeat. That rhythm alone cooled his concern.

The door chimed, and he stilled. Raising his gaze, he studied the sunlight painting patterns across the floor. One sun had begun to set. He'd sat there longer than he realized. A stack of garments rested on a chair close to the bed. He rose and sifted through the garments to select a pair of leggings similar to his sleeping pants. It was of dark blue fabric, thin, organic, and comfortable. There was also a tunic in white that he tugged on, leaving the feminine garments on the bed for Quin. The door chimed again, and he approached it, commanding it to open.

"How is she?" Illan demanded, his skin a gray tinge. In a weakened state, he clutched at the doorframe.

"She sleeps." Xan gestured to the bed.

Illan's gaze shot to where Quin's covered form lay—the bed visible from the doorway. "Awaken her," the Durn rasped. "Xan... Now."

At the urgency in his voice, Xan bolted across the room to kneel beside the bed. "*Ensa*, awaken for me," he whispered as he caressed her cheek and neck.

She stirred and rolled toward him. Her lips parted in invitation.

He crumbled under the temptation. After what he had endured in this one day, it amazed him that he hadn't found a secluded area in the cursed jungle and claimed her.

Sinking his fingers into her unraveling braid, he cupped the back of her head as he brought his lips to hers, slipping his tongue in to taste her. A breath lodged in his throat at her tart flavor, hating that his nipples hardened without stimulation or that his arousal throbbed. Her breathing altered, grew heavy, and her tongue stirred to challenge his. She embedded her fingers in his hair, tearing a deep throaty groan from him.

"Xan?" Her eyelids fluttered open. She blinked at him. "Kiss me again."

Leaning back to meet her hooded gaze, he grinned. He swooped down and crushed his mouth over hers, plunging his tongue in for a thorough exploration.

"Maker." He drew in a jagged breath as he pulled away, only then remembering they weren't alone. "She is awake, Illan."

"Illan?" She tried to sit up, clutching the blanket with one hand to maintain her modesty. "You found us?" She pressed her free hand to Xan's chest, keeping him close as if she needed his strength, warmth, or presence.

"I went to the *kuna*. If anyone could locate you, it would be his males." Illan's pale eyes traveled over her face with apparent concern. "How do you feel?"

"Exhausted." Her eyes widened then shimmered, with pain twisting her features.

Xan's heart tightened, and he inched closer to her, curling an arm around her shoulders.

"Eira," she moaned, scrambling to the edge of the bed. The blanket slipped, exposing bare limbs and curves.

"Please, Quin, I do not have the energy to shield your grief." Illan threw out a hand.

She froze and drew in a sharp breath, trying to rein in her emotion, though her face remained pale with her bottom lip trembling.

"Why the urgency to wake her, Illan?" Xan captured her hand where it rested on his chest, pinning it there.

"She was circling the *abyss*," Illan said. "Humans refer to it as *depression*. Once she falls into that, I would assume it is hard to return.

There is so little known of her species that I would prefer not to find out the hard way."

Darkness consumed Xan's soul for a moment. That he could have lost her so easily to an unknown and unseen force rattled him. How was he supposed to protect her? He cupped her cheek while tightening his hold over her hand. Etterians weren't trained to handle humans.

"I apologize, Supreme Commander." Illan dipped his head. "I was too intent on shielding myself that I was inattentive to her thoughts."

"She was asleep for a long time, what could have caused this? I verified her pulse was steady, her breathing even but was wary of waking her." Xan glanced at Quin, acknowledging how frail she had looked in his arms, despite knowing she had a core of inner strength.

"It could be the amalgamation of factors, emotional trauma, blood loss, pain." Illan shrugged. "I cannot know for certain."

"Um, Xan, Illan, where are we?" The awe in her voice had Xan glancing at her.

"We are guests of *Kuna* Sy'mar." Illan offered a small smile.

"The King of Lysara?" Her expressive mouth parted.

Xan groaned and leaned in for a quick kiss, snatching her breath from her. "Cease doing that." His voice was hoarse. He'd given up trying to control it. "Please, *ensa.*"

She frowned, her gaze meeting his.

"Now that you are awake, it is best not to keep the *Kuna* waiting." Illan gestured to the stack of garments. "Courtesy of the kuna. I suggest you wear it." He met Quin's gaze before leaving the chambers.

"Look at this room, Xan," she marveled while gathering the blanket around her with her free hand. Still, her shoulder remained bare, showing the med-patch.

"I held you in the cleanser, but if you wish to re-cleanse?"

"Thank you." She gave a gentle tug on her hand. When it didn't budge, she peeked at him, her eyes crinkling at the corners.

"I do not want to release you," he mumbled, as he cupped her cheek, threading his long fingers in the curls behind her ear. "I do not ever want to endure another day like today." He brushed his lips across hers, careful to show her tenderness. "Please, my Quin, have compassion for my heart."

HIS WORDS CAUGHT AND held her breath. The intense emotion in his voice and eyes had her frozen. Was he declaring he had *feelings* for her? Realizing he was waiting for a response, she offered a smile. "I promise I'll try, Xan."

His eyelids closed, showing his incredibly long eyelashes. They fluttered open, his bright blue eyes warm. "Thank you, Quin."

"You'll tell me when I mess up?" She bit her bottom lip, worried she had somehow offended this proud male, unintentionally hurt him, was disrespectful, or worse, dismissive.

He swooped in and nibbled on her lip, making her lean back on a chuckle. He buried his face in her neck to inhale deeply and stilled, releasing a throaty groan that must have damaged his vocal cords. "Your sweet, intoxicating scent has intensified. I scent blood, *ensa*."

She gritted her teeth. Cursed periods. Couldn't they wait one damn day?

"Now decide, cleanse or dress?" He released her hand and tucked a curl behind her ear.

"I'll dress." She gestured to the blanket and the doorway.

He grinned and strolled to the balcony doors, disappearing into the fading sunlight.

She wrapped the blanket around her body and rushed to the bathroom. While relieving herself, she cursed the fates or whatever madness had started her period today. *Damn. How am I supposed to deal with this now? On another planet? With no feminine hygiene products?* She straightened. *Replicator.*

While washing her hands, she glared at her reflection above the stone basin. Tendrils escaped her messy braid. Her skin was pale with shadows under her eyes. She released a controlled exhale. Eira was gone. She had to accept it and somehow deal with it, and Lord willing, maybe even breach the gap between her and Aiden. Drying her hands on the blanket, she twisted to study the patch on her back. Rolling her shoulder brought no pain. Huh. Healed by a black box.

Whipping the blanket around her, she opened the door and peeked out. With no Xan nearby, she darted for the replicator. As she scrolled through the selection of undergarments and sanitary pads, she snuck glances at the balcony while pulling the blanket tighter around her. Sure, she wore panties and a bra. Those didn't make her decent.

With products in hand, she bolted for the bedroom and threw off the blanket. After a quick change into new underwear and an application of sanitary pads, she sifted through the pile of clothing. She yanked out the only item small enough to fit her and grimaced. It was some sort of dress in a burnt umber color. *A dress?* She stretched the fabric, accepting that it would stick to her like a second skin. Even with sanitary pads and panties, the damn planet would know she was fertile. She grumbled about the stupidity of enhanced olfactory glands. Technically, she was at her most infertile, but there was no damn way she was going to explain it to every male, ad infinitum. Best to let them find out on their own.

Tugging on the dress had her gasping as it reacted to the heat of her body and conformed to her curves. *Yup. Painted.* The T-shirt-styled neckline was high, but that didn't matter when the fabric molded to her, enhancing the bra's contours, the stitching, and boning. She huffed, unclipped the bra, and wiggled it off without removing the dress. Throwing it onto the bed, she adjusted the dress, then sighed when it stuck to the underside of her breasts.

"Shit." She slid her hands from her waist to her hips, trying to peel the fabric off her. "Damned if I do, damned if I don't." Spinning, she swallowed a giggle when the skirt flared out from her hips into thousands of ribbons, all silk and feathery, ranging in lengths from her knee to her toes. No matter how she swayed, jerked, or paced, the fabric caressed her legs.

"There are no shoes, Xan?" She unbraided her hair, ran her fingers through to loosen the strands, then leaned upside down to fluff out the mass before flicking it back.

"Maker, Quin, do not do that," he rasped, gawking at her hair. His gaze caressed her curls when she swayed. She gathered it to one side, just to watch his reaction. His lips parted as his breathing rasped.

"Shoes?" She chuckled.

He blinked at her dress, then moaned. She was beginning to love that sound from him.

"You look...beautiful." He prowled closer to loop his hands around her waist, stroking the fabric as if he were touching her skin. "No shoes on Lysara."

She glanced down at his bare toes. Heat uncoiled in her belly. There was something personal about a man's toes.

Male.

Butt out, Illan.

Xan yanked her against his body and pressed an open-mouthed kiss to her neck. She gasped, wondering why that felt so good. She grasped his upper arms. He trailed his lips to hers, ravaging her mouth with a desperation that echoed within her. She clung to him, her knees weak, unable to keep her upright, not that it mattered with the way he pinned her against him.

He thrust her away, but his hands on her hips held her steady. He trembled as his gaze penetrated hers. "The *kuna* awaits, my Quinlan."

She blanked, dazed at the desire surging through her, the urge to burrow into his arms, and the intensity and variety of emotions crossing his swirling blue eyes. Her heart stuttered, and a realization dawned on her... *I'm falling for him.*

She glided her hands from his shoulders, down his arms to grab his hands, shivering at the texture of his muscles under her fingertips. Her nipples pebbled in reaction, and her stomach swirled with something hot and demanding. She didn't want to see the king...*kuna,* whatever. She wanted Xan to put his hands on her body. Not that it could lead anywhere. She snorted. *Typical. I swear the universe conspired with my guardians to keep me virginal.* "Lucas is laughing about this somewhere," she muttered.

"Lucas? Tell me about your guardians," Xan asked, snapping her out of her lust-filled thoughts.

"My...guardians?" Shit. He'd heard her.

He laced his fingers through hers and ushered her out the door.

Think, Quin. Brothers, guardians, general pains in your ass, re-member? "Um, Lucas you've seen, he's the oldest and is some sort of instructor. He's a know-it-all and a prankster." *Should get on well with you, Illan.* "Then it's Mason. He's a marine, um, uh...specialized military. I see him the least. Aiden's the youngest, the one you don't like. He's a tech specialist. He can work any hardware or software. Annoying genius."

The passage they were rushing along was of hand-carved gray stone, the floors, walls, and ceiling looked like the interior of a castle and yet not cold. Heat rose from the floor, warming her feet as Xan turned a corner. Beautiful tapestries lined the walls between flickering lights in square boxes.

"And with my brothers' friends, there's Garrett. I told you about him, he's the pilot. Charming, affectionate, sensitive."

Xan stopped so fast, she almost slammed into him. "You care for him."

She peeked around him, wondering what had halted their mad dash down the passage. "Yes, I love them."

Xan clasped her upper arms, forcing her to meet his gaze. "No, my Quin, Garrett is special to you."

She gasped at the pain in Xan's eyes. *Was this what he had meant when he asked me to have compassion?* She scrambled for the right words, never having had to choose them with such care. "Garrett was there when I needed friendship. I do love him, just not...like that." She released a slow breath. "He was *kind* to me, knew me and what I was going through. Not even my brothers understood. I was *so* lonely, Xan. I had no friends, no one..." Tears burned her eyes, and a lump strangled her throat. "No one *wanted* me." A tear escaped down her cheek. She flicked it away, fighting to gain control. *Silly emotions.*

"*Ensa.*" Xan drew her into his arms, sliding his hands up her back. "There is no one in all the known planets who wants you more than I do, my Quin. You will *never* be alone again." He wiped her cheek with the pad of his thumb. "You are mine as I am yours."

Her breath caught as time stood still. His gaze was intense, his voice thick with emotion. He was serious in his interest in her. Hot overwhelming joy burst through her. She'd never expected this to happen after the kidnapping. And by this, she meant finding him. *A precipice is at my feet, dare I jump?* She didn't hesitate. *Hell, yes.*

"You promise?" She studied his handsome features as she tried to memorize this moment.

"My vow." His smile was tender, then he grabbed her hand, pulling her behind him. "Your other guardians?"

"Joshua's in the Navy, specializing in submarines. Carter's in espionage, and Wyatt's a HALO jumper." She smiled, wondering what Wyatt was up to. "HALO stands for High Altitude Low Opening, which is why I'm always jumping out of helicopters, light aircraft, or hang gliding over a natural phenomenon."

"You did so willingly? From a craft in mid-air?" The horror on Xan's face was priceless.

She smothered a chuckle, in case her humor offended him. "Yes." She shrugged, accepting that not everyone understood the exhilaration. "I'd love to share the experience with you, Xan."

His cheeks darkened before he smiled. "I would share anything with you, my Quin."

She stilled, gazed into his stunning eyes, and leaned toward him as if to kiss him. "When we visit Earth," she said, focused on his lips.

He grunted, and once again, they were hurtling along the passage.

What would Wyatt say about skydiving with Xan? She grinned, anticipating that argument and the experience.

Now with Carter, he was the mysterious one, on some secret mission, though what a spy did when there was one global government, she had no idea. And she hadn't seen Josh in ages, the last she'd heard, he tested navigational software on the latest submarines.

Her smile faltered when they burst into the throne room. As they drew to a halt, the crowded court turned as one to gawk...at her.

Chapter Twenty-One

Xan tightened his hold on Quin as she scanned the stone throne room with its warm lamps and cream and gold tapestries. It was beautiful, luxuriant, and intimidating. She drew in a deep breath, trying to tamp down the various emotions churning inside her. Yes, sadness was still there in large quantities. She had only known Eira a day, but seeing him die in her arms, so to speak, brought back the loss of her parents and the Durn destruction. Combined, it had robbed her of her breath, of her self-control. And as exhausted as she'd been, the death of Eira was the last straw. She'd succumbed to the darkness where she could no longer feel.

Now, along with the sadness, arousal hummed through her, but she was hopeful, believing Xan wanted her more than short-term. *A gorgeous male wants me.* Her inner girl squealed. So, she was jubilant, as well. She was also nervous about meeting royalty. To say emotions roiled within her was an understatement. And on Lysara, with the way Bry-dar and Myn-ras had reacted, this wasn't good.

Breathe.

You breathe. She thrust her frustration at Illan. *I have to meet the king.*

Two, there is still King Xeus.

Shit. She gasped and blushed when Xan squeezed her hand.

Illan's chuckle reached from his position next to Oyaz.

I don't appreciate your flippancy. She tried to glare at him, but a familiar brown head snatched her attention. "Macy?"

Her friend peeked from behind Oyaz. She wore her leggings and a baggy T-shirt as usual.

Quin took a step, then glanced at Xan, who beamed at Oyaz. For a second, she blinked, dazzled by the male before her. He released her hand, and she hesitated before running across the court.

Macy weaved around Oyaz to hug her. "Oh, Quin, I'm so happy you're okay. Illan said you were, but I had to see for myself." Macy pulled back to run her gaze over Quin. "Whoa. Looking hot. What's the occasion?"

"Meeting the *kuna*." Quin winced.

Macy shivered as her eyes widened. "He's potent. I had Oyaz, so make sure Xan's at your side. And by potent, I mean your lady bits will explode." She giggled, her cheeks flushing pink. "I swear they release pheromones to dazzle us poor damsels."

Quin laughed. "I thought you wanted to snag a sexy alien?" She wiggled her eyebrows.

"Yeah, without being drugged or coerced, thank you very much."

Illan caught Quin by the shoulders and spun her to face Xan standing in the middle of the court. *Meet the kuna first.*

She huffed but darted across to where Xan waited. Lacing her fingers through his, she rested her temple on his upper bicep. "Sorry," she whispered.

He pressed a kiss to her temple and ushered them onward to the throne upon which sat a beautiful Lysaran male. He appeared tall, the way he had folded his legs. His skin was as caramel as Bry-dar's, but more muscle layered his body, perfectly in proportion with his broader shoulders. He was lithe more than bulky, and he had brown hair that fell to his mid-back, braided in some places with thin gold wire. Those attending court had the same brown hair. Even their eyes were an amber-gold. *Potent? Yes, Macy had been right.* He was so handsome he tipped the scales, and combined with his authority, his magnetism, he was sex on a stick.

That's a human saying?

Quin ignored Illan. She glanced at Xan and couldn't help but compare the two. It pleased her to say Xan won hands down. Her stomach fluttered as she studied his profile, wishing she could do more than look. His gaze dipped to her and caught her staring, making her stomach flip-flop. She glanced aside, wondering if a confident Quin would ever appear. Despite everything that had happened, deep inside, she remained a timid and blushing virgin.

With a predatorial grace, the *kuna* rose to his feet, gliding toward her. He moved like a caged panther. Xan's shoulders tensed as the Lysaran king approached them.

"This is another *human*, Supreme Commander?" The *kuna's* voice was thick, husky, his English accent educated. And he kept his amber gaze on Quin.

"Yes, my *kuna*. She is a human woman from the planet Earth," Xan said.

"May I?" *Kuna* Sy'mar requested permission.

She scowled, wondering why Xan had to agree. Surely the king should be asking her.

Xan clenched his jaw but nodded.

The king closed the distance between them. She dropped into her first curtsy, with her hand still in Xan's, using him as support. A murmur rippled through the court as she rose to face him.

"Lady Quinlan, is it?"

"Yes, Your Highness," she said, not ready to debate her peerage or lack thereof.

"Your Highness?" He glanced at Macy before holding his hand palm up.

Xan's grip tightened on her fingers, so she peeked at him before offering the king her other hand.

"It's how we address royalty on Earth. Your Majesty's also used." Not that he was listening. His gaze had focused on her fingers. He clasped her hand until it disappeared in his large grasp. He slid his fingers down her wrist and along her forearm before returning to her palm.

"The texture of her skin is exquisite, Supreme Commander." The king drew in a deep breath, and his eyes widened in delight. "Her emotional range is...magnificent." *Kuna* Sy'mar addressed Illan. "You spoke truth. Lady Macera I believed was an anomaly." He dipped his head at Macy in apology. "Although, I did not scent subterfuge either. This intrigues me, Lord Illan." The king raised a hand to lift a lock of Quin's hair as he peered into her eyes. "Lady Macera could pass for a Lysaran in some ways. You are not at all similar." He smiled, and Quin's heartbeat raced, fluttering in her chest. "I confess, your softness and emotional range are as intense."

"In truth, my *kuna*," Xan said. "Of the human females we have encountered, their hair colors range from black to sunlight to brown to that of your beaches. Their eyes are blues, browns, greens, and grays."

"And Prince Enyl's Dar Eth has red hair with green eyes, my *kuna*," Oyaz said.

"I see why Xeus insisted on protecting this planet." The *kuna* drew in another deep breath. His nostrils flared then his eyes widened. A sensual smile formed, and as Macy had predicted, heat burst outward in Quin's core. *Holy cow.* "You scent...fertile," he said.

Quin gritted her teeth, even as Xan's looped an arm around her to pull her against his side.

The Lysaran king gestured to them. "Come, let us dine. I scent that your Dar Eth hungers."

Xan's gaze dropped to hers just as she mouthed the words 'Dar Eth' with her eyebrow arching. He faced ahead but still clasped her hand, she followed like a puppy.

Glancing over her shoulder, she searched for Macy. But when her friend remained by Oyaz, Quin stumbled after Xan.

"I am pleased to see you so soon, Lady Quin," a male greeted her.

She gasped. "Bry, how'd you get here so fast?"

"Fast? It has been a day since we said farewell..." The Lysaran male fell into step beside her.

"True," she said.

The dining hall was a typical design—soaring ceilings, tall windows revealing the 'setting' sun with hidden lighting, and extended trestle tables. Long carpets lined the passages between the tables, and more tapestries adorned the stone walls.

"You serve the *kuna*?" Xan snapped as if Bry-dar had deceived him.

The Lysaran male frowned but strode ahead to lead them to the *kuna*'s table. "I wished to inform the *kuna* about humans. I am certain you would have done the same, Supreme Commander."

Xan grunted but said no more.

"Did you rescue us? Xan hasn't told me how we traveled from the jungle to here." She tried not to remember the last moment before she passed out.

"My testimony combined with Lord Illan and Lady Macy's plea for aid convinced the *kuna* to send one of his scouting units." He gestured to the bench.

Quin released Xan's hand to slide in. He did as well before crushing her to his side. Not that she minded.

"Your dealings with the Gracc impressed me."

Her head shot up. "You were watching?" She scowled. "Eira didn't have to die if your scouts reached us sooner." Fire burned through her, and she faced him. Instead of taking offense from her outburst, her anger, the Lysaran grinned. Her fingers curled into fists as she fought the urge to smack him. His charming smile wasn't the response she expected nor wanted.

"We have placed research cams throughout the jungle. I saw the Gracc incident just after you arrived here."

"Oh." Quin dropped her chin to hide her heated cheeks. "Sorry."

"Think nothing of it. I enjoyed that," Bry-dar said, his delight affirming his words. "Scouting units will include your approach as part of their techniques."

"Xan's males made it possible. Without their strength..." She shivered and placed her hand on Xan's thigh to squeeze it.

She might have lost him today. The pain that lanced through her chest forced her to look internally at how she felt about the big alien. *Falling for him? Hell, no.* She had hit the rock-hard floor, hadn't been able to dodge it, nor had she wanted to. It was quite evident to her dazed mind... She adored him. She glanced at him, tracing over his slashing eyebrows, his exquisite ice-blue eyes, his long nose to those tempting lips. She was head over heels in love with him.

Illan laughed. *At last.*

She gritted her teeth. *That's it, Illan, you need to teach me damn quick. There are thoughts I would like to keep private.* She huffed.

Xan closed the distance between them, his breath fanning her ear. She suppressed a shiver, then flashed him an apologetic look.

You couldn't have resisted for much longer. He knocks your socks off, sister.

She stilled. *Sister?*

Of course. A mind fuse naturally leads to this. You know me as well as my brother does.

Thank you, Illan. Smothering an unladylike sniff, she hurried to catch a tear before it slipped free. She blinked at her wet fingertips, growing angry with herself for being so uncharacteristically emotional even though it was understandable in her current *condition*.

"Quin?" Xan frowned. He lifted an arm to loop around her shoulders, drawing her into the safety of his embrace.

She met his gaze, then crumbled under his care. "Illan called me his sister." She hadn't expected Xan to scowl nor for him to rub his chest as if he was experiencing indigestion. Her revelation didn't please him, but she couldn't understand why.

"You have seven brothers, why would you need another?" he snapped.

"He said it was inevitable with our fusing." She beamed at Illan, who strode toward them.

"You would think you have exhausted your capacity to love more brothers," Xan said.

"That's not how love works." She caressed his cheek, unable to resist. "I have an immense capacity for my brothers. My children will draw from another source, just as my husband will have his own." His eyelids fluttered as the O.D.I. instructed him, she knew not on what. She snatched her hand back to accept the goblet of dark purple liquid a server offered her. "Love comes in different forms."

"Your...*husband's* source? What would that look like?" Xan lingered on her lips as she sipped from the goblet.

She savored the way her body burst into flame at his heated expression. "I'd love him with all my being, with my every thought and breath. He'd be my rock, my solid foundation. I'd draw from his strength, his confidence. But without his love in return, I'd cease to exist as myself. A loveless union would kill me." She nodded, pleased with her words. That kind of relationship was what she had searched for, and settling on Xan's attentive face, she may have found it.

"You have given this thought?" He rubbed his chest again.

"Oh, yes. I've looked for love for a long time." She smiled at him, unable to cease doing so now that she loved him. "Isn't it the same for you?"

"Yes, it is the same," he rumbled. "You are a strong female and do not need a male to protect and care for you."

"I'm not strong at all, Xan." She placed her goblet on the table and faced him. "What I did on the slave ship my guardians drilled into me. It's instinctual now. But I'm an emotional creature as a human woman. I react based on how I feel. My anger and fear fueled my desperation to seize that ship. The Yithians had me scared shitless." She brushed aside his hand still resting on his chest to replace it with hers, just over his heart. Twirling her thumb across the shirt's fabric left her wishing she could touch his skin. "Your recapture of a ship would've been methodical no matter how you felt."

"You did it well, despite your emotions," he said, his voice hoarse.

What had she said to deepen his voice, or was it her touch?

Tell him, Quin. Warmth crossed their connection as if Illan shared his courage.

She shook her head. *I don't know if he feels the same way.*

He does. He cannot stop touching you.

She chuckled. *Oh, Illan, we must get you laid.* Silence met her thoughts, and she grinned, delighted to find a subject that silenced Illan-know-it-all.

"All she needs from a husband is his love." Illan sank onto the bench to the right of Xan.

She threw her new brother a warning look.

"That is too little to ask for," Xan grumbled.

"Not for human women. It's everything." She picked up a sliver of fruit from the feast spread before them. Its tart flavor exploded in her mouth. She moaned, chewing with relish. The fleshy orange fruit was more like a peach but tasted like a tangerine. "What is this, Xan? It's delicious."

"It is a *lemte*," he said before lifting his goblet to his lips. He emptied it and returned it to the table. Grasping her free hand in his, he pressed a long kiss to her palm. Suppressing a shiver, she stared at his lips, amazed at how they affected her.

"Supreme Commander Xan," Oyaz said from behind them, Macy clinging to his side. "Lady Quin." He dipped his head in acknowledgment. "I am pleased to find you both well."

"Oyaz, welcome, my battle-bond." Xan grinned.

"I have Kemt expecting a comm later this evening." Oyaz glanced at a bouncing Macy and smiled. "Until then."

Quin gaped, having wanted Macy to join her. When her friend waved and skipped after Oyaz, she slumped, then squared her shoulders. She could play the diplomat for a little longer.

Kuna Sy'mar sat beside her. She offered him a polite smile in greeting. Xan slid his hand over her hip to press against her lower back. His warmth penetrated the dress and filled her with a sense of peace and security.

"How do you find Lysara, Lady Quinlan?" The *kuna* offered her a sliver of pale pink meat.

She hesitated, not sure she should take it with her fingers or open her mouth like a good little girl. He lifted it to her lips, and she parted them obediently. The succulent meat was spicy and sweet.

She hummed her appreciation. "Dangerous, though I adored those white flowers on the jungle floor."

"*Myameru*. They blossom to receive the sunlight for that time before withdrawing only to appear at the next retraction."

Now offer him a sliver of meat, as well.

She peeked at Illan and winked. "*Myameru*." She rolled the word over her tongue as she chose the choicest sliver of meat before holding it to the king's lips.

He *was* handsome, textbook gorgeous. His vampiric teeth pressed sexily on his bottom lip, not that she feared them. He had fuller lips than Xan's, and they were pale against his caramel skin almost as if he wore lip balm. She smothered a laugh.

The king's gaze met hers as he smiled, the sensuality skittering across her skin in a wave of goosebumps. "I can scent your humor, *sali*," he said, his voice dropping an octave.

She gaped. "You can?"

"Yes, it is why we find humans fascinating."

"I must admit, I didn't understand when you said emotional range." She glared at Illan. *Why don't you have this information on Lysaran culture?*

He shrugged. *The destruction of my homeworld ended my studies. Don't mourn, sister. There will be no sadness this evening.*

She drew in a calming breath.

"We struggle with emotions as a species. Yet here you are, a unique creature with so many passionate responses," the *kuna* said before he raised his gaze to search his court. "Lady Macera more so. You are far more reserved."

He had the right of it. Macy was a bundle of joy. Quin was far from it. "We are often accused of being too emotional or irrational." She accepted his goblet before offering him hers. "Many wars have started due to emotions. People have died and lives ruined for the slightest offenses."

"On Lysara, these emotions bring the rain to nourish the soil."

She gaped. Beside her, Xan grumbled something. She glanced at him to find his gaze on her mouth.

He pressed a kiss to her parted lips, sweet and short.

She released her breath with a whoosh. "What was that for?"

"You tempt me when your lips part." At his blatant admiration, heat stained her cheeks, and for a moment, she forgot about the *kuna* sitting next to her. "I cannot resist."

"I shall 'part my lips' more often," she said with a mischievous grin.

"As long as you accept the consequences," Xan said, despite his top lip curling upward.

"Accept it? I look forward to them." She smirked before facing a fascinated king. "I understand your planet is dying, Your Highness."

"Yes, without emotions, our people are not finding their mates. Without the act of mating, we receive no rain. It is frustrating to be so helpless." He jerked back, his eyes widening. Perhaps he hadn't meant to reveal so much to her.

"Then getting you some humans might be the first step. Though, perhaps not by abduction. We tend to view that in a negative light." She chuckled. "Our males are just as passionate." She then leaned in to whisper like they didn't have enhanced hearing. "But if you need females, they'll adore Lysarans as much as they'd love Etterians. We do have men like yours, they're just rare."

"Thank you for the encouragement, Lady Quin," the *kuna* chuckled.

"I suggest meeting with King Xeus and forming a coalition." Illan rested his elbows on the table, the goblet clasped in his hands.

"A joint venture would aid Lysarans immensely." Iddan peered around Illan. "Why send so many battleships when Etteria has more than enough capacity."

"If you would excuse us, my *kuna*?" Xan's request was met with Sy'mar's dismissive gesture. Like they were late for something, Xan hoisted her off the bench and out of the throne room.

"What? Did you think he'd change his mind?" she teased while clinging to Xan.

He drew to a halt and gazed at her. A slow smile formed. "Yes. You are intoxicating, my Quin. Any male would want to keep you."

She laughed. *Right. Sweet talker.* "And what if I wasn't finished with my food?"

"Our chambers have a rehydrator." He looped an arm around her shoulders and steered her down a passage. "Besides, I am tired."

She pouted her lips. "Oh, poor Xan. Want me to tuck you into bed?"

The heat in his eyes melted her laughter into desire, and she wished he'd say yes. Him in a bed would be the stuff of dreams. Instead, he gathered her close and said no more.

Chapter Twenty-Two

Planet Lysara

The city of Sosu, their chamber

STILL IN HER FORMFITTING dress but with a blanket draped over her shoulders, Quin gazed at the purple-hued sky. It glowed like a Borealis through the second sun's pale rays.

"You cannot sleep." Xan stepped onto the balcony.

She faced him, her heart swelling, almost choking her. She couldn't help running her gaze over his length. Oyaz had collected Xan to comm Kemt in a communications tower *Kuna* Sy'mar used.

"No, but I expected it after our crazy day." She shrugged, though she didn't trivialize the events. Admiring the view, she leaned her elbows on the chilled stone balustrade.

Xan came up behind her and slipped his arms around her, hugging her against his chest. She moaned as his warmth seeped through her thin blanket. Her bare feet on the cold stone of the balcony floor didn't help, but she couldn't stand on the chamber's heated floor and still view the sky. He kissed the crown of her head while shifting her hands to hold onto his forearms.

"Come, *ensa*." He drew her toward a tall plant growing up the side of the wall. Its appearance was that of an arum lily with yellowy-green petals double the height of an Etterian male. He rubbed its stem and stepped back. An elongated petal unfurled to open across the balcony's floor. Climbing onto it, he sprawled along its length and held out his hand to her.

She hesitated, but at his warm smile, she slid her fingers into his hand and allowed him to pull her onto the petal. As she lay beside him, the heat of him saturated her. The yellow petal cocooned them as it curled along its sides but didn't enclose them.

"What is this, Xan?" Quin stroked the petal's velvety texture. It shivered under her fingers. With a gasp, she snatched her hand back.

"It's a *d'nastu*, a plant seeking our body heat." He cuddled her closer so she could rest her head on his shoulder.

"It's wonderful." She placed her hand on his chest, quite content to lie there with him, to admire the star-studded sky together. "Two things." She rubbed her nose across his chest, trying to warm the still-cold tip. "What did Oyaz have to say?"

"Maloidians fired upon the shuttle, and it may be linked to Pannos's signal. But that is nothing more than speculation. Data Officer Kemt is investigating. The second thing?" His voice reverberated through him where she pressed her ear.

"*Kuna* Sy'mar called me your Dar Eth?" She shifted to push off him, needing to see his expressions. Her gaze caressed the angles and dents of his handsome face.

"When an Etterian male finds his Dar Eth, his life force, he experiences what we call the Ethera." He paused to smile. The softness in his gaze made her heart skip beats and her breathing stutter. But she couldn't say what that look meant. "The Ethera is painful, my Quin, and pleasurable."

"How is that possible?" she teased while tracing a pattern across his collarbone.

"It is. I have experienced this, but I am joyful, above all the sensations bombarding my mind and body. To find my Dar Eth is something I have longed for."

"You longed to find me?" She stilled, settling her gaze on him rather than on his glorious skin her fingers exposed.

"I *needed* to find you, *ensa*. If a male does not find his Dar Eth, he lives a life where loneliness will drive him to forsake all hope as Eira did."

She frowned. Eira had succumbed without fighting for his life? "That's horrible, Xan. I'm glad you won't be lonely anymore, but are you sure I'm your Dar Eth? Could you be wrong?"

His eyes narrowed, and a dark scowl formed. "The Ethera compels me to claim you, my Quin, but if you need something tangible, my eyes changed color."

"Your beautiful eyes?" She traced his eyebrow. "So, what happens now that I'm your Dar Eth?" She lowered herself onto his chest, seeking his warmth against the chill of the night.

"You are mine as I am yours," he said as if that explained it. It didn't.

"For how long?" she mumbled.

"It is forever," he said.

She gasped and pushed off him again. "Forever? What if you don't like me anymore? What if you find another Dar Eth?"

He chuckled and sat up too, wrapping his arms around her to lie down again with her sprawled on top of him. He pulled the petal around them, trapping her.

"There is only one Dar Eth per Etterian male. And you are mine, Quinlan Walsh."

"Like an arranged marriage?" She twisted to study him but only caught his angular jawline. *Holy shit. What were they talking about? What was he saying?* She blinked, trying to clear her thoughts, but they buzzed with happiness, images of forever after with Xan, and this unshakable lassitude.

Illan? She hummed, snuggling into Xan's embrace. *Did you know about this* Ethera *thing?*

Yes.

She tried to growl but instead found herself sighing. Anger dissipated as fast as it had formed. *You should have told me.*

And have you run from the inevitable? Don't be silly, sister. You're his forever; his to adore and care for.

She shook her head, struggling to understand. She wanted to rant at Illan for keeping this from her, but she couldn't gather the energy to do so. She drew in gasping breaths, hoping the fresh air would help. The fog in her mind cleared and one fact formed. She loved Xan. So this was good, right? And despite the shock coursing through her, excitement and joy exploded in her chest like confetti. She hated it when Illan was right, but still, no bended knee? No I-love-yous; just wham-bam-forever with no hope of parole? And what about dates, getting to know each other? Didn't the Ethera think of that? What if she hated Xan and was now stuck in an arranged marriage? What if he hated her? Ice curled around her heart and squeezed.

"No, you are my world, my reason for existing. If you die, I die. Yet, as a human, you may choose another non-Etterian male." He winced, but that he told her the truth settled within her heart, unpeeling those icy fingers and warming her. He could have omitted that, and she would never have known. *Wait, did he say die?*

Illan? Xan dies if I don't choose him, doesn't he?

Yes.

She met Xan's gaze, assessing the concern in his eyes. He didn't beg her to stay with him, almost like he needed her to decide for herself. *He trusts me to save him?* Her chest swelled as tears pressed against her eyes. Not even Garrett had trusted her this much. She raised her chin, determination stiffening her body. *I'll trust him with my heart.*

"No, I'm quite fond of this Etterian male, thank you." She tapped his chest with her fingers.

He relaxed, and a sensual smile curled his sinful mouth. "As I am fond of you."

Not a love confession but a start. She lowered herself to snuggle against his warmth, the crown of her head brushing his chin. "Do Etterians marry then? Is that a thing in your culture?" She didn't bother to lift her head, too comfortable to make eye contact.

"By Etterian law, the Ethera joins us the moment it occurs."

"You're my husband?" she squeaked, then melted, finding she didn't care about it now that she had accepted a forever with him. She rubbed her cheek back and forth. His scent rose to greet her, and she greedily inhaled it. Her vision swam, and her limbs felt leaden.

"Yes. I could not inform you when it occurred. I did not believe you would accept me." His voice was rougher now.

She mumbled how damn right he was about her not accepting marriage when they met but didn't bother to vocalize her words better.

"You are not displeased with me?"

"No." She sank into him, heat traveling from her toes to the tips of her ears. Sleep teased the edges of her mind, promising blessed restoration. And his scent added to the paradise engulfing her. His arms around her and the feeling of safety also drove her eyelids down. "Maybe tomorrow..."

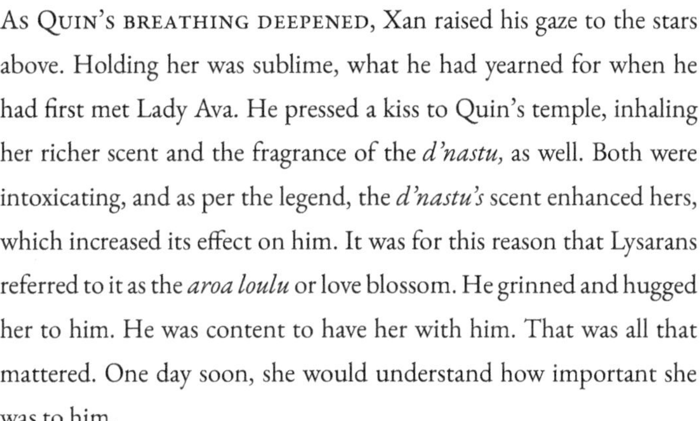

As Quin's breathing deepened, Xan raised his gaze to the stars above. Holding her was sublime, what he had yearned for when he had first met Lady Ava. He pressed a kiss to Quin's temple, inhaling her richer scent and the fragrance of the *d'nastu,* as well. Both were intoxicating, and as per the legend, the *d'nastu's* scent enhanced hers, which increased its effect on him. It was for this reason that Lysarans referred to it as the *aroa loulu* or love blossom. He grinned and hugged her to him. He was content to have her with him. That was all that mattered. One day soon, she would understand how important she was to him.

After watching *Kuna* Sy'mar ogle her, Xan had to admit, had the male met Quin first, perhaps the Ethera wouldn't have occurred. Had Xan simply been lucky? He didn't like that. He far preferred the notion that the Maker had chosen her as the perfect match. It implied their union was blessed.

He'd been arrogant, believing that bringing her along to see Lysara would please her. Not once had he considered he'd endanger her. As an Eth, he had to do better. He shifted, twisting to take the brunt of the cool breeze sneaking between the petals. First, he would learn about her species, how to make her happy and how to bring her to fulfillment. He'd assumed the Ethera would choose physiology similar to Etterian. It cost him nothing to learn either way. He had expected his Dar Eth to be weaker and reliant on him for protection. Quin needed neither from him. Entering into their future at a disadvantage didn't sit well with him.

He tapped his O.D.I and navigated to the data they had on Earth and its people. It didn't take him long to find articles on her fertility which led to vids on how to please her. With the images flashing before him, he paid attention on where to touch her. The humans had an extensive library on pleasuring each other. Their males had to be incredible at it. Xan didn't delve too deeply into the cornucopia of information, skimming the basics. The rest, he hoped Quin would guide him. Experience had taught him that no two females were the same. He assumed that applied to humans too. Macy was nothing like Quin, which proved it.

He deactivated his O.D.I. as the dawn's light bathed the night's sky. Perhaps today, they would return to the *Phoenix*. He wanted off this planet and en route to Etteria. He snorted. What he wanted was Quin far from these Lysarans. Now, if he could only leave Illan behind. He smiled, imagining doing just that. Then he could have his Dar Eth to himself. He yearned to learn everything about her and how her mind worked. The Gracc rescue had been a stroke of brilliance. His chest constricted. He'd thought he'd die, missing out on a life spent with her. Then the wilanegy had attacked. He had no doubt killing them in the pool had been her idea too.

To have a Dar Eth such as she would make any warrior proud.

And he was.

He just wished she needed him as much as he did her. There lay the crux of the matter.

She could survive without him. Flourish even. Mate someone else, bare them *damu*. He nodded, pressing a kiss to her temple. He'd find what she needed the most and be the one to give it to her.

Illan had said to love her. That was all. Yet, it was too little to ask for when she meant so much to Xan. She'd described what loving her mate would be like, and he'd ached to be that male.

She moaned in her sleep, so he gathered her closer.

Activating his O.D.I., he searched for 'love' and examples of it, vowing to show her how choosing him would benefit her.

Quin drifted awake, well-rested, safe, and protected in her electric blanket. Even the weight of it was comforting. She inhaled a spicy scent, elusive yet enticing. She drew in a deeper breath, attempting to capture it within her lungs. With a moan, she gave up and rubbed her nose across the velvety texture of the mattress. This released fresh scent, delighting her so she inhaled again. Satisfied, she hummed and snuggled deeper into her bed. She loved her bed, then giggled, wondering if it was legal to marry furniture.

But she was already married.

To Xan.

Nope. She'd dreamed it. No way a man fell to a knee, and bam, she was married. What happened to witnesses, signing the marriage certificate, and sharing the day with friends and family? Well, in her case, guardians. Cyn and Macy were her new friends, and she'd invite them for sure.

Then her mind went there. What if Xan was her husband for real. She smiled when joy flooded her. Gorgeous, sexy-as-hell Xan hers forever? She could get used to it. Being with him wouldn't be a hardship. And hell, he was the first man...male she wanted to sleep with. There'd been a guy or two she'd gushed over, but none of them could compare to the sheer masculinity of an Etterian Supreme Commander.

"What are you thinking, my Quin?" A deep voice reached through her lethargy.

She fluttered her eyes open to drown in his ice-blue gaze. "Morning, my Xan." She snuggled into him again, brushing a kiss across his chin.

Cinching her chest like a vise were his arms, cradling her—smashing her nose into his chest, and her body gathered close to him as if he cherished her. Whoa, this male was textbook perfect. Her lower stomach rubbed against his hip where she'd thrown her leg over his thighs. The yellow petal still curled around them. The sky was lemony-yellow again, pale and bright.

"What thoughts summoned your beautiful smile?" He buried his face in her hair, his arms tightening.

She stilled. What could she say? That she dreamed he was her husband? That he adored every inch of her? He'd run for the hills.

"Um, just slept well." She dipped her gaze, not used to lying. Well, it wasn't a complete lie. The most believable had kernels of truth.

"I was worried my confession would disturb your rest."

She met his gaze, trying to remember everything they'd discussed. As memories bombarded her, she froze. It was true. She was married. Lucas was going to kill her. "We're married?" she rasped.

"We are." Xan watched her, probably expecting her to lose her shit.

She should, but her mind reeled while her heart did the hula. What she wanted was to speak to Mace or Cyn, but that wasn't an option. She opened her mouth then snapped it shut. What could she say? It was a done deal by Etterian law, and by the sounds of it, divorce didn't exist. He was as stuck with her, as she was with him.

The problem wasn't that she didn't mind. What bothered her was how he felt about this. Was he happy? He'd said as much, spouting something about longing for her. But that could just be the saved-him-from-dying angle. Still, starting on the right foot mattered.

"That I have a wonderful husband," she said and pushed up, asking him to remove his arms. He loosened his hold only, giving her sufficient space to rise and glance at him.

"Wonderful?" Humor and hope crinkled his eyes.

"Oh, yes," she gasped before kissing him. She meant to brush his mouth with hers, but he groaned and crushed her to him.

Before she could think the words "morning breath," he plundered her mouth. He rubbed his hands up and down her back. She melted into him, embedding her fingers in his hair at the nape of his neck. The heated taste of him was so addictive. She couldn't think, couldn't stop craving this male.

"Quinlan," he whispered into her mouth. "Your scent, your taste drives me wild."

"I feel the same." She struggled to keep air in her lungs.

I do not. Illan's words froze her.

Go away. Not appreciating the interruption, she shoved anger at him before claiming Xan's lips for another deep and thorough kiss.

You will not make love to him in your current condition, Quinny.

Sucking in a sharp breath, she pressed her temple to Xan's. She hated it when Illan was right but raiding her mind again was unacceptable.

"Can we kill a Durn?" she said to Xan before brushing her lips across his parted mouth.

I heard that.

I'm planning your murder here so butt out. Her thoughts were petulant. *I can't believe I have an annoying brother in my mind. Yesterday, it was so sweet of him calling me his sister. Now? Not so much.*

"I suppose if we left Iddan alive?" Xan chuckled. "Believe me, *ensa*, I am tempted."

"You too?" She blinked at this revelation. "Why? What did he say or do to you?"

"He shares my Dar Eth. I do not have kind thoughts toward him."

At his words, heat unfurled in her stomach, and a giddiness stole her breath. "Are you...jealous?"

He frowned. "Etterians are trained not to feel, and if they should suffer any intense emotion, it would not be something as trivial as jealousy."

"So, if Illan stormed in and kissed me, what would you feel then?"

"Anger. No male is to touch what is mine."

She sat up while trying not to smile, but damn, being cherished was better than kicking Aiden's ass at poker.

"Yes, you're right, that's not jealousy at all." She hid her smirk as she climbed out of the petal. Xan followed her, then did the sweetest thing. After the petal had furled, he stroked the stem as if to offer thanks.

"I hear your humor, *ensa*. Etterians struggle with emotions. Jealousy, infatuation, love, and hate are rarely experienced. I do not believe we can recognize them should we experience them."

Proving my point, she snorted. Illan's chuckle carried through their connection. She stilled. He'd said *love*.

"Are you saying you'll never love me?" *A forever of unrequited love?* She glanced away, trying to hide her horror. *No, the universe couldn't be that cruel, could it?*

"No, I am not saying I will never love you, my Quin. What I am saying is that I will need your assistance to classify emotions when I experience them."

She studied him. The possibility of love was better than none. "That intense, irrational anger you *feel* when someone takes what is yours... That's jealousy." She patted him on his chest before crossing the chamber. One last glance revealed he grinned like an idiot.

She chuckled, shaking her head before disappearing into the bathroom.

"Can you order clothes for me?" she called, expecting him to hear her through the walls.

"What would you like to wear?" he asked as she stepped into the cubicle.

"Your choice," she said, "but with underwear, please."

It was strange not to soap, but she stood there, allowing the water to wash her body and hair, and with a quick gargle, her teeth. So efficient, yet she missed the taste of toothpaste. With the chore of bathing done for her, she stepped out and activated the drier. Yes, it was easier but rubbing a towel down your back was like scratching an itch. The Etterians missed out on so much. She cracked the door open and held out a hand, not willing to use a toweling robe when she could just put on whatever Xan had ordered for her.

When she met his gaze, his face glowed with pure joy. Had she asked him to perform something wonderful? Clothing her delighted him? She would find out more soon enough. He grabbed her hand and pressed a kiss to her palm, skittering sensations up her arm. He draped one garment across her hand before she could tease him over the kiss. Yanking her hand inside the bathroom, she blinked at the well-made kimono in black and gold and as soft as silk.

"Xan? Is this sleepwear?" It looked like a dressing gown, designed to reveal a negligee.

"It is an Etterian ceremonial dress in my bloodline colors," he said from just outside the door.

As in his family's traditional colors? "I assume it serves a purpose?"

"Yes. It tells everyone you are mine," he said.

Her breath whooshed out of her. She wanted to belong to him, and if this meant he wanted the same, who was she to gainsay him? She smiled, slid it on, and clasped the lapels together. The magnetized garment clicked, then adjusted around her body, caressing her as the fabric shifted and shrank. Gathering her hair from underneath the collar, she exited the bathroom.

Xan's gaze roamed her body like a starved male. It *was* good that he liked it on her, right?

"No shoes again?" she teased.

"No," he said before clearing his throat.

She headed for the replicator, needing a brush. As she pulled it through her hair and worked on the tangles, Xan grunted before closing the bathroom door behind him.

Quin grinned, liking the kimono-style garment he had picked for her, especially if it elicited such a response from him. She imagined what a negligee would do. Oh, the possibilities were endless.

The door chimed, and she granted access. Jokta marched through the chambers as if ninja assassins hid in the walls.

"Greetings, milady." He stood to the side of the doorway like he was on guard duty.

"Morning, Jokta." She offered him a smile that altered into a full-blown grin when his gaze traveled the length of her before he nodded, agreeing with Xan's taste. *Typical Etterian male,* she chuckled. "Would you like anything from the rehydrator?"

He glanced at her, opened his mouth, snapped it shut, hesitated, then muttered, "Chocolate."

She widened her eyes and arched both eyebrows. "For breakfast?"

"It has a specific time when it may be consumed?" Jokta gaped. Wait till she told him about the antiquated tradition of tea and biscuits at four o'clock in the afternoon.

"I suppose not. You've eaten already?" She strode to the rehydrator to order a slab of plain chocolate. He hadn't mentioned a preference, so she'd assumed the standard was fine.

"No, milady."

"Then may I interest you in a human breakfast?" She dipped her chin to smile when he grumbled something. She ordered a toasted bacon and cheese sandwich and his chocolate before placing it on the table in front of a massive chair that didn't cup her backside. "Would you like coffee with this?"

He stared at the food, but didn't sit, just stood guard.

When he didn't answer, she folded her arms across her chest. "Okay, explain. Why are you at the door and not eating the food I've requested for you?"

"I owe you a life debt," he said.

She frowned. Like she knew what that meant?

"It was Eira's last request." Xan stepped through the bathroom door in a white robe.

Damn. She blinked for a moment, her mind not yet fully understanding that he'd spoken. The robe left a gaping deep V, revealing his molded-caramel chest beneath. She was tempted to tug apart the robe to expose all of him. The hair on the back of her neck rose, and heat uncoiled in her core, sending out waves of goosebumps.

"Last request?" She struggled to gather her thoughts. Eira hadn't said anything.

"I owed Eira a life debt, which he transferred to you," Jokta said.

"The hell you say?" she gasped, dropping into the comfy a little alarmed. "And what does this life debt entail?"

"Your protection until I save your life, then the debt is paid in full."

"You're my bodyguard for as long as it takes?" She curled her fingers into her palms, forming crescents with her nails, while she waited for their O.D.I. to explain.

"Yes," Jokta said.

She pointed at the food. "Come, eat." When he hesitated, she drew in a calming breath, fighting the urge to smack him upside his head. "Listen here, Jokta. You've just told me I'm stuck with you for hours each day. This means we're going to spend time together. The best approach is to become friends. Get your backside here and eat, or else, so help me, I'll make your debt service hell."

Jokta lowered his stiff body into the comfy but was seconds later groaning in delight. She nodded. Bacon had the same effect on her. "And you..." She approached Xan. "Unless this is also a ceremonial dress, I would suggest you put some clothes on." Along the edges of his robe, she dipped her fingers into the V to touch his bare chest. She realized she baited the dragon, especially when his gaze narrowed and his hands twitched at his sides. In a blatant challenge, she met his gaze, but he too grumbled before striding toward the replicator to order another suit of armor.

"Hungry?" she asked when he disappeared into the bathroom again.

"I will have what you have chosen for Jokta," he said.

She ordered the same meal and had it ready for him when he returned in his armor.

"What is this, *ensa*?"

She sank into a comfy and scooped her plate onto her lap. "Bacon and cheese grilled sandwich and a cappuccino with cream."

In mid-chew, Illan intruded. *Are you ready to return to the ship?*

She huffed. *Duh.*

Sarcasm? At this hour? he teased.

Where do you need us? she asked while watching Xan devour his sandwich before scooping a dollop of cream off his cappuccino. She may be a virgin, but there was so much she could do with cream.

Focus, Quinny. Illan sighed. *Head for the royal court. We require Kuna Sy'mar's permission to depart.*

Acknowledged. On our way. But she didn't jump up, choosing instead to watch Xan lick cream off his lips.

Chapter Twenty-Three

Kuna Sy'mar clasped Quin's hand for longer than Xan liked. The male bowed his head at Xan and moved along to Lady Macy, who bounced on her toes, her hair swaying as she teased Oyaz.

The *kuna* drew in a deep breath, gathered Macy's hands in his, and grinned. "It has been a pleasure to meet you, Lady Macera. Are you certain I cannot convince you to stay?"

Oyaz stiffened, his shoulders brushing Xan's.

"As I told Bry-dar, it would be rude of me not to travel to Etteria first, after all, they rescued us."

The *kuna* smiled. "A diplomatic answer, milady. I will schedule a visit with King Xeus and hope to persuade you then."

She slumped and sidled closer to Oyaz, casting him a pleading glance, though what she hoped he would do, Xan couldn't fathom.

Within half an hour, the kuta Illan and Oyaz had utilized shuttled them to the *Phoenix*. Xan had to comm King Xeus, but he trailed Quin instead when she returned to her quarters. She and Macy hugged Cyndi like they'd been apart for months. Xan shook his head and settled into the comfy to observe them. Their delicious scents filled the room. Oyaz grinned and assumed the comfy next to him.

Xan couldn't drag his gaze from Quin in his colors. *Maker. Am I insane to do this to myself?* Her hair glowed like a bright yellow flame, and her pale skin contrasted with the black. The garment clung to her as a cleansing wrap did. That thought alone took him down other mental paths. He adjusted his arousal in his pants, ignoring its demand to be freed.

Macy handed Quin a long, tall glass that held a transparent liquid similar in color to Cyndi's hair. They clinked their glasses together before downing the liquid. It was an unusual mannerism, one he would eventually learn about. But for the moment, he was content to bask in the excitement filling the room.

Quin rushed to the replicator, trailing her fingers along his shoulders in passing, snatching his breath. She returned a few minutes later, shoving ice-cold brown bottles in his and Oyaz's hands. Xan sniffed it, but before he could take a tentative sip, Oyaz tapped the bottles together. Maybe it was a form of thank you? Oyaz grinned and took a long pull with no hesitancy. When had he become familiar with the beverage?

Xan did the same. Cold, bitter liquid filled his mouth, and an incredible, smoky flavor followed. He rumbled in approval, studied the bottle, and glanced at Oyaz. "What is it?"

"Beer."

"And more intriguing is how do you know it?"

Oyaz shrugged. "Macy is an incredible ambassador and introduces our males to Earthian delights every evening meal."

Xan jerked. "Why was I not—?"

"You have been preoccupied." Oyaz gestured with his bottle at Quin.

She had ordered more of the bubbly liquid, flashing him a sensual smile as she sipped. Her gaze darted between him and Lady Macy, who, while bouncing with ceaseless energy, burst into birdsong. The unexpected connection of words to flow in a pleasant rhythm froze him, and again when Quin and Cyndi joined in the singing. They were jumping up and down, laughing, their hips swaying at different rhythms. Beside him, Oyaz bobbed his head side-to-side and mouthed the words. *Alodon's balls.*

At the meaning of the birdsong, Xan tensed as unbearable heat scorched through him. A female lying in wait for her lover. The fulfillment like fire, desire killing her. The male in fever, aching to touch and taste her.

Did Quin not realize what she was saying?

He gripped his knees, willing himself to stay seated when her joyful and husky laughter filled the room, along with the scent of her arousal. Her hooded and intense gaze focused on him as she sang the words, crumbling his control. His O.D.I. buzzed up his arm. With trembling fingers, he activated it, his breathing coming in gasps.

A comm from King Xeus waited. *Thank the Maker.*

Xan rushed out of the room, not glancing at Quin lest she tempt him to drag her with him and thus ignore the king's summons. He paused in the passage to draw in much-needed air—it seemed cooler than the air within her quarters. He could, at least, breathe a little easier.

He headed to his quarters, adjusting his pants around his arousal as he strode. With a start, he realized he still held the bottle. He shoved it to a passing male before lengthening his strides to reach his quarters faster. In front of the display vid, he took a moment to gather his thoughts. He accepted the king's request and squared his shoulders when Xeus's image appeared before him.

"My king." Xan cleared his throat. That he had lost control of his vocal cords was the least of his problems.

"You crashed onto a planet with a sensitive biome, killed three migrating wilanegy males, lost a valued male in Eira, and still managed to have King Sy'mar praise you. The how is beyond me." Xeus chuckled. "I have never seen Sy this animated."

Xan blinked at his uncle, not knowing how to react to his joviality. "Maloidians attacked us without provocation. The situation was unavoidable."

"Yes, I have read Kemt's report," Xeus said with a dismissive flick of his fingers. "Your Dar Eth made such an impression that Sy'mar has scheduled a diplomatic visit to Issneen."

Xan scowled. *Didn't Xeus mean Macy?*

"I am most pleased, Xan, despite missing meeting her by a few hours."

"You were on Lysara?" Xan gritted his teeth. Quin distracted him so well that he hadn't noticed his king's presence.

Xeus's gaze turned inward. A slow smile spread his lips, and for the first time in a long while, his posture relaxed, almost as if he was at peace. "Yes," he rasped. "A fortuitous visit." Raising his chin, he focused on Xan. "Yet you are not pleased."

Xan paced in front of the display vid—his agitation clear as restlessness flooded his body. Perhaps a sparring session later would assist, but his instincts whispered doubt.

"No, I am not...*pleased*. These human females lack control. Their emotions are so varied there is no possibility of dealing with them successfully. An Etterian male is not equipped to handle this intensity and still retain his honor and self-worth."

"You are displeased with your Dar Eth?" Xeus's arched brows almost brushed his hairline.

Xan grunted, understanding that *Eths* never found their giftings displeasing. "No, I am not ungrateful for such a gift. I am angry, frustrated, in some instances, powerless. Her mind works in fascinating ways, and yet her emotions override logic. She reacts in haste and endangers herself. That there are successful resolutions is by pure chance."

"Perhaps she reacts by faith?" Xeus's words silenced Xan's tirade.

She acts by faith... "She *trusts* it will end well..." He replayed the events from the past few days. "Like a youngin."

"You may be accurate in that assessment, Xan. As a species, they have not learned self-control. Would we not be as emotional had we followed a different path?"

"True, my king. And yet their emotional capacity is what draws us."

"That and the Ethera?" Xeus teased. "What is the underlying issue?"

Xan frowned at his grinning king. "I cannot control my responses." He gritted his teeth at having to admit this weakness.

"Xan, do you wish to?"

"I wish to honor Etteria, to retain what has made me a good male."

"And with your Dar Eth, none of that matters?" Xeus asked, his dark-blue eyes as penetrating as usual. Xan scowled. How could he reveal to his king that his allegiance had shifted? "Why not do as your human would do and take a leap of faith?"

He stared at Xeus, his mind, the ache in his chest all coalescing into one thought—to claim her and have faith it would end well. That he could keep her forever.

"Thank you,...Uncle." Xan grinned at the king, who jerked back, then grinned. "I will take this leap of faith."

"Excellent and do inform me if it goes well." And with that, Xeus ended the comm.

Xan glanced around his quarters and entered the cleansing room, choosing to test out the cold-shower he'd read about in this morning's research. He needed to be calm and focused when he took his faith-leap and claimed his Dar Eth at last.

XAN SCOWLED AS HE activated the blue button. The air-dryer attempted to dry a frustrated Etterian male, but he couldn't stand there for its full cycle. His patience was non-existent. He strode across to his bedroom, yanking out a spare uniform. The cold shower had been effective, but the moment he'd deactivated the water, the Ethera had flooded his body again. As aroused as when he'd stepped into the cleanser, the fiery burn of anger now coursed through him at having wasted time.

"Supreme Commander, comm room now," Oyaz said through his O.D.I.

Xan yanked on his boots and left his quarters. His long forceful strides revealed his agitation, a rare occurrence for an Etterian male with such a reputation as his. His males avoided him, but he didn't have it in him to alter his emotional state.

He burst into the comm room and halted. A Yithian filled the display vid. Xan's anger deepened into a barely contained rage. *They are not taking my Dar Eth.*

"Yithian," he said in greeting.

"Supreme Commander. I am Commander Pyo, I assume your King Xeus has mentioned our previous discussion," Pyo lisped in a thick-accented Galactic.

"I require validation as to your identity," Xan said.

The Yithian hissed at him in anger.

This display of pseudo-outrage was wasted on Xan. "If you are Pyo, a validation would not offend. You could be a pretender. I will not take the risk and jeopardize Etteria."

Pyo glared at Xan before raising his chin. "Very well, what validation do you require?"

"Name of the battleship you communicated with?" Xan asked.

Pyo smirked. "Too easy, Etterian. The *Kushin*."

"The names of the Supreme Commander and his Sub-Commander?"

"Ulriq and Nerx." Pyo curled his wide mouth upward, exposing his elongated teeth.

"The final question. What is the color of Ulriq's eyes?" Xan folded his arms across his chest and waited.

Pyo hiss-laughed. "Dark blue as per all Etterians. That was a trick question."

"Pilot Msar, fire the chokaar," Xan said.

Msar didn't hesitate, punching the black button while Pyo sputtered. The display vid blanked. "Target destroyed, Supreme Commander," Msar said into the silent comm room.

"Comm the king." Xan didn't glance at Oyaz. What he'd done, he wasn't comfortable with. He may have taken many Yithian lives. And yet he had no doubt he'd saved the lives of his males, of the human females, and more specifically, his Dar Eth.

"Supreme Commander Xan?" Adviser Cales answered the comm request. In the background of the display vid, Xeus strode into his office. He was bare-chested and wearing his loose pants so prepared for sleep.

"Adviser, my king, I may have ended the Yithian rebellion. A Yithian claiming to be Pyo did not pass the validation checks." He squared his shoulders, prepared to accept any punishment Xeus deemed fit.

"Are we firing chokaars as if they're blaster stuns?" Xeus boomed, his strides angry and forceful as he approached the display vid.

Everything within Xan stated he'd done the right thing. The decision had nothing to do with what Quin invoked within him. "You have read Kemt's report, my king."

Xeus scowled before running a hand over his face in frustration. "Maloidians are on the offensive. Yithians are rebelling against King Urio. What in Alodon's hell is going on?"

"How certain are you that it was entrapment?" Adviser Cales asked.

"He could not state Ulriq's eye color. He was therefore, either a pretender, unobservant, or with poor intel. None of those promise a trustworthy alliance."

"And if he was not Pyo, destroying the vessel would not bring war." Xeus pursed his lips. "The pretender meant to deceive."

"War is inevitable, my king, since they insist on targeting Earth." Oyaz stood beside Xan and clasped his hands behind his back.

"Return to Etteria for a war council," Xeus said, his tone brooking no argument. "I must notify the ambassadors, advisers, and lima kuu of these underwater ships you have discovered."

A glance at the console confirmed their journey. "We are en route. Estimated arrival in four days."

"I will schedule the council for your arrival," Cales said.

"Xan, since your Dar Eth mentioned these *submarines*, does she have in-depth knowledge that might assist?" Xeus's eyes twinkled with excitement.

Xan scowled, only now noticing its absence of late. "I am uncertain, though her bonds may be of assistance. Reaching out to them would be fortuitous should Malo's negotiations be successful and our only option should Malo fail. I will ensure she attends the council, my king."

"Assistance from Earth would indeed aid this war. To construct such a vessel from the schematics will take time." Xeus gave Xan a pointed look. "No more chokaars. All of Etteria is with you."

And the display vid went blank.

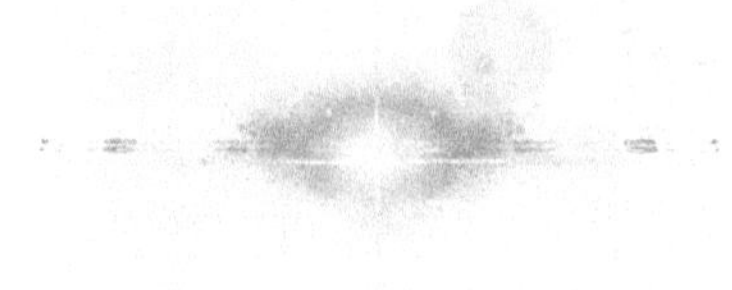

XAN REPEATED HIS CALMING routine to rein in his arousal and tighten his control. Doing so naked meant nothing touched his hypersensitive skin. Sweat ran down his chest and dripped in his eyes, yet his malehood still throbbed, and his control remained elusive. The Ethera was demanding appeasement. It urged him to collect Quin, bring her to his bed, and bury himself in her. And he wanted to, with an obsession that bordered on madness. It had already been four days since Lysara, four days of hell being near her, allowed to touch her yet to do no more. Her fertile scent was driving him senseless. He didn't care that she was bleeding, he just *needed* her.

"Supreme Commander Xan," Pilot Msar's voice came through his O.D.I.

"Msar." Xan grunted as he restarted his routine for the eighth time.

"Another Pyo requests your presence," the pilot said.

Xan groaned and jumped up, yanking on his uniform with more violence than he needed to, his hands trembling. Angry again, he stormed to the comm room, expecting to destroy yet another Yithian ship.

"Supreme Commander," a Yithian greeted from the display vid the moment he entered.

"Yithian, what do you require?" Xan scowled at Oyaz's absence.

"I require a secure comm." The Yithian's request snapped Xan's gaze to the vid.

He nodded to Msar to secure it.

"Comm secure, Supreme Commander," Msar announced.

"My lord Kbal requests a converse with your King Xeus," Pyo said.

"You need to pass the validation checks, Yithian," Xan squared his shoulders, preparing to order the kill shot. Msar powered the chokaar in anticipation.

"Proceed," the Yithian's unwavering confidence caught Xan off guard.

"Name of the battleship you initially communicated with?" he asked.

"The *Kushin*. Ulriq is the Supreme Commander. As I recall, he was overly aggressive though I did sense he was not himself." The Yithian hiss-laughed before continuing, "Sub-Commander Nerx remained calm, however. Pilot Ksal commed King Xeus and somehow altered the source of my comm. That male *was* impressive."

Xan grunted. "Very well, Pyo, present Kbal while Msar comms our king," Xan gestured to Msar, who requested a comm with Adviser Cales on a side vid.

"Truly, Xan, this is becoming a habit," Cales groaned as he accepted the request. The scene around him was of his chambers. The magnus sun had yet to rise.

"Greetings, Adviser. I assumed King Xeus would speak with Kbal, or would you prefer I destroy this ship as well?"

"It is good that Pyo remains alive, Xan. I have alerted Xeus," Cales said, not taking offense at Xan's irritable tone, for which he was thankful. It would do him no good to anger Xeus's closest battle-bond. Another Yithian now occupied the left panel on the display vid, with Cales occupying the right.

"Greetings, Supreme Commander." This Yithian was taller and bulkier than most of the Yithians Xan had encountered. Both species considered this a good trait.

"Greetings, Lord Kbal. King Xeus is en route." Xan bowed his head.

"Thank you, Supreme Commander." Kbal's Galactic was elegant with no hint of an O.D.I accent.

"Greetings, Kbal." King Xeus strode toward the display vid. Cales slid out of view as Xeus dominated the screen, large and intimidating, even bare-chested.

"King Xeus, I appreciate the time and apologize for the intrusion." Kbal gestured to his bare chest.

"What assistance do you have in mind?" Xeus asked.

Xan hid a smile, appreciating his uncle's directness.

"Simply your support," Kbal lisped, his twitching lips revealing his long canines. It was a Yithian's version of a smile.

"The word *support* is vague. What are your exact requirements?" Xeus stared down the soulless black eyes of the usurper with stony resolve. "The current buzz mentions war. Are you aware of this?" At Xeus's question, Kbal nodded. "War is imminent. I would prefer you resolve this before the destruction of your homeworld. The death of innocents does not sit well with my males, yet we have prepared for it."

"You cannot use your world-taker on Yithia, King Xeus. They cannot penetrate our oceans." Kbal's voice warbled as lines furrowed his brow.

"True, but my enemies should not believe I am without other weaponry in my arsenal."

"A true leader prepares for everything," Kbal stated.

"Tell me, Kbal, under your leadership, how will you govern Yithia? How will your rule be an improvement?"

"I cannot anticipate that the transition will be smooth. Our people have become greedy, selfish, cold, and arrogant. We survive on the downfall of others like true savages. The first thing I shall do is promote trade. Mining our precious minerals would allow me to disband the arena. Of course, there will be much displeasure, this I *can* anticipate."

"I am certain you will do what's best for Yithia." Xeus leaned in. "However, my warriors will kill Yithians on sight. My concern is for your followers caught in the crossfire."

"A problem easily remedied, King Xeus."

"Have you the support of the Global Council?" Xeus asked.

"A few of its members. I have approached this with caution. If the buzz should reach Urio's ears, he would boil my family."

"A valid fear." Xeus glanced at Xan before settling on Kbal. "We must assume Urio knows and act accordingly. I require a list of your blood-bonds. We shall safeguard them on Etteria until such a time that they may return to Yithia."

"Thank you, King Xeus. This is...unexpected."

"Should it come to intergalactic war, if your soldiers strike from within and Etteria assaults from without, I hope to resolve this with minimal sacrifices." Xeus scowled. "In addition, Yithians have targeted a small blue planet. This must cease at once."

"Earth?" Kbal jerked.

"It has significance to many planets in the universe. Their people, not their resources. A mid-grade planet such as this requires protection not exploitation."

"Yithia will cease unsavory dealings with this planet, King Xeus," Kbal vowed.

"I apologize for the intrusion. I have a personal matter to discuss with Kbal regarding a captive," Xan said.

Xeus nodded. "Very well, Lord Kbal. My first choice would be a peaceful resolution without civil war and, therefore, avoiding an intergalactic war. I pray to the Maker you will see great success. Regardless, you will have my full support, not only in war but in the reconstruction of your new Yithia and at the Global Council."

"Thank you, King Xeus. This is more than I hoped for."

Xeus ended the comm, and the display vid filled with Kbal's face.

He flashed his canines. "Thank you, Supreme Commander. Now, how may I be of assistance?"

"You have a Maloidian in Yithian captivity. I require his release and safe delivery to his homeworld."

"And this Maloidian's crime?" Kbal frowned, then shook his head. "Never mind, it was probably an imagined slight. My apologies, Supreme Commander, my people are petulant children. The name of this captive?"

"Mannx, son of Pannos," Xan said. "I believe he serves you."

"Indeed. I shall use all that I have in my power to release him, Supreme Commander. On this, you have my word, such as it is."

"Excellent, Lord Kbal. The release of this male would go a long way to securing the support of the Maloidians, as well."

"True, but war costs tokens. The Maloidians will deal with all sides."

Xan spared the Yithian a small smile. "And the cost of Maloidian steel will triple."

"I will have the Maloidian captive inform you of his release."

"My thanks." Xan arched a brow when the comm didn't end.

The Yithian hesitated. "We intercepted a signal coming from your battleship, Supreme Commander. It conveyed images of your females." Kbal's lips turned downward. "This using of innocents for personal gain is abhorrent to me. We scrambled it and pray no other Yithian ship encountered it."

And the screen went blank. Xan released a long-drawn-out sigh. That was one less thing to worry about. "Msar, inform Kemt of this but have him continue to monitor. Location of Oyaz?"

"With the human females, Supreme Commander."

Xan grunted. "Should a different Pyo comm you, fire the chokaar…"

"Truth?" Msar gaped.

"Said in jest, Pilot." Xan left the comm room and headed for his quarters. He didn't once consider collecting Quin en route. The temptation to do so would win out. Once in his quarters, he stripped off his armor, discarded his garments, and began the exercise routine for the ninth time.

Chapter
Twenty-Four

Etterian Battleship, Phoenix
The Comm Room

OYAZ ENTERED THE COMM room to continue his shift. His thoughts returned to the past day, a little alarmed at his commander's uncharacteristic reactions. Xan had destroyed a Yithian ship. His actions were decisive as expected of a supreme commander. Oyaz wasn't certain if he should be proud or concerned over such behavior.

He'd just come from issuing Quin her quarters. Macy had shared that the human woman struggled to sleep at night and would keep her and Lady Cyndi awake. They'd requested separate quarters with humancentric training equipment. The delight on Quin's face was a pleasure to behold. Said woman's voice echoed through the comm room's display vids.

"Msar, you get your ass down here this instant. No, you two, stay." She addressed someone off-screen before facing the pilot. Her commanding tone was one Xan would have been proud of. She wore a tight white sleeveless tunic soaked with perspiration, with her breasts

240

heaving from her agitated breathing. He couldn't help but notice. "Msar. Now." And the comm ended.

"Alodon's balls, what did you do to anger her so?" Oyaz asked the pilot, who bounded out of his seat.

"Unusual sounds emanated from an unallocated officer's quarters. I tasked two sec warriors to investigate," Msar said before racing out of the comm room.

Unusual sounds? Oyaz laughed. He'd yet to inform the logs of Quin's new quarters and the modifications done to it. He approached the console to amend his error before activating the sec vids and the audio for her quarters. Then he notified Xan that his Dar Eth was likely to kill a male this evening in her quarters and the location thereof. Oyaz dropped into Msar's seat to observe the interaction. His grin reflected off the display vids.

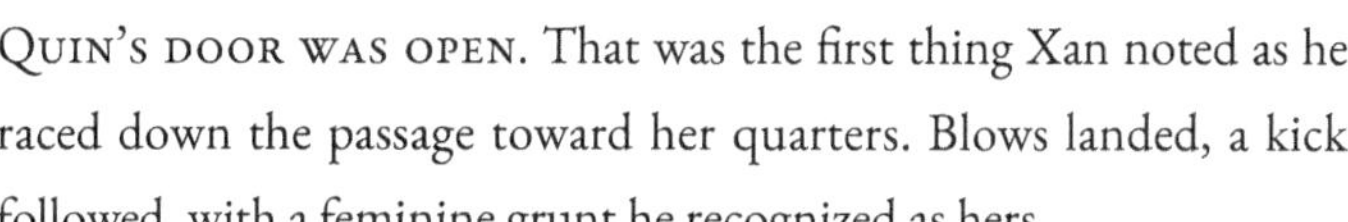

QUIN'S DOOR WAS OPEN. That was the first thing Xan noted as he raced down the passage toward her quarters. Blows landed, a kick followed, with a feminine grunt he recognized as hers.

He burst into the room expecting to fight, even to kill the male who had dared to harm her. The scent of her hit him. Her usual intense fruity scent had returned, without the fertile temptation he'd endured since Lysara. Added to this were the salty tang of her perspiration and the smoky rich fragrance of her arousal. He swallowed a groan and tried to focus on the situation at hand. She hadn't noticed his entrance since her back was to the door.

"This is a roundhouse." She swung her leg, twisting on the ball of her left foot as she connected with the bag hanging from the ceiling. It careened from the force of her kick. "Are you paying attention, Msar?" she asked in a tone that rivaled Remi's. "This is a teep," she said, kicking forward, her foot smacking and recoiling. "Now, do either sound like I need assistance?" She glared at the male, putting her in profile. "On Earth, if I were in danger, I'd scream. Did you hear any screaming?"

Xan refused to blink, needing to savor everything about her—her angry stance, her tight blue leggings halting just below her backside and leaving her beautiful legs bare. Even her feet were unadorned.

I've touched those tiny toes.

"My apologies, Lady Quin. Thank you for demonstrating the source of the sounds," Msar said with all seriousness.

Xan smiled. His gaze flew back to Quin, only to lose his focus at the sight of her damp tunic clinging to her, emphasizing her small waist and heaving breasts.

"What is that used for, milady?" A sec warrior gestured to a bar hanging from the ceiling.

"That?" She launched herself up and caught the bar with her hands. "It's a pull-up bar." She pulled herself up until her hips rested against the bar, then swung herself backward, looping her legs through her arms and the bar to hook it behind her knees. She released her grip to hang upside-down. She folded her body until her nose almost touched her knees before lowering herself again. Only to repeat the movement, keeping her muscles tight and controlled. Catching the bar, she released her knees and dropped to the mat.

"Want to try?" Her offer implied her anger had dissipated. "It will hold your weight. Oyaz tested it."

Oyaz? Xan scowled. *That son of a kreso.*

"Have the Sub-Commander install one in the common," Xan said.

His males nodded. They left the room. Xan checked the door, glaring into a hidden sec-cam before deactivating it.

"Hello, Etterian," Quin said, her gaze riveted on his bare chest. "To what do I owe the pleasure?" She purred the word *pleasure*.

He shivered and folded his arms across his chest. "What do you think you are doing allowing males into your quarters?"

"I'm *so* dressed to entertain," she snorted.

He brushed his fingertips along the fabric of her tunic, trailing down her arm to press her taut stomach. She was unaware that her tunic had slid up, exposing her smooth and muscled abdomen.

"You cannot sleep," Xan said.

"No." A pained expression twisted her features.

Xan stepped closer. Her heated scent saturated his lungs with every breath he took. He kept his palm on her stomach, burning from touching her at last. Reacting on instinct, he looped an arm around her backside, just below her hips, lifted her off the floor, and held her against his chest. She hummed before gazing into his upturned face. The unknown emotion in her eyes snatched his breath.

"Come, *thamani*." He pressed a kiss to her damp neck.

When she grabbed his shoulders, elation burst through him, at her silent agreement and trust. He released her and caught her as quickly, his arm now around her back, just above her waist. Sliding his other hand under her braid, he splayed out his fingers between her shoulder blades, crushing her against his chest.

"Xan?" She peered into his eyes, tiny lines furrowing her forehead.

He didn't respond, instead, he brushed his lips across hers, pausing to inhale her essence, to meld their souls for eternity. Not bothering to smother his shudder, he strolled to the cleansing room. He stepped into the cubicle and allowed the water to drench them. Brushing his lips over hers again called forth her deep sigh, one he echoed to the depths of his soul.

She looped her arms around his neck, pressing her chest tighter against his. In slow motion, she dipped her chin and latched onto his bottom lip to suck it into her mouth. At the same time, she hooked a leg around his hip. He groaned, spinning to pin her back against the white bulkhead, his hips holding her in place.

This position freed his hands to tear off her tunic and undergarment—the thin fabric unable to resist the force of his fingers. Her breasts bounced free, her nipples taut and begging for him to touch and taste them, as per the words of her birdsong.

"Maker." He slipped a hand beneath her, along her back, arching her upward to meet him halfway.

The moment he drew her nipple into his mouth, a moan tore from her. She gripped his shoulders, clinging to him. He cupped her other breast, thumbing her nipple. She chanted his name, her head thrashing against the onslaught. Her reactions were unrestrained, driving his need until it clamored for immediate attention.

He released her breast to slide a hand over her ribs, along her waist to mold to her backside. Squeezing the cheek, he groaned at how the softness filled his palm.

"Xan, please," she begged.

"What do you need, *thamani*?" he asked into her breast, his words breathing across her nipple, making her shiver. "Tell me," he ground out, uncaring that he could barely speak.

"So help me, Xan, if you don't do…I don't know, something, there will be hell to pay." Her gaze reflected the truth—her desire and confusion. Her innocence was in her wide eyes, her yearning in her flushed cheeks.

He deactivated the water and pressed the blue button. While they dried, he lowered her to her feet, allowing her to feel how much he wanted her. And she did, judging by her gasp.

He grasped her hips and the fabric of her pants before tugging and tossing the torn garment to the floor. His gaze lingered on her, so beautiful and naked before him. He grabbed her backside and raised her to brush a kiss along her jaw, to her chin, then across her mouth. She moaned, draped her arms around his neck, and clung to him, her tongue delving into his mouth, meeting his challenge, tasting him, claiming him.

Her approach was bold and warrior-like.

Ignoring the air-dryer, he strode to her bedroom, ravaging her mouth, drowning in her sweetness, softness, and essence. He spread her out on the bed and removed his semi-dried pants, not allowing her the time to admire his body. Her need called to his, enhancing the intensity. He was fast losing what little control he had. He rested a knee onto the bed, between her knees, forcing her to part her thighs, exposing the deep pink of her feminine folds among the dark gold curls guarding her sex.

He raised a trembling hand to run a path from her collarbone, between her breasts, over her stomach to brush the curls. She moaned and writhed under his touch, her responses true and passionate. As soon as he dipped a finger between her folds, her eyes flew open. She was so wet, so ready for him. Her rich aroused scent filled his chest, and his arousal bobbed with eagerness. Then he flicked a finger over her nub as instructed. She arched off the bed, thrusting her breasts toward him, her deep penetrating groan of pleasure pierced his resolve. He slid his hands down her inner thighs, parting her legs, her feminine folds blossoming for him. His breath hitched. He paused to admire such beauty. *Maker.*

He tucked a thumb into her channel and shuddered. She was tight, soft, so hot. He had never experienced anything as incredible. He flicked his forefinger over her nub and raised his gaze to watch her expressions. Her moans intensified, her hips rose as if begging him to take her, and her mouth parted in that tempting way he adored. She was close to finding her fulfillment.

Her nipples puckered, and tiny bumps formed across her skin. She screamed his name. Her body trembled and twitched as she clawed the bedding. With a grin, he removed his fingers, positioned the tip of his arousal at her channel, and worked his way in an inch at a time. Waiting for her body to adapt to his intrusion was killing him.

"So tight," he moaned, biting on his bottom lip.

She looped her legs around his hips and thrust upward, crying out.

Xan froze. Scenting blood, he bent over her in dismay at having harmed her. Anger and self-recrimination were swift to strike. He made to withdraw, but she shook her head.

"Don't move," she whispered.

He stilled again, trying not to focus on how the silkiness and heat squeezed his malehood. He trembled with the urge to withdraw and plunge in again or die from the exquisite sensations coursing through him.

"It had to be quick, Xan. I didn't mean to startle you."

"*Thamani.*" He cupped her cheek. "Are you well? Do you need a medic?"

"No, I'm fine. Please proceed." At her command, he nearly chuckled.

"Xan." She met his gaze with her lust-filled eyes. "You can move now. The pain is gone."

He hesitated. She wiggled her hips, and her mouth parted. Pleasure tore through him at her movements. He withdrew with care and slid forward with a guttural groan escaping him.

"Maker, you feel so good." He pistoned out and into her again.

Increasing the pace had sensations bombarding him, consuming his focus. She screamed his name again, launching herself over the precipice, her fulfillment contracting around him and dragging him over the edge with her. Cool tingles slithered down his spine to nestle in his balls before exploding. He crushed his mouth to hers and moaned his pleasure.

He collapsed on top of her, careful not to smother her. Sprawled across her, he relished her body against his, her pounding heartbeat, her breathlessness, her scent surrounding him. He rolled onto his back, taking her with him so that she lay over him, and yet, he managed to ensure his arousal remained inside her.

"You are precious to me, Quinlan." He pressed a kiss to her temple. "I apologize for harming you." He tilted her face up toward his. "I vow to not harm you next time."

"I did it, remember? So, don't feel guilty. And there's no need to go slowly, Xan. You've taken my virginity. There won't be any blood or pain next time."

He gaped, replayed her words, then kissed her hard, drowning in her taste once again. "Truth?"

She smiled.

He ravaged her mouth again, now free to kiss and taste her whenever he wanted to. "I cannot wait to claim you again, my Quin."

"I like it when you claim me, my Xan." Her eyes drifted shut as she nestled into him.

He embraced her, keeping her close.

She sighed. "Don't leave. Please stay here with me," she whispered, rolling her chin to press a kiss to his skin.

His breath caught. The ache in his chest intensified and burned. He couldn't discern what it was or explain how it made him *feel* toward her.

"I am yours for eternity," he answered despite knowing she'd fallen asleep, that she wouldn't hear him. He needed to speak them regardless. Peace descended and settled over him. No more darkness reigned in his soul. Only light bloomed. The Ethera was, at last, appeased.

Chapter Twenty-Five

THE BUZZ BOTHERED QUIN'S sleep, calling her from a delicious lassitude. She had never slept so well, not since the *d'nastu*. That had been the best sleep she'd had in months. Nor could she hope to replicate such an evening in her new quarters. So, she'd exercised for hours, yet exhaustion had remained elusive. Xan was the tormentor of her thoughts and dreams.

Then he was there, in her quarters, in nothing but a low-riding pair of yoga pants in a thin gray fabric that enhanced every inch of him, from his hips to his thighs. Her breath caught at the sight of his carved torso. His muscles rippled as he folded his arms across his expansive chest. She'd only seen him in his military gear and a Lysaran tunic. *Hot damn.* That man ought to be declared illegal.

"*Thamani.*"

"So tired." She swatted the intruder away.

The dream was too good to abandon. The buzz bothered her again, and she mumbled, rubbing her cheek against the velvet smoothness of Xan's chest. Her dream male was amazingly lifelike. Images of last night flooded her mind like photos rising out of the fog. And with her heart fluttering, excitement was swift to follow, snatching her breath. The urge to squeal like a girl gripped her, but thankfully, her breathlessness wouldn't allow for that. Breaking through her lethargy, she snuck a glance at his face and squeaked.

She snuggled deeper into his embrace, trying not to focus on her nudity and that she rubbed herself against his chest. Heat stained her cheeks at her brazen behavior. But damn, last night had blown her mind. Despite the shyness now fighting for supremacy, happiness consumed her and morphed her cheeks into a wide smile. He crushed her to him, his lips plucking at hers until they parted for his full intrusion.

"Good morning, Xan," she said when he drew back to let her breathe.

"I need my arm back," he teased, wiggling said appendage trapped under her.

"Pay me first," she said, lifting her mouth to his.

He paid and then some, kissing her until her toes curled. With a sigh, she rolled away from him, freeing his arm before snuggling against his side. He glanced at her; his eyes swirling with intensity, but then he activated his O.D.I. to read the message.

"You have a comm." He swung his legs over the side of the bed.

"For me?" She gasped. The sight of his smooth bronze back was a temptation she couldn't resist. She wrapped her arms across his shoulders, pressing her breasts against him. He groaned and shuddered, spinning on the spot to sprawl her across the bed, sliding his body over hers.

"If we hurry…" He buried his face in her neck to press a wet kiss there. "It is a human male called Joshua."

"Joshua?" She squealed and shoved at his chest, demanding he get off her.

He flipped to his side and chuckled as she stumbled off the bed to find the sleepshirt she'd ordered yesterday. He folded his arms behind his head and watched her.

"If *you* hurry, you can meet him." She pulled the shirt on and raced to the display vid.

"Do I have to?" Xan teased.

She tried not to ogle him when he pulled on his military pants and strode toward her. Wow, all that bronzed skin needed a good licking. She swallowed a giggle and touched the display vid. But nothing happened other than the usual menu. Panic gripped her, that she had taken too long to respond. Who knew when Joshua might call again?

"It's not activating. Did I break it?" she asked Xan.

He held one hand at the base of her spine and touched the vid with the other.

Msar's face appeared. "Supreme Commander, the comm will take a moment." The male tapped away on something. So like Aiden. With Xan's warmth alongside her, she pressed her face to his chest, brushing kisses along his skin, feathering her fingers across his right nipple. He growled and imprisoned her against him, trying to capture her questing fingers.

"Did you select the porn channel?" Joshua chuckled.

"Yip, this is *exactly* how I want to imagine my sister," Carter said, his tone playful.

"Josh *and* Carter?" She faced them. "How's this possible?"

"Carter got stranded, and I had to fetch him," Joshua said. "Had to take the sub out. The captain doesn't know yet." His laugh was robust with Carter looking chagrined.

"I miss you guys," she sniffed, wishing they were there for her to hug. She tightened her arm around Xan's waist, pleased to use him as a substitute.

"Miss you too, babe." Carter grinned in that suave way of his. That he had nondescript brown hair and eyes with a face that could be handsome or not, made him excellent at his profession. He was oozing charm now.

"I got the strangest news," Josh teased, his green eyes mischievous as they roamed Xan's expansive chest. "Aiden's message said you got probed by aliens."

There it is. I'm going to kill him.

"Probed by one alien only." She patted Xan's right pec.

"Probed?" He scowled. "The O.D.I.—"

"—doesn't understand human jokes." She beamed at him. "I'll explain later when you're probing me again."

"I look forward to your...explanation," he said. His arousal did some preliminary probing at the juncture of her thighs.

Thank the Lord, it was off-screen. She snuck a peek anyway and sighed. "Josh, Carter, this is Supreme Commander Xan and my...?" She frowned. *Husband? Lover? Opposite to Dar Eth?*

"Eth." His two-dimpled smile melted her socks, whether she was wearing them or not.

"My Eth," she said to her guardians.

"Eth?" Josh's brows twitched.

"The man who won your heart is on my need-to-know," Carter said, drowning out Josh's grumblings.

"Eth?" Josh asked again, his gaze darting between Xan and her.

"My husband." Her grin was beyond her control. She leaned into Xan's arms, twisting a little to place a kiss on his chest.

"Shit." Josh sat there for a few stunned moments. "Shit. Lucas is going to...blow a gasket."

"Congratulations, sweetheart." Carter smiled. At least one of her guardians was happy for her. "Welcome to the family, Xan." He gave Josh a wicked grin. "We know before Lucas. That's really what's going to get to him."

"But I thought you and Garrett would eventually...merge," Josh said.

She glanced at Xan and released a satisfied sigh. *Garrett schmarrett.*

"Garrett cannot have her." Xan's tone brooked no argument. "Quinlan is mine." The authority in Xan's voice had them both sitting up. They blinked at him.

She laughed. Only certain types of men would be acceptable to her guardians, and a supreme commander was top on their list. "Do you record these comms?" she asked Xan.

"Yes."

"Excellent, I want to frame their reaction," she teased before smothering her face in his chest again, inhaling his heated scent like a criminal looking for their next fix. "Later, I'll do that much...*much* later."

"When will you be in our neck of the woods?" Carter ran a hand through his brown locks, disheveling them further.

"I don't know..." Quin shrugged.

"When my Quin wants to be," Xan said. "She determines where we live."

Carter jerked back. "It's that simple?"

"She is my Dar Eth." Xan kissed her temple. "Everything she requires to be joyful is my honor and pleasure to see to."

Her breath hitched as she raised her gaze to meet his. "Why don't you two run along and tell Lucas the good news," she said to her guardians and ended the comm on their idiotic grins. She rose on her toes to press a sweet kiss to Xan's lips. "How about you show your Dar Eth what an *honor* and a *pleasure* it will be to see to her needs?" She trailed her nails over his chest, scraping his nipples.

He hissed and scooped her into his arms, carrying her to the bedroom. "Would this be the probing you were referring to?" His chuckle warmed her heart.

"Extensive and repeated probing." She closed her eyes on his descending kiss.

Chapter Twenty-Six

Planet Etteria

The Royal City of Issneen

Quin leaned over Msar's shoulder as they approached the landing pad just outside the royal gardens of the Royal City on Etteria. *Damn.* Pink skies stretched before them. It was a cloudless day, so the sky almost merged with the red ocean. The beaches were a pale gray, strange against the crimson waves. The gardens surrounding a large white building held blue bushes with flowers in pink, white, and green. It was as if someone had taken images of Earth and played with the color settings.

Various white buildings sprawled outward from the central Royal Court, lessening in height the closer they were to the markets. The outdoor stalls had colorful tents—striped, patterned, but blue was predominant. There was something significant about the dark blue with hints of gold included. Xan escorted her to a hovering shuttle, the top open to enjoy the fine weather. She settled in a seat but gripped and released her knees, intermittently sliding her palms down her thighs.

They were en route to what Xan had called the War Council. King Xeus had requested her attendance, so there was no escaping this. He had taken the information about Earth's submarines to the council, and they were excited to learn more. Typical males to find war exciting.

Breathe, Illan commanded her, summoning her smile. Wait till she told Lucas about her new brother. She faced him and Iddan. The council wanted to see the Durns too. Illan wasn't concerned. His nonchalance calmed her across their link.

She regulated her breathing, deep inhale, slow exhale. *I don't see the point of me being there.*

Illan snorted, meeting her gaze across the open shuttle. *The human female who retook a slave ship?*

How would they know about that? Her heart froze mid-beat, alarmed at the thought of yet another bout of males staring at her.

Sec vids from the slave ship's data cube, perhaps? Illan teased her to put her at ease.

She snuggled closer to Xan, pressing her thigh against his. He glanced at her and smiled—one single dimple appearing—before lacing his fingers through hers. She squeezed his hand, drawing strength from him. Jokta shifted in the seat next to her. She frowned. That male hadn't left her side unless Xan was with her. She wriggled in her seat, embarrassment burning her cheeks. Even when Jokta guarded her from the passage, could he hear everything that happened within her quarters?

Every male had to know exactly how well Xan pleased her.

Every male including me.

Her blush deepened. *Quit listening in, pervert.* She sent him a teasing warmth through their connection.

Illan grinned but didn't comment any further.

The hover shuttle docked. Xan escorted her off it and down a long white-stone passage lined with blue and gold banners. They approached massive doors, which opened as soon as they reached them. She squeezed Xan's hand, revealing how nervous she was. Meeting *Kuna* Sy'mar paled in comparison to meeting her new king.

At least she felt beautiful, having decided to honor Xan by wearing the ceremonial dress he had ordered for her on Lysara. She had checked with Illan to ensure she didn't offend anyone by doing so. And judging by Xan's reaction when he had collected her, he was pleased with her choice. She had added gladiator pumps that the garment hid well. The added height gave her confidence. The strappings around her calves gave her courage.

"Supreme Commander Xan and his Dar Eth, Lady Quinlan." The announcement boomed through the great white hall. As per *Kuna* Sy'mar's court, everyone watched them. She drew in a deep breath and squared her shoulders before stepping into her new world.

"Finally, another woman I can talk to," a red-haired woman strolled toward her. "Welcome to Etteria, Quin." She gave her a hug, her temple brushing Quin's chin. She too wore a ceremonial dress but in dark blue and gold. Her red hair hung down her back, wild and free.

"My Quin, this is Princess Oriana, the first human Dar Eth," Xan said.

Quin stiffened. *Princess?*

"Ori is fine," the princess said. "The whole milady and princess nonsense gets tiresome." She settled beside Quin to observe the crowd. "I saw your sec vids, impressive." Quin dipped her chin to hide her surprise. "Now relax, Xeus is a big old teddy bear."

Two Etterian males approached, both in dark blue and gold cloaks over their black armor, like Xan in his black and gold cloak. Their stride and their mannerisms showed they were family.

"Oriana, beating us to the guest of honor?" the younger male teased as he ran a heated gaze over the princess.

"That's my Eth, Prince Enyl," Ori whispered.

"Your Highness." Quin dropped into a curtsey she hadn't had a chance to do for Ori, though she was thankful for the whispered introduction.

"Lady Quinlan, a pleasure to meet you." Prince Enyl held out his hand.

She accepted it as she rose and was surprised when he shook it twice before gesturing to the older male beside him. "This is my father, King Xeus."

She sank into another curtsey. "Your Highness," she said before rising to accept his offered hand. He cupped hers, his grip firm yet comfortable.

"Welcome to Etteria, Lady Quinlan. I am pleased Xan found his Dar Eth. I am also delighted at the skills you have demonstrated. Ori insists not all human women are the same, this I find to be true. However, the same core of strength in her runs through you."

"It's strength under adversity, King Xeus." Quin sighed when Xan joined her to press his hand to her lower back.

The strength must come from somewhere. It cannot just appear whenever adversity presents itself. Illan harrumphed.

She stiffened. *Your timing sucks, Illan. Can't we have this chat later?*

Avoiding my observation only delays the inevitable.

She gritted her teeth before asking him the question he waited for. *What's inevitable?*

The realization that you are a strong, capable woman. Xan believes it, fears it, why do you deny it then?

She scoffed. *Xan fears it? He's scared of nothing.*

He fears you do not need him. It is a valid concern for a strong Etterian male.

She frowned. *But I do need him.*

Yet you have not told him this.

She twisted to scowl at Illan, who hovered behind her. *Is the blue bastard right? Does Xan not know how much I adore him?*

"She communicates with the Durn, my king. She is not intentionally insolent," Xan's words snapped her attention forward.

She squeaked and fell into another curtsey. 'Off with her head' came to mind. "I'm so sorry, Your Highness. Illan-idiot insists on talking to me at inopportune times."

"Idiot?" Xeus sputtered.

"Her candor is what I value most, my king." Illan stepped forward wearing a smile

She glared at him. *See?*

"As do I. It is not often someone disrespects my blood-bond. I cherish every occurrence." Iddan dipped in a formal bow.

She gaped, torn between hiding in a hole or kneeing Illan in the balls.

"I wish to confirm you are prepared to answer a few questions we may have regarding these *submarines*?" Xeus asked.

"I will try, but my guardian Joshua would be better equipped to answer." *Shit. A question and answer session? An alien version of a pop quiz?*

"This is not an interrogation," Xan whispered. The brush of his lips along the shell of her ear made her shiver.

He led her into a large room dominated by an oval table in the center. There were no chairs. The war room had display vids on every wall, like black eyes waiting to be awoken. The solid doors closed, calling forth more anxiety within Quin. She stiffened, heat prickled her skin, and she struggled to breathe.

Xeus activated his O.D.I. The vids flickered images of submarines through various stages of development. Some of the images were downright archaic.

"You would need to build your own," she whispered to Xan as she crowded him. "These are designed for minimal space, to be fast, sleek, and silent. Your males are too big to use any of ours."

"I anticipated as much, Lady Quinlan." King Xeus gestured to the males gathered.

She dipped her chin, chastising herself for forgetting about their preternatural hearing. "If time's an issue, an alliance with Earth including several deliveries of their subs and crewmen would be advantageous," she stammered on to hide her faux pas. "Even more awesome would be the acquisition of their engineers, designers, and builders."

"That would be *awesome*," Xeus teased. "And your guardian Joshua? Would he advise?"

"Oh, yes. He's currently testing navigational systems for the subs. He would know what expertise you would need, who to consult...," Quin said.

"And your missiles? They fire true?" another male asked her.

"Yes, we call them torpedoes. They have various purposes. They can target other submarines, surface ships, and air crafts. Some of them are homing torpedoes that use passive or active guidance, or a combination of both, allowing you to deploy a torpedo, and it will wait for a specific signature before detonating."

"Alodon's balls." The intensity swirling in Xan's eyes said he liked what she was saying.

She flashed him a heated glance in return before facing the king. "There are also several types of propulsions. Like I said, Joshua would be better able to assist."

"And would your guardian be willing to do so?" Xeus's gaze rested on her face, waiting, watching.

"If you explain the situation with an intergalactic war on the horizon and Earth caught in the middle...then yes."

Xeus nodded. "Thank you, Lady Quinlan, for your guidance. I may need your assistance further should Joshua not wish to aid us."

"I'm happy to help, Your Highness. After all, this is my fault." She assumed the blame. If this was to be her home, then her new king ought to know how much it cost him to welcome her.

Xeus grabbed her hand to pat it. "You did what you needed to do, to survive. We do not hold you accountable."

"I have said as much, my king." Xan pulled her into his arms.

"Lady Quin, look around the room, please. Observe that none of the males present show any animosity or resentment toward you," the prince said. She hesitated but did as asked, and he was right, no one was angry with her. Yet that seemed wrong, cold, unemotional.

They are not human. Illan reminded her.

She offered Prince Enyl a small smile. "At the time, I didn't regret killing him. I should have. To take a life is a serious matter. But now, I do regret it. I truly am sorry."

Your words prove how stubborn you are, not to see the truth, to doubt the king's sincerity.

She grimaced. *Ah, that would explain the scowl.*

"We do not regret your decisiveness. They insisted on targeting Earth, despite all the warnings from Etteria and the Global Council. That Prince Yada was on the slave ship with kidnapped humans means the royal house condoned it. Thus is the war inevitable."

So all sides made mistakes is what Xeus tried to convey. But as far as she could see, Etteria was innocent in this. However, Earth would need them in the coming war. Without their strength and abilities, Yithia would decimate the planet. She didn't point this out to Xeus on the off chance he withdrew his support.

"I received word from Kbal that a Mannx has been delivered to his uncle in the Maloidian city of Argaxx. The Maloidian Pannos has confirmed this," Xeus said to Xan.

Wait. What? She fought the urge to kiss him. That he had done something so magnanimous made her love him more. *Macy's going to flip.*

"This is good news, my king." Xan nodded.

"Yes, it shows this Kbal has influence. It is imperative you know of Urio's attempt to kidnap Enyl. This happened shortly after Yada's death. Leave at once for Earth, and with Malo, secure the assistance we need to build our submarines."

"Yes, my king."

"Tomorrow morning will suffice. All of Etteria is with you," Xeus said. "Now, if you will excuse me, the Durns must tour our extensive archives." He escorted Illan and Iddan out of the war room. Prince Enyl and Princess Oriana trailed the king. A strange light shimmered around the royal couple.

"Are they...glowing?" Quin whispered, staring until her eyes watered.

"Yes, it is an unexplained phenomenon," Xan smiled as he led her into the hall.

"Will *we* glow?" She held up her forearm as if it would, at that precise moment, begin to glow.

"We would have after our first union if we were meant to."

"Oh, thank goodness." She slumped.

He escorted her out of the hall and down a covered walkway, only pausing once he'd reached a blue door. "This is ours." He opened the door.

"Ours?" She peeked inside at the expansive room with décor themes similar to the battleship.

"Yes, as my Dar Eth—"

"We're going to live together?" She blinked at him, assessing his twitching fingers yet warm gaze.

"If it pleases you."

"How do I feel about living with my husband? Um, let me think about it." She clasped his hands and dragged him into their new home. Releasing him, she twirled, plastered herself along his length, and smiled. "It pleases me, Xan."

White stone was everywhere. Eight colorful comfys occupied the central room with a 'kitchen' to the side. There was an actual counter around the replicator and rehydrator, and tall windows formed the wall behind the kitchen. Bright light spilled into the room, throwing blinding shapes on the white floor.

"Keeping this clean must be a nightmare," she said as she skipped to the only door in the room.

"We have auto-servos." Xan followed at a more leisurely pace. The bedroom had a massive bed almost exactly the size and shape of the beds on the battleships. There was a cleansing room off to the side, which was much more convenient than in her quarters.

"Do you have any plans for today, my Xan?" She peeked at him where he reclined against the door frame. Without waiting for his response, she touched the lock mechanism on the robe, and it parted. His breath hitched. She blew him a kiss before shrugging out of the garment. It pooled on the floor like an ink stain on the crisp white stone.

She'd seen the lingerie on the replicator and had ordered them in black and gold. Judging by his reaction, she'd chosen well. The black bustier hugged her torso, thrusting her breasts up and promising to free her nipples. The matching lace cheeky panties hugged her backside like a second skin. Added to this were the gladiator pumps, crisscrossing around her calves.

"Alodon's balls, Quin...," he rasped, pushing off the wall to reach for her. "What are you wearing?" he whispered as he touched the silk of the bustier.

"It's lingerie, and we wear it to entice." She raised her arms to unravel her braid. As she shook her curls out, he curved his hands around her waist and yanked her against his chest.

"I am enticed," he growled. "Take everything off, lest I tear it."

She smirked and slipped the front buttons on her bustier through their holes, allowing it to part, leaving it gaping. A strip of her stomach and cleavage was visible, enough to tease. She slipped her thumbs into the waistband of her panties and shimmied them down her thighs, letting them fall to the floor before shoving them aside. Shrugging the bustier off, she raised her foot onto the bed to undo the straps.

He plastered his pelvis to her backside, his fingers embedding in her hips, keeping her still against his hard erection. "Leave the footwear on."

Within seconds, his cloak and armor lay discarded, his boots tossed haphazardly. His velvety skin warmed her backside at the same time he cupped her unbound breasts. He pressed a heated, wet kiss on her neck.

"*Maker*," he rasped as he caressed the inner thigh of her raised leg. "You tempt me to be uncivilized, my Quin."

Her core spasmed as he slid his hand toward her sex.

"We have time now. Show me how uncivilized you can be," she said.

The guttural groan he released was animalistic, but it increased her need, her craving for him. And for the next few hours, he accepted her challenge, conquering her in more ways than one, leaving her breathless and satiated.

Now may I intrude?

Sleep lured her where she lay in Xan's arms, his ever-present arousal still buried within her. *You may, Illan.*

An intense emotion exploded through the link. She stiffened until she realized it was unadulterated joy.

These archives have our entire history, everything documented. Our techniques, our culture. His tears of gratitude flowed freely. He'd believed this knowledge lost in his planet's destruction.

I am happy for you, brother. She opened her heart to share her excitement for him.

If you do not hear from me, please do not be offended.

Have fun, Illan. She chuckled and snuggled against Xan, letting sleep claim her.

Chapter Twenty-Seven

"Your smiles come more frequently," Oyaz said as they strolled through the gardens. "I must assume you are receiving regular exercise?"

Xan chuckled, relishing the fire in his veins, as if the pulse of life had taken up residence deep within him. "Yes, I am often exhausted. Though, that is not the reason why I smile. I almost perished on Lysara, Oyaz. I realized then that every moment should be enjoyed, each emotion savored."

"I am pleased for you, Xan. Your reactions are as expected from an Eth," Oyaz said.

Illan strode toward them with more energy than usual.

"Lord Illan," Oyaz greeted as the Durn stopped in front of them, bringing Xan to a halt, as well.

Xan frowned as Illan lifted one finger and pressed its tip to his forehead. He dragged a line from the bridge of Xan's nose to his hairline while whispering words in an unknown language.

"What are you—?" Pain lanced through Xan, and he clutched his temple, agony exploding and pinging behind his eyes. He swayed, his knees weakening.

"It is done, Xan." The Durn strode away with the parting words, "I will miss her."

"Xan? What just happened?" Oyaz gripped Xan's shoulders, keeping him upright.

Xan glared at the Durn's departing back. *What in Alodon's hell?*

Across his mind, Quin's sweet voice whispered, *Illan?*

Xan jerked back. *How is this possible? That is Quin's voice.* He breathed her name. *Quin.* He didn't expect a response, but when she gasped, the full realization of their mental connection shot joy through him.

Xan? How's this possible?

He grinned. *Illan touched my temple.*

She chuckled, her humor blossoming across his mind. It was blinding. *Hurts like hell, right?* She faltered. *Illan's gone? I can't feel him anymore.* Then her sadness engulfed him, the force of it snatched his breath.

"Xan? Do you require a medic?" Oyaz's question drew Xan's gaze.

"I am well. Illan mind-fused me to Quin."

Oyaz blinked, then leaned back. "Oh. Still, I recommend—"

Xan ignored a scowling Oyaz. His battle-bond's mouth moved, but Xan couldn't focus on him. *He transferred the bond to me, my Quin.*

His chest swelled at the knowledge that she was his alone. That he need no longer share her. Illan had gifted them with unparalleled intimacy, one never experienced. Perhaps now, the constant craving would abate. *Maker, how I do love you, my Quin.* Silence reigned. He stilled. He shouldn't have told her.

Her response was breathless. *Come find me and tell me that again.* A rush of desire that wasn't his bolted through him, shooting heat to his groin. Was she touching herself? *And don't take too long.*

"I have to...go," Xan cut Oyaz off mid-sentence. "I'll explain later." He abandoned Oyaz on the pathway, sprinting to their chambers.

She waited for him, in the leggings and shirt she'd requested this morning. Not that he could take the time to admire her. She launched herself at him the moment he drew to a halt. Crushing her to him, he buried his face in her neck like a starving male.

Her breath warmed his ear. *I love you too.*

Emotions swelled in his heart and soul, breaking over him in a vibrant crescendo. She loved him? Now he understood why she only needed his love. Having hers empowered him. He could conquer the known universe with her beside him.

She leaned back to meet his gaze before brushing a tender kiss across his lips. Strange emotions exploded through him. What she invoked within him with her soft lips was there as usual, but along with it was her reaction to kissing him.

What was that? She gasped, twisting to meet his gaze.

He gaped. *You feel it too?*

She nodded, her awe crossing the link. Reaching between them, she stroked his arousal through his military pants. The influx of sensations now shared overwhelmed his senses.

Strip, she commanded as she stepped out of his arms to yank off her shirt and leggings, taking the time to admire his body as he revealed more and more with each removed piece of armor.

His focus was on her naked before him and the emotions crossing their bond. *I can feel your admiration, your need pounding at you.*

She smirked. *You're a beautiful male, Xan, and I do desire you. Smell that I'm ready for you.*

He drew in a deep breath, inhaling her rich, smoky scent.

Holy crap, no wonder you're always aroused.

I am and have been from the moment you stepped onto the viewing deck. He thrust images at her, his memories of his time with her.

Tears shimmered in her eyes. *Is that how you see me?*

He pulled her closer, gliding his hand down her taut stomach to dip his fingers into her wet feminine folds. Her throaty moan widened his eyes in delight. Her intense pleasure exploded colors across his vision and made his arousal throb. He scooped her into his arms and shivered when her skin brushed his, pebbling his nipples in response to her reactions flooding the connection.

He growled. *Maker.* He followed her down to the bed and pressed his arousal at her entrance. She writhed beneath him, reacting to the bombardment of his emotions, his imagery. And as he slid into her welcoming heat, her impending fulfillment slammed into her. She contracted around him, sparks settling in her core just as tingles rippled along the length of his malehood. Sharp bolts of need drove her senseless, and in so doing, fogged his thoughts. Fire rushed down his spine to pool in his loins. The sensation of his arousal rubbing the inside of her channel and her potent, glorious fulfillment gushing over him had him finding his own. He roared her name and almost released again when she reacted and exploded again.

"This is going to take some getting used to." She panted as she kissed his shoulder.

"As long as we love each other, nothing else matters." He brushed his lips across hers before dipping his tongue in for a brief plundering. "And I will love you forever, my Quin." Sincerity, truth, and an all-encompassing love poured through the link. His heart ached to have found such a love.

"Forever with you is not enough, my Xan," she said.

He grinned. *Agreed.* And he caught her mouth with his to convey how much she did mean to him, by deed and thought.

His O.D.I buzzed, but he ignored the four attempts to intrude. He far preferred to spend a lifetime kissing her while nestled between her thighs.

"My apologies, Supreme Commander, but Lady Quinlan's *'oldest brother'* requests a comm."

Xan growled at the intrusion but succumbed when happiness poured off Quin.

"Josh and Carter must have told Lucas." She grinned. "This's going to be good." She kissed Xan's chin. *Now get off me, and come meet your new family.*

GLOSSARY

ETTERIANS WORSHIP ONE GOD, one Maker, since the universes have only His fingerprint on all of it, a single golden thread through all of creation.

Tokens: intergalactic form of currency

Kliks: predetermined length of distance.

Hatimaye – To bring an end (Hutt-ee-my-ee)

Etterian

Alodon (A-low-donn): who accidentally shot his balls off with his own blaster.

Teacher: lima (lee-ma)

Great teacher: lima kuu: (lee-ma koo)

Directions: semit (semm-it)

Lemon: giyua (gee-you-a)

Young one: damu (daa-moo)

Heart: ensa (enn-sa)

Heart of my heart: ensa ra ensa (enn-sa raa enn-sa)

Beloved: thamani (ta-mar-nee)

Little joy: minus susa (mee-nas soo-sa)

Little cat: minus cesu (mee-nas sess-oo)

Large: magnus (mag-nis)

Orgasm: fulfillment/deite asteri (see stars) / released (day-ta ass-tare-ree)

Starfighter: asteri peju (ass-tare-ree pear-joo)

Collection of glass vials: virak (vee-ruck)

Scum of the galaxies: xemi (ze-mee)

Hair up: malia pa (Mar-lee-a par)

Hair down: malia pado (Mar-lee-a par-dow)

Lysaran

Visitor: kashi (Kaa-shee)

God: Kaiha (Kigh-haa)

King: Kuna (Koo-na)

Orange fleshy fruit: Lemte (Lem-ta)

White flowers: Myameru (My-a-me-roo)

Precious: Delica (Dell-ee-ka)

Sweetheart: Sali (Saa-lee)

Arum Lily-type flower: D'nastu (D-nass-too)

Love Blossom: aroa loulu (A-row-a low-loo)

Maloidian

Title of respect: lommia (Lomm-ee-a)

Stubborn, lethal tree: tewaa (Tee-wah)

Tokauri/Kulai

Blade – Sulac (soo-lack)

Bone – Ukog (you-cog) - bone from some dumb animal, probably an ukog.

Braided – Gisul (gee-sool)

Father – Danno (dan-no)

Heart – Kassu (cass-soo)

Maker – Mugbu (Mug-boo)

Mother – Manno (man-no)

Sapphires – Buha (boo-ha)

Shit – Saho (sa-ho)

Star - stuon (stoo-on)

Stupid – Ungog (oon-gog)

Vessel/ship - sakay (sa-kay)

Pronunciations

Names

Aaro - Ah-row

Adda – Ay-dah

Aldur - Al-durr

Alllero - A-le-row

Balllio – Bah-leee-oh

Bos - Boss

Bry-dar - Brigh-darr

Brynr - Brin-ner

Cales - Cale-es

Cento - Sen-tow

Citus - Sigh-tuss

Coldar - Coal-daar

Cria - Kree-ah

Eriz - Sigh-low

Danic - Dan-eek

Deeezo – Dee-zoh

Der - Durr

Diso - Dee-sow

Diyo - Die-oh

Eira - Eye-raa

Enyl - E-neel

Eriz - E-rizz

Garix - Ga-ricks

Gayn - Gain

Iddan - Ee-dann

Idon - Eye-donn

Illan - Ee-lann

Jarg – Jar-g

Jokta - Jock-tar

Kanzo - Can-zow

Keelu – Key-loo

Keryr – Kerr-eer

Ksal - Ka-sell

Lazu – Lah-zoo

Lurz - Lurr-z

Malo - Mail-oh

Matir - Mat-teer

Myan - My-ann

Myn-ras - Min-russ

Naio – Nay-oh

Nerx - Nurcks

Nuos - New-oss

Oyaz - Oh-yaz

Prex - Precks

Ronin - Row-nin

Saan - Sarn

Sena - See-na

Sy'mar - Sigh-marr

Syna - Sigh-na

Tamra – Tum-rah

Taro - Tah-row

Tenu - Ten-oo

Trav - Trahv

Tinh - Tin

Vytus - Vie-tuss

Vodin - Vo-din

Ulriq - Yule-rick

Vorn - Vawn

Vyar - Vie-arr

Xan - Zan

Xeus – Zeus

Zaro - Zah-row

Ziot - Zye-ott

Places

Argaxx – Are-jax
    Crustiiu – Criss-tee-oo
    Dyuqa - Dee-you-ka
    Etteria – E-tare-rea
    Galaza – Gah-Lar-Zah
    Gikaet – Gee-ka-ett
    Iphara = Ee-far-ra
    Kulai – koo-ligh
    Lysara – Liss-saa-ra
    Mascroba – Mus-crow-ba
    Resia Cay – Ress-Ee-ahh Kay
    Sarvis – Sarr-viss
    Sosu – Sow-soo
    Tokauri – Too-cow-ree
    Yithia – Yith-ee-a

Battleships

Chikara – Chee-kar-a - Force
    Gladio – Glad-ee-oh - Sword
    Kushin – Cush-shin - To Pierce
    Surata – Soo-ra-tah – Beginning
    Usaha – Oo-saa-hah - Endeavor

Shuttles

Celeeri – See-lee-ree - swift

    Denessi – Denn-ess-ee - sodge

    Eshima – Ee-shee-ma - respect

    Kevol – Kev-oll - agony

    Kuta – Koo-tah - modular shuttle.

    Liri-ny – Lee-ree-nye – freedom

    Misaia – Miss-aye-a - memory

    Sasay – Sass-ay - whispers

    Yakin – Yuck-kin - belief

Creatures

Asnu – Ass-Noo – buffalo/donkey

    Eiltur – Ale-turr

    Gracc – Grrr-ack

    Ilag – Ee-Lug– leggy slugs that feast on sol.

    Kreso – Kreh-soo

    Omeika – Oh-may-ka

    Pagsu – Pug-Soo - cocksuckers

    Reshy – Resh-Ee - huge, like the size of a kuta shuttle, with massive jaws and rows of sharp teeth.

    Sogair – Sow-gare

    Wilanegy – Will-anna-jee

About the Author

Sevannah Storm is a fiction writer who immerses herself in fantastical worlds both magical and science fiction. She has a flair for the creative having studied art and interior architecture and spends her time drawing, oil painting, and writing. An avid reader from an early age, Sevannah finds her inspiration from various sources: games, novels, music, and the land of make-believe. The unique versus the practical has brought on numerous debates.

In her spare time, she does Krav Maga, CrossFit, and rereads novels that snatch her breath away. Having embraced the social media world, you can find her on most platforms.

Her home is a land south of Wakanda, where animals roam free. Born in Zimbabwe, she grew up in South Africa. The crisp blue skies with cotton-candy sunsets expand her heart and soul, encapsulating a sense of freedom.

Words she lives by: "Know your pothole and dodge it. Don't work in a pencil factory if you're a vampire."

Sevannah loves to hear from her readers. You can find and connect with her at the links below.

Website/Newsletter:

https://www.sevannahstorm.com/

Facebook:

https://www.facebook.com/sevannah.storm

Instagram:

https://www.instagram.com/sevannah.storm/

Twitter:

https://twitter.com/sevannah_storm

Thank you for taking the time to read Earth Forged. If you enjoyed the story, please tell your friends and leave a review. Reviews support authors and ensure they continue to bring readers books to love and enjoy.

https://sevannahstorm.com

SOUL FORGED

Know-it-all Oriana agreed to travel with aliens who need women. But she didn't agree to abduction, life/death battles, and escaping with a bossy, arrogant man. She was sabotaged, attacked, and kidnapped, but she is far from beaten. Forced to participate in an alien battle arena with no promise of freedom, she has to forget the loss of her family and focus on surviving.

Enyl has given up hope. His people are dying due to a genetic modification gone awry. Darkness is consuming his warriors, and his world, as he knows it, will end. His father, the king, has rolled out a plan to save them all. But Enyl doubts a solution will be found in time.

And when a compatible female is found...and lost, he must rescue her, a human female capable of surviving despite all odds. However, freeing Oriana serves to anger the aliens holding her captive. Ensuring she is cared for—as per Etterian protocol—he is stunned by the strong connection between the two of them. Such a bond was only experienced between Etterian mates.

Is she his salvation or is that wishful thinking on his part?

Read it here:

https://books2read.com/u/mlAWr9

FATE FORGED

SUN FORGED

The Gifting Series #3

Meeting a drop-dead gorgeous man, who falls onto a knee the first time they meet, sounded too good to be true for Ava. Of course, with her luck, he had to be an alien. Thrust into an unknown alien world, meeting weird and scary creatures, and fearing for her life, Ava tries to survive as best as a hairstylist can.

Kanzo never expected to find a life mate, a Dar Eth. Since he was young, he was taught that pairings were rare with fewer females born. The statistics on finding his Dar Eth would be slim to none. Instead of dreaming and longing for companionship, he focused on being the best male possible, to end his life on a battlefield with honor. But when he experiences the Ethera—the life mate force, and is blessed with his female, he isn't prepared for the level of pain, pleasure, and need she invokes within him.

Unable to save her as she's teleported from him, the dark consuming pain in his chest drives him into a blinding rage. With no idea who stole her or where to begin the search, he will scour the known universe to find her, to hold the female he never wanted.

Read it here:

https://books2read.com/u/3n5vaB

STAR FORGED

THE GIFTING SERIES #5

Macy is feeling a little left out, as usual. Who would have thought moving from one planet to another wouldn't change that loneliness? She is never alone these days since Etterians guard human women with an urgency she understands. But the lack of companionship is like a dark aching abyss inside her chest. On some days, it threatens to implode, and Macy Mitchell would cease to exist. Looming is her impending meeting with King Xeus of Etteria. How is she supposed to keep her shit together when presented to royalty? Not after she ran from the last king she met.

For Xeus, the void expands daily. Duty, honor, concern for his dying people, and endless loneliness fill his life. Having decided to search for pairings among other worlds, he is pleased his son found his soulmate among human women. It doesn't mean that Xeus's loneliness and longing haven't ended until he stumbles upon a crying female. Meaning only to soothe, he is spellbound when her presence brings him peace. Unable to resist, he forms an attachment to a female he can never have

Read it here:

https://books2read.com/u/3nXgp5

SHADOW FORGED

The Gifting Series #6

Forty-year-old Caroline is too old to start dating and too bored with her vibrator, but what other choices does she have. On the day she burns her shirt and breaks a fingernail, she meets Etterian warriors. As part of her job at E.S.A. (Earth Space Association,) she must 'entertain' the hot-as-apple-pie Chief Engineer she suspects isn't who he claims to be.

Operations Commander Malo, Head of Espionage, must act as an engineer and ambassador, hoping to invite human females to visit Etteria and save his dying race. From Princess Oriana, he has strict instructions to distrust humans. What he finds he cannot trust are his emotions and his body whenever in the presence of the human ambassador, Caroline. She does not believe in soulmates or in a forever with him. Convincing her to choose him is the greatest task ever set before him, one he cannot afford to fail.

Until she is stolen from him. He calls in favors, utilizes all his resources to find her. And *when* he does, he is never letting her off his battleship...or his bed.

Read it here:

https://books2read.com/u/bPNd8j

EARTH FORGED

THE GIFTING SERIES #7

Guilt hounds Izzy, who caused her sister's injury and subsequent blindness. But no matter how she cares for Simone or what she sacrifices, it doesn't ease the ache in her chest. With Simone and naive Caro, her best friend, Izzy's role as protector is fully realized. The cost? Hiding behind quirkiness, pseudo-joy, and giving up her hopes and dreams. What she needs is a knight in any armor. After all, beggars can't be fussy. She has no idea that armor, in her case, means black military and that a knight could come in any color, specifically bronze.

Oyaz wants to find his life force, his soulmate, and he'd like her to be human. Earth's females are soft, amusing, passionate, and their scents rival a garden of hahyt blossoms. His task is to guard their planet that promises so many salvations for his males. It's a duty he's pleased to perform, one he would die for. When Operations Commander Malo orders Oyaz to retrieve a human female, he's eager to oblige. That it would lead to his salvation is something he couldn't anticipate. What he hadn't planned for is an ambush that costs him more than his memory, the loss of his soulmate.

Now what? Nothing in their training prepared him for this.

And yet, despite not remembering kneeling for Izzy, he longs to claim her with every inch of his soul.

Read it here:

https://books2read.com/u/31V82D

LUST FORGED

The Gifting Series #8

Ex-socialite Leona wants nothing more than to enhance the mechanics within sex-cybs, not to mention improve their performances with their 'lovers.' It's a job where she's safe in an all-woman factory on Callisto, and far from her matchmaking mama. When the chief engineer is incapacitated, Leona's required to gift—her term would be pimp—sex-cyborgs to prospective clients. On an Etterian battleship, surrounded by gorgeous males, she tries not to think of sex when it's her work, especially with the Sub-Commander Aaro whose neon-blue eyes are the stuff of her erotic dreams.

As a diplomatic favor, Aaro must abandon his task to guard Earth, and perhaps find his Dar Eth or soulmate, all to protect cargo en route to many worlds, including the dangerous and unpredictable Yithia. Princess Oriana is most concerned for the two human female engineers determined to ensure the deliveries are successful. A simple enough mission until one human enters Aaro's cargo bay, dropping him to his knees.

But revealing to independent Leona that she's now trapped in a marriage isn't something Aaro can bring himself to do. He violates all he stands for, every ounce of honor by not telling her the truth. All in the hopes that she will choose to love him.

Read it here:

https://books2read.com/u/3LdA1w